"If you're worried about your precious so-called virtue, believe me, you've nothing to fear," Malachi snapped

"I'm so damned cold and tired that I couldn't take advantage of you even if I wanted to!"

Anna went rigid in his arms. He could feel the rage pulsing through her body as she groped for a retort that would hurt him as much as he had just hurt her. "What was it I called you earlier?" she asked in a raw-edged whisper.

"As I recall, you called me a cold-blooded, self-righteous prig," Malachi said.

"So I did." Anna's eyes glinted like an angry bobcat's. "Well, I was wrong, and I would like to apologize."

"Apologize?" Malachi raised his guard.

"Yes." She spoke in brittle phrases, veiling the sentiment that if she'd had a knife, she would have cheerfully buried it to the hilt in his gut. "I feel I was guilty of gross understatement!"

Dear Reader,

With the passing of the true millennium, Harlequin Historicals is putting on a fresh face! We hope you enjoyed our special inside front cover art from recent months. We plan to bring this wonderful "extra" to you every month! You may also have noticed our new branding—a maroon stripe that runs along the right side of the front cover. Hopefully, this will help you find our books more easily in the crowded marketplace. And thanks to those of you who participated in our reader survey. We truly appreciate the feedback you provided, which enables us to bring you more of the stories and authors that you like!

We have four terrific books for you this month. The talented Carolyn Davidson returns with a new Western, *Maggie's Beau,* a tender tale of love between experienced rancher Beau Jackson—whom you might recognize from *The Wedding Promise*—and the young woman he finds hiding in his barn. Catherine Archer brings us her third medieval SEASONS' BRIDES story, *Summer's Bride,* an engaging romance about two willful nobles who finally succumb to a love they've long denied.

The Sea Nymph by bestselling author Ruth Langan marks the second book in the SIRENS OF THE SEA series. Here, a proper English lady, who is secretly a privateer, falls in love with a highwayman—only to learn he is really an earl *and* the richest man in Cornwall! And don't miss *Bride on the Run,* an awesome new Western by Elizabeth Lane. True to the title, a woman fleeing from crooked lawmen becomes the mail-order bride of a sexy widower with two kids.

Enjoy! And come back again next month for four more choices of the best in historical romance.

Sincerely,

Tracy Farrell
Senior Editor

BRIDE
ON THE
RUN

ELIZABETH
LANE

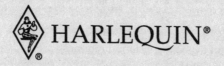

HARLEQUIN®

TORONTO • NEW YORK • LONDON
AMSTERDAM • PARIS • SYDNEY • HAMBURG
STOCKHOLM • ATHENS • TOKYO • MILAN • MADRID
PRAGUE • WARSAW • BUDAPEST • AUCKLAND

ISBN 0-373-29146-9

BRIDE ON THE RUN

Copyright © 2001 by Elizabeth Lane

This edition published by arrangement with Harlequin Books S.A.

Visit us at www.eHarlequin.com

Printed in U.S.A.

Please address questions and book requests to:
Harlequin Reader Service
U.S.: 3010 Walden Ave., P.O. Box 1325, Buffalo, NY 14269
Canadian: P.O. Box 609, Fort Erie, Ont. L2A 5X3

For my parents,
who gave me a love for rocky canyons and rushing rivers,
and for Tanya.

Prologue

St. Joseph, Missouri
January 4, 1889

> "Love, oh, love, oh careless love,
> Love, oh, love, oh careless love,
> Love, oh, love, oh careless love,
> Just see what careless love has done...."

Anna DeCarlo sat on the edge of the tiny stage in a cross-legged pose that offered her audience a tantalizing glimpse of silk-stockinged ankle. Lamplight gleamed on her tawny, upswept hair and glittered on the paste-diamond choker that encircled her creamy throat. Her low, velvety voice flowed like dark honey through the smoky haze that filled the grand salon of the Jack of Diamonds, rising above the piano to mingle with the clink of crystal, the whir of roulette wheels and the low murmur of men's voices.

From the ring of tables that surrounded the stage, she could feel hungry eyes on her, feel them devouring her small, voluptuous body through the clinging peacock satin gown. *Go ahead and look,* Anna thought fiercely. *You'll* never get another chance!

"Love, oh, love, oh, careless love…"

Did she love Harry Solomon? Anna was not prepared to answer that question. She had stopped believing in love a long time ago. But she liked the dapper, silver-haired owner of the Jack of Diamonds. He was kind and generous and treated her like the lady she had always longed to be. Last week he had asked her to be his wife. Tonight he would get his answer. It would be yes.

"Just see what careless love has done…"

Anna lowered her gaze as the song ended, letting her head fall forward like a wilted blossom. For a long moment silence filled the lamplit circle. Then, as she lifted her face the audience burst into cheers. Smiling radiantly now, she took her bows. It was all over— the smoke-filled rooms, the leering eyes and pawing hands, the haggling over contracts and payment, the endless packing and unpacking. As Mrs. Harry Solomon, she would have a home. She would have the respect and security she had hungered for all her life.

As the applause died away she slipped backstage, pausing only to take up her white merino shawl from its hook on the wall. Wrapping the shawl around her bare shoulders, she hurried through the draughty corridor and up the back stairs. Harry would be in his sumptuous second-floor office now, waiting for her answer. She had kept him on tenterhooks long enough.

For all Anna's resolve, doubts gnawed at her as she

mounted the dark stairway. Harry Solomon was old enough to be her father. Was she doing the right thing by him and by herself? Could she be a loving wife to him? Share his bed? Even give him children?

But she was being foolish now, Anna lectured herself. Harry was the best thing that had ever come into her rough, miserable life. He had offered her the world of her dreams, and she would be generous with her gratitude. She would make him proud, and she would make him happy. Harry Solomon would never be sorry he had married her.

Lost in thought, Anna climbed upward. From the salon, the lusty chords of the grand piano, playing "Beautiful Dreamer," echoed eerily up the stairwell. Above her, on the landing, she could see the thin crack of light beneath Harry's door. He would be waiting for her, she knew, with iced champagne and two crystal goblets on the sideboard. Minutes from now they would be toasting their future together.

She was a half dozen steps short of the top when the door flew open and two dark figures burst out onto the landing. They were cloaked against the winter night, their low-brimmed hats shadowing their faces, but she recognized them both. The shorter of the two was Louis Caswell, chief of police in the riverfront precinct and a frequent patron of the Jack of Diamonds. Yes—she could see the black high-heeled boots he wore, custom-made to increase his height. The taller, darker man was little more than a stranger, a shadowy man known to her only as The Russian.

What business would Caswell have with Harry at this hour of the night? Anna was weighing the wisdom of asking when the two men pushed past her without a word and hurried on. Only the startled flash of Caswell's eyes in his sharp little weasel face indicated that he had seen her at all.

Partway down the stairs she saw The Russian hesitate, glancing up at her. For an instant the light from the open doorway fell on his long, pockmarked face, and Anna felt her heart contract with a sudden, nameless fear. He turned, as if to start back toward her, but then Caswell seized his arm, said something in a low voice, and the two of them vanished into the dark corridor.

"Harry?" Anna's elegant kidskin boots clicked across the landing as she hurried toward the open door. "Harry, what on earth—"

The words died in her throat as she stepped into the room. Harry Solomon was lying facedown in a spreading pool of blood, among the papers that had spilled from his open safe. A large, bone-handled butcher knife protruded from his back, right over the spot where his heart would be.

Chapter One

Arizona Territory, May, 1889

They would never find her here.

Anna's lips moved in silent reassurance of that fact as the buckboard creaked down the narrow dugway that had been blasted into the sun-colored sandstone cliff. The silent man who sat beside her, his massive fists keeping a tight rein on the mules, probably thought she was praying. She wasn't. Anna had given up on God at roughly the same time God had given up on her. By what she judged to be mutual consent, she no longer asked heaven for favors. Not even at times like this.

Above the towering canyon walls, the sky was a blinding turquoise gash. Two great, dark birds, which Anna guessed to be vultures, drifted back and forth, circling and descending on the hot spirals of air. Infinitely patient, they seemed to be waiting for a misstep. For the man. For the mules. For her.

The man glanced coldly at Anna. His name was

Malachi, like the last book in the Old Testament. Malachi Stone—a hard-hewn, righteous-sounding name if she'd ever heard one. Malachi's lead-colored eyes flickered upward in the direction of her gaze. "Ravens," he said. "You'll see a lot of them here."

Anna nodded, twisting the unfamiliar gold band that encircled her left ring finger. This was nothing but a bizarre and frightening dream, she told herself. Any minute now, she would wake up in St. Joseph, warm and secure in her cozy hotel suite. Harry would still be alive, and she would be planning their wedding, not fleeing from town to town in a constant state of terror.

Louis Caswell had known what he was doing that January night when he'd stopped his sinister cohort from killing her. By the time she'd realized her mistake, her clothes, shoes and hands were streaked with Harry's blood. She had left bloody footprints all over the Persian rug, bloody fingerprints on the knife handle and on Harry's once immaculate pearl-gray suit. She had wiped her hands on the papers that lay scattered on the rug. She had even left her bloodstained merino shawl at the scene as she fled, panic-stricken, from the room. No jury on earth, she knew, would believe her version of what had happened. She'd had no choice except to run or hang.

Anna had snatched up what little money and valuables she could lay her hands on, packed a few necessities and hired a driver to take her to the railway station. Omaha…Denver…no place was safe for more than a few weeks. She had planned to head for California or perhaps Mexico where no one had ever heard of Anna DeCarlo. But in Salt Lake City her money had run out. She'd been scanning the *Salt Lake Tribune,* looking for any kind of employment she could find, when she'd spotted the advertisement one Mr. Stuart Wilkinson, Attorney at Law, had placed on behalf of his widowed cousin: "Wife Wanted: Remote ferry location on Colorado River. Must get on well with children and be accustomed to hard work...."

The front wheel of the buckboard lurched over a rock, jarring Anna's thoughts back to the present. From hundreds of feet below, hidden by rocky ledges, she could hear the rushing sound of the Colorado. Spring was high-water time. Malachi Stone had told her that while they were still trying to make polite conversation. Swollen with runoff from melting mountain snows, the current was too dangerous for any kind of crossing. Having planned for such a time, he had lashed the ferry to the bank, hitched up the mules and turned the buckboard toward the ranch where his nearest neighbors lived. All night he had hunched over the reins, arriving at dawn to meet the stranger who, by virtue of proxy marriage, was already his legal wife.

Anna studied him furtively from under her parasol. Malachi Stone was a big man. Big shoulders, big arms, hands like sledgehammers and, beneath the dusty felt hat, a face that could have been hewn from hickory with the blade of an ax. She liked big men. Always had. Not that it made any difference in this case. The contract she'd signed in Salt Lake City did not include marital duties. She was hired help, plain and simple. The so-called marriage existed only to suit Malachi Stone's rigid sense of propriety.

That arrangement was fine with her, Anna reminded herself as the buckboard swayed around a stomach-twisting curve. She was not looking for love or permanence, only safety. And Malachi Stone looked as if he could fend off an army of Caswell's thugs with his big, bare fists.

She ran the tip of her tongue across her front teeth, tasting gritty sand. "How much farther?"

"Not far." He did not look at her.

"You left your children alone at the ferry?"

His hard gaze flickered in her direction, then returned to the road. "Didn't have much choice. Not that they can't look after themselves if need be. Carrie's eleven, old enough to see to the boy for a couple of days. And the dog's with them. Good protection in case a cougar or bobcat comes sniffing around. All the same, it'll be a relief to get home."

"How long has it been since their mother passed away?"

The silence that followed Anna's question was broken only by the sound of plodding hooves and the low hiss of the river far below. "A year come this summer," he said in a flat voice. "We've gotten by as well as you might expect. But the two young ones need more care than I can give them on my own. That's why you're here."

"Of course." Anna gazed past him toward the next bend in the road, where the long, thorny spears of an ocotillo, each one tipped with a bloodred blossom, rose from behind a clump of prickly pear.

Yes, it was all about the children. She had known that from the beginning, but now, hearing his words, she felt the truth sink home and settle in like a spell of gray weather. A man like Malachi Stone could live alone on the moon without wanting for love or companionship. But his two young children were different. They needed a mother.

And what did she know about mothering? Her own mother had died of typhoid when Anna was still in diapers; and there'd been nothing motherly about the rod-wielding women who'd run the orphanage where she'd lived until the age of fifteen. She knew more about faro and five-card stud than she did about children, a fact that wouldn't buy her much with a man like Malachi Stone.

The buckboard lurched through a flooded spot in the road, its wheels splattering water that was the color of cheap Mexican pottery. The Colorado would be the same—too thick to drink and too thin to plow, the locals said of it. A river of mud, sunk into a canyon as deep as the mouth of hell itself.

Would she be safe here? Even now, a shudder passed through her body as she thought of Louis Caswell and his pockmarked companion. For a time she had hoped that, having blamed her for Harry's murder, the police chief would allow her to disappear. By now she knew better. Caswell would not rest as long as she was free. He wanted her dead.

Anna's eyes ranged up and down the sheer, rocky walls. No, she decided, feeling better, Caswell's hired thugs would never find her here. She could lose herself in the great, twisting canyon and its maze of arroyos and tributaries. She could vanish from the earth as the wife of an unknown ferryman, safe and secure until she was ready to move on to California and start a new life.

As for the children, she would manage somehow. After all, how difficult could her job be? When they were hungry, you fed them. When they were dirty, you washed them. When they were tired, you sent them to bed. What could be simpler? Now, their father, on the other hand...

Anna shot another sidelong glance at her companion's rough-hewn profile. The straitlaced Mr. Stone would give her no trouble, she reassured herself. The man was no more open to entanglements than she was. Theirs was a business arrangement, with a contract that could be canceled at any time by either party. That, too, was all for the best. It would make things that much easier when the time came for her to leave.

What the bloody hell had Stuart been thinking?

Malachi stared at the dust-caked rumps of the mules, his spirits growing darker with each turn of the wheels. He should have known better than to trust his city-bred cousin to find the kind of wife he needed—a strong, plain, practical woman who would take to the rigors of running the ferry and managing two active youngsters. A woman of impeccable moral character. Stuart Wilkinson may have studied law, but that was no substitute for common sense. The fool had succumbed to the first pretty face that came along, and now there would be the devil to pay.

He glanced furtively at her hands, which were clasped tensely around the handle of her lace-trimmed parasol. They were like creamy bisque porcelain, each fingernail a perfect, ivory-rimmed oval. He could see no sign of a scratch or callus on those hands. Not a mark to show that she had ever done a lick of work in her pampered life.

But that wasn't the worst of his concerns—not by a damned sight. A woman that pretty and self-assured could get any man she wanted. Why should she settle for a mail-order marriage to a stranger with nothing to offer except solitude and hard work?

Why, indeed—unless she was running away from something?

He remembered his first sight of her, standing on the porch of the Jepsons' ranch house where the freight wagon had left her, wearing a demure lavender gown that, for all its modest cut, clung to the curves of her lush little body in a way that made his breath stop. She had watched him in silence as he swung out of the wagon and hitched the mules to the rail. He remembered the tilt of her small head as her gaze swept upward from his muddy boots to his sweat-soaked shirt, then paused to linger on his face. He had stood there clutching his hat, feeling big and awkward and dirty, desperately hoping there had been a mistake and she was waiting for someone else.

Her hair, gathered into a crocheted snood at the back of her neck, was like a swirl of molasses taffy, each strand a different shade of gold. Her eyes, set in a square, sharp-boned face, were a rich, startling shade of amber, flecked with bits of gold and brown. They had regarded him boldly, as if he were a prize hog she had just won at a church raffle. "Well," she had said in a husky contralto voice that seemed much too big for the rest of her. "Well, well, so it's Mr. Stone, is it?"

Malachi's heart had dropped like a plumb bob.

He should have turned away right then and there, he lashed himself as he leaned hard into the brake to slow the careening wheels. He should have tossed her a few dollars for fare back to Salt Lake, climbed into the buckboard and driven off without a backward glance. Instead here he was, wondering how he was going to make do with the last kind of female he wanted on his hands.

Malachi's inner grumblings were cut short by the crack of splintering wood. His bride gave a little yelp as the wagon lurched sideways, its momentum pitching her out of her seat. The parasol flew from her hands and vanished into the wide, rocky void of the canyon. She might have gone the same way if he had not grabbed her arm and wrenched her back toward him.

"What on earth—?" Her eyes were as wide as a startled fawn's, her arm taut through the thin fabric of her sleeve.

"It's all right," he growled, "I've got you."

"I can see that, but it doesn't explain what happened." Annoyance formed a furrow between the golden wings of her eyebrows. Close up, she smelled of clean sweat and cheap hotel soap.

"Broken axle." Malachi bit back a curse as he released her. "Happens now and again on this road."

"So what do we do now?"

"We unhitch the mules and ride them down to the ferry. Unless you'd rather walk, that is."

"What—about my things?" Her eyes flickered uncertainly toward her leather-bound trunk. It was of modest size as trunks go, but Malachi was in no frame of mind to lug the woman's useless finery down six miles of rough road.

He scowled at her. "No reason it shouldn't be safe where it is. Nobody comes this way when the river's in flood."

"We can't take it with us?" The eyes she turned on him would have reduced a lot of men to quivering putty, and probably had.

"There are two mules," Malachi swung out of the seat and dropped to the ground. "I plan to ride one of them. The other one can carry you or the trunk. Not both. Take your pick."

Still she seemed to hesitate. Resolving to ignore her, he strode to the front of the rig and began unbuckling the double harness from the traces. One of the mules raised its tail and dropped a steaming pile of manure in the orange dust. Yes, that about summed things up, Malachi reflected dourly. Stuck on the road with a useless city female, an hour from darkness, with the children alone and waiting for him. He hoped to blazes the woman could ride a mule.

"Aren't you going to help me down?" Her raspy little voice, as mellow as southern bourbon, penetrated Malachi's awareness. He glanced back to see her watching him with eyes as bright and curious as a wren's. There was a birdlike quality about her small frame, the quickness of her movements and the way she sat forward on the wagon seat, as if she were about to spread her wings and take flight. Anna. A good, simple name. But something told him there was nothing simple about this woman.

"Well, Mr. Stone?" Was she demanding or only teasing him? Malachi was tempted to ignore her, forc-

ing her to climb down on her own, but then he noticed
the narrowness of her skirt and realized she could not
get down except, perhaps, by jumping. How in blazes
was she supposed to ride a mule? He hadn't brought
along a damned sidesaddle.

With a sigh of resignation, he walked back to the
side of the wagon and extended his arms. The corners
of her mouth lifted in a tight little smile as she leaned
toward him, letting his big hands encircle her ridic-
ulously tiny waist. He lifted her without effort, bracing his senses against the onslaught of her nearness
as he swung her over the edge. This was a business
arrangement, Malachi reminded himself. It would remain just that until she got tired of the sand, the bugs,
the isolation and the unending work, and lit out for
greener pastures. That wouldn't take long, he reckoned. A week, a month, surely no more, and he would
be faced with the dismal prospect of starting over—
if it wasn't already too late by then.

Anna.

Her hands lingered on his shoulders as he lowered
her to the dusty roadway. Close up, her skin was
warm apricot in tone, luminous beneath the smudges
of rust-colored dirt. Her eyes were the color of aged
brandy, her body warm through the fabric of her dress
and soft, he sensed, beneath the tightly laced corset.
Malachi felt the all too familiar tightening in the hollow of his groin. He cursed silently. No, this wasn't
going to work out. Not for a week. Not for a day.
Not for a damn-blasted minute. He'd have been better
off alone.

Determinedly, he stepped away from her. "I'd better get these mules unhitched,'' he muttered, feeling sweaty and awkward.

"Can I do anything to help?" she asked all too innocently.

"Just stay out of the way. A skittish mule can kick hard enough to kill you." He turned aside and began fumbling with the buckles, which seemed unusually stubborn. Anna stood where he had left her, glancing up and down the road as if she were expecting company.

At last she cleared her throat. "Well, if you don't need me, I'm going to find a convenient bush," she announced. "Heaven knows I've been needing one."

Malachi choked on his own spit. He wasn't used to having a woman speak so frankly about her bodily functions. There was hell of a lot he didn't know about this woman who'd given her maiden name as Anna Creer. But one thing was already certain—his new wife was no lady.

"Watch out for rattlesnakes," he said. She shot him a startled glance, then turned and stalked up the road toward a big clump of sagebrush, lifting her skirt to keep the hem from trailing in the dust.

Malachi's mood darkened as he finished unhitching the mules. He could feel his whole plan unraveling like a badly made wool stocking—not that it had been a great plan to begin with. He had grown desperate over the past eleven months, with Elise gone and the children so sorely in need of a mother. Every day he had lived with that need—watching Carrie grow toward womanhood without a mother's guidance, seeing the lost look in little Josh's eyes. His heart had ached for them. But there were no eligible women within a day's ride, and it was all he could do to manage the ferry and the stock and the household chores, let alone go off courting.

He had let the months pass without taking action. Then the letter had come—the letter that even now threatened to rip his whole world apart—and Malachi had known he could not wait any longer.

One desperate night he had hit on the idea of ordering a wife—a plain, good-hearted woman with no illusions about romance, a woman who would be content to stay in the canyon, care for the children and work at his side. Before dawn he had written the letter to Stuart and the plan was in motion.

The terms of the contract had been set up to protect both himself and his prospective bride from hurt if things didn't work out. But it had been Malachi's hope that over time, mutual respect would ripen into a semblance of love, and the awkward arrangement would become a true marriage. Now—he swore under his breath as he struggled with the harness. What a calamity he had brought down—upon himself, upon his innocent children, and upon this willful bit of fluff who seemed to have no notion what was in store for her.

Anna emerged from behind the sage clump, brushing twigs and flecks of dirt from her skirt. "No rattlesnakes," she said. "But I did meet a very curious lizard. I ordered him to turn his back, but the little imp just sat there and stared at me the whole time. Most ungentlemanly of him."

Malachi kept his eyes on the mules, ignoring her attempt at ribaldry. "There are a lot of animals in the canyon," he said. "You'll get used to them in time."

What in blazes was he saying? The woman wouldn't likely stick around long enough to get used to anything!

He glanced back to find her a few paces behind him, watching as he freed the harness from the traces. She was older than he'd first thought, Malachi reckoned, twenty-five or twenty-six, perhaps. That part was fine, since he was almost thirty-five himself. But even though she was trying her best to be pleasant, something about her just didn't set right. She was too bold, too worldly; too much like the women he had known in that other long-ago life, the life before Elise and the children.

How could he bring such a woman home to care for his son and his impressionable eleven-year-old daughter?

"Can you ride?" he asked her.

"Some."

"Then climb aboard."

He waited, deliberately standing with folded arms as she glanced from the broad-backed mules to her narrow skirt. For a long moment she hesitated, then shrugged and, to Malachi's consternation, reached down, gathered up her skirt and petticoat, and hitched them above her knees.

"I'll need a leg up," she said.

Malachi swallowed, then bent down without a word and made a cup of his linked hands. The black high-button shoe she placed between his palms was expensively made, as were her fine-knit white stockings and the lace edging on the bottoms of her drawers. The woman had clearly lived well. She'd had money for nice things—or someone to give those things to

her. So what in the devil was she doing here, headed
for the bottom of the Grand Canyon with a man she'd
only met that morning?

It was high time he found out.

Malachi held his breath, steeling himself as she
pressed her weight into his hands, gripped the harness
and, with a little gasp of effort, flung her free leg over
the back of the mule. The scent of her clothes swept
over him as her skirts flew up, flooding his senses
with the light, sweet odor of musk. He bit back a
groan, averting his eyes as she straddled the mule and
wriggled into place, tugging her rucked skirts down
over the lace-trimmed hems of her drawers.

Would she tell him the truth if he asked her?

What a damn-fool question! The woman would tell
him the first story that came into her head and expect
him to believe it! But he was no fool. There had to
be other ways to learn what this so-called Anna Creer
was hiding.

Then again, Malachi reminded himself, why should
he bother? He knew her kind well enough, and the
thought of where and what she had been filled him
with a deep, simmering anger. When he'd paid his
cousin to find him a wife, he'd known better than to
ask for a virgin. A widow lady would have been fine,
even one who'd made a few mistakes, as long as she
had a good heart. But he hadn't counted on a woman
like Anna. He had never expected that Stuart would
send him a whore.

Chapter Two

The mule wheezed and laid back its ears as Anna settled her tender buttocks atop the bony ridge of its spine. "There now," she murmured, struggling to soothe the nervous beast. "Take it easy, old boy. You got the best of the deal here. You could be carrying that big hulk of a man instead of me."

But the mule did not appreciate her logic. It rolled its eyes, shook its dusty hide and began kicking out at the buckboard with its hind legs. Anna groped frantically for reins to control the creature. There were none.

Malachi had mounted the other mule—a much calmer animal than the one he had chosen for her, Anna noted wryly. If he was concerned for her safety, he did not show it. "Just hang on to the collar and give Lucifer his head," he told her. "He knows the way home."

"Lucifer?" She shot him a sidelong glare, struck by the aptness of the name. "And, pray tell, who might you be riding? Saint Peter?"

"Beelzebub." He nudged the flanks of his long-

eared mount and moved ahead of her on the trail.
With a contemptuous wheeze, Lucifer fell into line.
Anna clung grimly to the padded leather collar as the
massive beast swayed down the road. She'd lied to
Malachi about being able to ride—just as she'd lied
about other things to Stuart Wilkinson and to the
kindly couple who'd let her wait at their ranch for
Malachi to arrive. Lies had come more and more easily to her since that shattering night in St. Joseph. By
now they were almost second nature.

A fresh breeze, smelling of rain, ruffled Anna's
sweat-dampened hair. She glanced up to see clouds
sliding across the jagged gash of sky. In the depths
of the canyon the shadows had deepened from mauve
to purple. Fear twisted the knot in her stomach as she
realized the daylight would soon be gone. They would
have to pick their way down the narrow, dizzying
roadway in full darkness.

Even now she could feel twilight closing around
her. Its bluish haze blended with the back of Malachi's faded chambray work shirt as he moved in and
out of the shadows like a ghost, keeping well ahead
of her. He had fallen as silent as the great stone buttresses that lined the canyon. Oh, but she knew what
he was thinking. Disappointment had been etched all
over his big, craggy face from the first time he looked
at her. She was not what he had expected, let alone
what he had wanted.

But then, what difference did it make? Anna reminded herself harshly. If she had anything to say
about it, the dour Mr. Stone wouldn't have to put up
with her for long. She could only hope that when the

time came for goodbyes, he would be decent enough to buy her passage to California.

As the sky deepened a coyote sang out from a distant ridge top. The sharp crescendo of yips climaxing in a long, mournful wail, puckered the skin at the back of Anna's neck. Malachi's broad-shouldered back was no more than a flicker in the gathering murk. He was deliberately leaving her farther and farther behind. She could pitch off this accursed beast, tumble into some bottomless ravine, and he would not know—or likely care—until the mule wandered into the corral without her.

"Get up, Lucifer!" She kicked at the mule's flanks with her sharp little boot heels, but the stubborn animal only wheezed and stopped to nibble at a trailside plant. Anna clung to the harness, kicking and cursing under her breath as the collar slid forward. Malachi had not even glanced back to make sure she was all right. The big, sullen wretch was more than disappointed, she realized with a sinking heart. He was angry. It was almost as if he'd hated her on sight.

Maybe she should have invested her last dollar in a set of itchy woolen long johns and a flour-sack dress. Yes, and braided her hair in scraggly pigtails tied up with rags. Maybe she should have smeared a little mud on her face and practiced belching out loud and saying *ain't* and *gol-darnit*. Would that have elevated her in Malachi Stone's esteem? Or was this just the way men treated women in these parts?

"Wait up, blast it!" she shouted after Malachi's vanishing form. "Lucifer won't budge, and you're leaving me behind!"

Malachi paused, glancing back over his shoulder.

Putting his fingers to his mouth he gave a long, shrill whistle.

Lucifer's huge, bony head shot up like a catapult, throwing Anna backward as the animal plunged onto the road and broke into a spine-jarring trot. She gripped the collar for dear life, her hips alternately bouncing into the air and slamming down on the mule's rock-hard back. Malachi sat and watched her, his face hidden by the deepening shadows. If he was laughing at her, Anna vowed, she would kill him for it!

"I thought you told me you could ride," he said as Lucifer came abreast of his own mount and slowed to a swaying walk.

"I did," Anna muttered, tugging her skirts over her knees. "I just didn't specify *what* I could ride."

He rewarded her witticism with a scowl. "It's clouding up. Let's get moving," he said, nudging his mule to a brisk trot. This time Lucifer fell into line, bounding down the rutted road like a nine-hundred-pound jackrabbit. Anna clenched her teeth as her raw buttocks pounded the bumpy ridge of Lucifer's spine. Misery rankled and roiled in her, festering until she could keep her silence no longer.

"You—don't like—me, do—you?" she muttered, spitting out the words between bounces.

"Did I say that?" Malachi did not look at her.

"You didn't—have to! Damn it, I'm not stupid!"

"I never said you were."

"Then slow down, for mercy's sake!" She seized Lucifer's harness and by sheer force of will wrenched the big, lumbering animal to a halt. "No matter what you might think of me, I won't be treated this way!"

she said. "Either we come to some kind of under-standing here and now, or I'm not budging another inch!"

Malachi, who had already gained half a furlong on her, hesitated, then wheeled his mount and rode back to where she waited. "All right," he said in a cold voice, "have it your way. Your call."

Anna's breath hissed out in a ragged exhalation as she prodded Lucifer to a slow walk and waited for Malachi to fall in alongside her. She swallowed hard, steeling her nerves before she spoke.

"You desperately wanted me here," she said. "At least that's what your cousin, Mr. Wilkinson, led me to believe. And I did believe it, or I would not have come such a distance. So why are you treating me as if I'd brought in the plague?"

Malachi's silence was as long and deep as the shad-ows that flowed through the craggy hollows of the canyon. The haunting cry of a desert owl shattered the darkness. As the sound echoed across the gorge, Anna realized how alone she was in this place, how helpless, how utterly dependent on this hostile stranger who was her lawful husband. It was too late, this time, to go flouncing off and climb aboard the next train out of town. She was stranded in this alien landscape with no money, no food and no one else who would help her.

"You've asked a fair question. I'll give you that." Malachi's voice rumbled out of the shadows, almost startling her. "But not even you can believe this is going to work. I asked Stuart to find me a woman who could survive and pull her own weight in this wild, hard place—a woman who could run the ferry and drive the mules and—"

"You could have hired a man for that," Anna said curtly.

"Could I have hired a man to help an eleven-year-old girl grow up to be a good woman?" His voice rasped with emotion reined in too tightly for too long. "Could I have hired a man to dry the tears of an eight-year-old boy who still misses his mother?"

Anna let the damp evening wind cool her face for a moment before she spoke into the awkward silence. "So I'm not a fit candidate for the job. Is that what you're saying?"

Malachi's answer was a disdainful snort. "Look at you! Your clothes, your hands, the very size of you! Have you ever milked a cow on a morning so cold that the ice froze in the bucket? Have you ever plucked a duck and singed off the pinfeathers over an open fire?"

"As a matter of fact, I have." That much, at least, was true. The orphanage had had its own dairy barn and kitchen, and Anna had worked long, drudging hours in both.

"Could you pull a pig out of the quicksand or stick a calf that's bloated on too much spring clover?"

"Could your wife do those things?"

Malachi's breath sucked in as if he'd been gut-punched. "This has nothing to do with Elise," he said in a raw-edged voice. "I was asking about you."

Anna drew herself up, fueled by a slow-welling anger. "Whatever else you may think of me, Mr. Stone, I haven't had an easy life. There are a good many things I can do if I have to."

"Yes, I can well imagine." His cold voice dripped innuendo. Anna recoiled as if he had struck her. She had surmised what he thought of her, but hearing the words spoken, and with such contempt, stung her like an openhanded slap in the face.

She was still groping for a retort when he cleared his throat and continued his assault on her character. "The message Stuart telegraphed to Kanab mentioned you were widowed in a Comanche attack. Is any part of that story true?"

"No." Anna was too angry to lie. "I thought the story might win Mr. Wilkinson's sympathy, and I suppose it did. I'm here."

His eyes narrowed as if he were looking at her down the barrel of a rifle. "So what's the real story, Anna, or whatever the blazes your real name is?"

"It's Anna." She stared between the dark *V* of Lucifer's ears, biting back the urge to spill out the whole truth. How could she tell this man that her face was on Wanted posters in three states, and that Louis Caswell himself had put up one thousand dollars of the reward money? How could she tell him about the lawmen and bounty hunters that dogged her trail, the fear-filled days, the sleepless nights?

"I was desperate," she said, settling on a half truth. "I was out of money, out of work, had no place to go."

Malachi sighed, his powerful shoulders shifting in the deep indigo twilight. "I wish I could believe you," he said. "But your kind isn't exactly known for veracity."

"My kind?" Anna glared at him, her stomach churning.

"I think you know what I'm talking about."

She fought the nauseating rage that rose like bile in her throat. "Would it make any difference if I told you I'm not a—" She hesitated, staring down at her pale hands. No, she could not even bring herself to say the word *whore*. She had known too many of those poor, lost girls. And she had come all too close to sharing their fate. In those homeless, hungry days, only the gift of her voice had saved her from the hell of those upstairs rooms.

"I'm not what you think I am," she said, recovering her poise. "But of course, I can't expect you to believe that, can I?"

His silence answered her question, and for the space of a heartbeat Anna was tempted once more to tell this man the whole true story and beg for his protection. But no, she reminded herself, he would not believe her. And even if he did, he would not like what he heard. The upright Malachi Stone would not take kindly to the fact that the woman on his hands was wanted for murder.

Beyond the winding, narrow thread of the road, the canyon was a darkening wonderland of castle-shaped buttes, spires and buttresses. Colors changed with the changing light, deepening from sienna to violet, from indigo to midnight. The wind moaned as it funneled down the arroyos, a lonely, haunting sound that was broken only by the rush of the river and the steady, plodding hoofbeats of the two mules.

Anna gazed upward at the darkening gap of sky. Her spirits sank even deeper as she saw the flicker of lightning and heard, a heartbeat later, the distant roll of thunder.

Malachi had not spoken. Glancing at his stubborn profile, she knew that this was one contest of wills she could not win. Her breath slid out in a long sigh of defeat. "Very well," she said. "I understand and accept your position, Mr. Stone. If you'll consent to give me shelter until your wagon is repaired, I'll be on my way. I assume your cousin Mr. Wilkinson will take care of the contract cancellation…and the divorce." How strange to say the word, when there had been no semblance of a marriage between them. They were strangers to one another, and would remain so until the end of their days.

Malachi stirred at last, as if awakening from sleep. He shifted his seat on the mule, cleared his throat and spoke. "Where will you go?"

"California, as soon as I can manage the fare. There are plenty of opportunities there for my kind, as you so generously described me."

She sensed the tightening of his jaw as the irony sank home. "The buckboard shouldn't take more than a day or two to fix," he said wearily. "Then I'll take you as far as Kanab and put you on the stage for Salt Lake. It's the least I can do to compensate you for your trouble."

"That's very kind. Thank you." Anna spoke through a haze of disappointment. If only he would offer to pay her way to California. She could get work there, maybe even a singing engagement if she changed her name and dyed her hair. If things went well, she could save her money and go anywhere she wished—Mexico, even Europe. But Salt Lake City was too small, too isolated for safety. Sooner or later, she was bound to be noticed. Her face would be matched with the face on the poster, and then the bounty hunters would come.

The wind had picked up, carrying the first elusive drops of rain. Anna licked the moisture from her dusty lips, savoring the coolness as Malachi pushed ahead of her once more. "Let's get moving," he said. "Storm's going to break soon, and this stretch of the road is prone to slides."

He kneed his mule to a brisk trot. Not wanting to be left behind, Anna jabbed her heels into Lucifer's flanks and was rewarded by a sudden burst of speed. She gripped the collar, her teeth clenched against the pain that jarred her pelvis and chafed her thighs with every bounce. Walking would be agony tomorrow— if she survived that long.

Lightning cracked across the sky, casting buttes and mesas into stark blue relief. The earsplitting boom of thunder echoed across the canyon, and in the next instant the rain began to fall. Not a gentle shower but a stinging, lashing torrent. Within seconds it had plastered Anna's clothes to her body and turned the road into a seething river of mud.

Startled by nature's sudden savagery, the perverse Lucifer stopped dead in his tracks and began wheezing like a ruptured steam calliope.

"Come on!" Malachi swung back toward Anna and yanked the frightened animal into motion again. "There's an overhang about a mile down the road!" he shouted above the rain. "We can stop there till the worst of this passes!"

He swung ahead of her to lead the way and was at once swallowed up by darkness and rain. All but blinded by the stinging raindrops, Anna gripped Lucifer's collar, trusting her life to the erratic beast. The mule knew the way home, she reminded herself. As long as she stayed on its back, she would be safe. All the same, it was hard not to be terrified when water was gushing over the road with a force that threatened to wash away the entire hillside.

"Keep him away from the edge!" She could hear Malachi's voice shouting from somewhere off to her left. "This way!"

Another lightning bolt split the sky above the gorge. In its ghostly flash she saw him plunging toward her, one arm outstretched in an effort to grasp her mount's harness. Then thunder broke like the roar of cannon fire, and Lucifer lost his footing. Squalling and kicking, the mule went down and began to slide.

Anna screamed as she felt herself flying through the black rain, felt the twisting jerk as Malachi's powerful hand caught her wrist, wrenching her upright. She slammed into the side of his mule and hung there, her breath coming in hard little sobs.

"We've got to get out of here!" Malachi was hauling her upward. Wild with terror she fought against the pull of his arm.

"Lucifer!" she gasped. "We've got to save him!"

"He'll have to save himself! Get up here, damn you!" He was dragging her alongside the mule, almost twisting her arm out of its socket.

"Please—" she started to argue. Then she heard it—a roar of sound that rose out of the rain like a demon out of the sea, growing, building until it became the scream of the earth itself.

Landslide!

Malachi bent down and caught her waist, sweeping

her off her feet as the mule shot forward. Anna used the harness to clamber up behind him, and they rocketed down the road, skidding around curves, dodging boulders and exploding through mud pits.

Too terrified to think, Anna pressed against Malachi's back, her arms encircling his lean, muscular waist, her knees spoon-cupped against the backs of his thighs. From behind them she could hear the rush of water and the rumble of falling earth. She could hear it gaining on them, moving closer with every breath, every heartbeat.

Malachi's body strained forward against her clasping hands. His muscles bunched and lengthened through the rain-soaked shirt as he lashed the mule's flanks with a loose harness buckle. Startled by a crashing boulder, the mule skidded sideways, giving Anna a fleeting glimpse of a whitish rock outcrop that loomed perhaps a quarter mile down the road. It had to be the overhang Malachi had mentioned earlier. They had seconds to reach it.

Malachi cursed as the mule wheeled in sudden panic and stopped still, braying and rolling its eyes. "Give me your petticoat!" he shouted. "We've got to blindfold him or he won't move!"

Clinging on with one hand, Anna tugged at the stubborn muslin. When it failed to come free, Malachi reached back, seized a fistful of cloth and yanked hard. The sodden fabric ripped, almost jerking her off the mule as it tore loose.

A fist-size chunk of sandstone bounced off Anna's shoulder and skittered down the slope. Malachi had dismounted and flung the petticoat over the head of the screaming mule. They were moving forward now, at the leaden speed of a nightmare chase. She could hear his voice through the rain, urging the animal forward.

"Come on, you stubborn old devil! It's all right! Just let loose and run!"

Anna could hear the sucking sound of the earth washing away behind them. Just ahead the huge, pale outcrop jutted over the road like the bow of an ocean-going ship. She could see the hollow beneath it, their only chance of safety.

"Get up, damn you!" She slapped the mule's haunch with the flat of her hand. Startled, the animal bolted forward, almost running Malachi down in its haste. Anna lay low against its neck as they passed under the edge of the overhang, and then, miraculously they were beneath solid rock, safe for the moment.

The air was dark here and strangely quiet. Without waiting for Malachi to help her, Anna slid wearily down the mule's wet side, her hand catching the petticoat on the way down. The ground was solid and dry beneath her feet, but her quivering legs refused to support her. With a little moan she folded onto the sand and huddled there in a sodden ball, her knees drawn tight against her chest.

Malachi had come inside, his presence filling the small space beneath the outcrop. Anna could hear his breath coming in raw gasps as he leaned against the rocky wall. His wet clothes steamed in the darkness.

The mule had ambled off to one side. It snorted and shook its dripping hide, spraying muddy water. Anna thought of the stubborn, cantankerous Lucifer and how he had gone flailing off the road at the worst possible time. She remembered the soft rabbity ears, the wheezy bray, the patient back. The accursed beast had meant nothing to her, but suddenly Anna found herself weeping—not in ladylike sniffles, but in ugly, body-racking sobs. She cried as she had not cried since her teens. She cried for the loveless years of her youth, for poor, dear Harry, for today's hideous misadventure and for all the rough and lonely times ahead. Her tears gushed like water through a bursting dam, and try as she might, Anna could not make them stop.

"What the devil is wrong with you?"

She glanced up to find Malachi looming over her, his eyes glowing silver in the eerie light of the storm. "I can understand a few tears," he growled, "but enough is enough, lady! For the love of heaven, you're alive! You ought to be kissing the ground in gratitude instead of bawling your damn-fool eyes out! What's gotten into you?"

Anna raised her swollen face, too distraught to care how she looked or what this man thought of her. "Lu-Lucifer," she hiccuped. "The slide—he—"

"Bloody hell, woman, you don't have to tell me! I know what happened to the blasted animal!" He furrowed impatient fingers through his wet hair, making it stand up in spikes. "That's the luck of the draw in a place like this. You lose stock. Sometimes you even lose people, and the sooner you get used to that, the better off you'll be. So stop your sniveling, lady! If anything, I'm the one who ought to be upset. I paid top dollar for that idiot mule!"

Anna stiffened as her distress congealed into a wintry rage. Slowly she rose to her feet, her clothes dripping mud, her hair streaming in her tear-blotched face.

"How dare you?" She forced each word past the barricade of her chattering teeth. "How dare you speak to me like that—as if I were *nothing,* a piece of livestock, bought and paid for?" She took a step closer, her eyes drilling holes in his face. "I've known some cold-blooded, self-righteous prigs in my day, but you, Mr. Malachi Stone—you deserve the blue ribbon! You take the all-time first prize!"

Chapter Three

The darkness shimmered with the storm's electric glow as Malachi stared down at her—this small, hysterical creature who had suddenly flown at him like a bantam hen defending her nest.

Cold-blooded? Self-righteous? Priggish? Lord, how his friends from the old days would have laughed at her description of him. Malachi didn't much like the names she was calling him, but for the moment, at least, he was too bone-tired to respond.

"So you paid top dollar for that mule, did you?" she lashed him "How much did you pay for *me*, Mr. Stone? And what would you have said if I'd been the one to tumble off the side of the road and disappear in the storm?" She squared her shoulders and thrust out her trembling chin in imitation of a male swagger. "Paid top dollar for that fool woman!" she drawled in a voice that was startlingly deep for the size of her. "Damned shame she's gone, but I reckon it can't be helped. 'Luck of the draw in these parts.' But what the hell, there's always more where she came from. Maybe I'll order a taller one next time."

Under different circumstances, Malachi would have laughed. But there was nothing funny about anything that had happened today. She was making too much of his words, and he was becoming irritated. "That's a low blow," he growled. "You don't know enough about me to go making snap judgments, lady, and as for—"

"My name is Anna," she said, cutting him off, "and you've already made it quite clear that I'm no lady in your eyes! As for making snap judgments, I haven't a patch on a certain so-called gentleman I could name. Talk about the pot calling the kettle black—"

"Now, listen—" Malachi took a tentative step toward her. In that same instant lightning flashed behind him, illuminating her face to reveal wet strings of hair, bloodshot eyes and a full lower lip that was quivering like a little girl's. Only then did he realize how cold and miserable she must be.

"No, you listen!" Her teeth were chattering now. "To hear you talk, one would think that anyone— anything—is expendable!"

"To hear me talk? That's a joke! I can't get a word in edgewise!"

She went on as if he hadn't spoken. "Break an axle, lose a mule—fine! You just pick up a replacement the next time you're in town! Lose a woman—" She struggled to finish the sentence, but cold and exhaustion were clearly winning out. "Lose a woman, and all you have to do is wire your efficient Mr. Wilkinson to send you another! It's that…simple to you, isn't it?" She was shaking uncontrollably now, fueled only by her own anger. Malachi knew that if he didn't do something to ward off her chills she would be sick, if she wasn't sick already.

Hellfire, what he wouldn't give for a flask of good whiskey!

"How many others have there been?" she raged. "How many other mail-order brides before me? Did they run off, or have you got them all locked up down there in your—"

Her tirade ended in a startled gasp as he caught her shoulders, jerked her against his chest and wrapped her tightly in his arms.

"What do you think you're doing?" She fought like a wet cat, squirming and twisting in protest. Malachi could feel her small, shivering body through his clothes. He tightened his none too gentle embrace.

"I'm trying to keep you warm. Hold still, damn it!"

"I will not! This is outrageous!" she hissed, craning her neck to glare up at him. "Let me go this instant!"

Malachi did not loosen his grip on her. "Listen to me for a change," he ordered. "You've taken a bad chill. If we don't get you warmed up fast, you're going to be down with double pneumonia, and the last thing I need is a sick, whining female on my hands. Is that clear?"

"Clear?" She gave a disdainful little snort that could have meant either yes or no. "What a question! After the way you've treated me, I'd rather snuggle up to Beelzebub over there!"

Malachi swallowed the temptation to let her try exactly that. She was so cold it frightened him, and her teeth were chattering like Spanish castanets.

He dredged the well of his patience, his arms tightening around her as he spoke. "I wouldn't recommend that. Beelzebub is covered with mud, and even when he's dry he has a disposition like a snapping turtle's. So unless you want to catch your death, Anna, I'm afraid I'm your last and only resort."

Even then she resisted, triggering a burr of annoyance that rankled Malachi beyond the point of self-control. "If you're worried about your precious so-called virtue, believe me, you've nothing to fear," he snapped. "I'm so damned cold and tired myself that I couldn't take advantage of you even if I wanted to!"

Anna had gone rigid in his arms. He could feel the rage pulsing through her body, the ragged intake of breath as she groped for a retort that would hurt him as much as he had just hurt her. "What was it I called you earlier?" she asked in a raw-edged whisper.

"As I recall, you called me a cold-blooded, self-righteous prig," Malachi said.

"So I did." Anna's eyes glinted like an angry bobcat's. "Well, I was wrong, and I would like to apologize."

"Apologize?" Malachi raised his guard.

"Yes." She spoke in brittle phrases, not quite veiling the sentiment that if she'd had a knife she would have cheerfully buried it to the hilt in his gut. "I fear that I was guilty of gross understatement. If the truth be told, Mr. Stone, you are the most sanctimonious, high-handed, hypocritical bast—"

"Shut up, Anna." He jerked his arms tight, crushing her against him so abruptly that the breath whooshed out of her lungs. Her throat made incoherent little grunts of anger as she wriggled and squirmed against his vise-like grasp. Malachi felt the sudden gush of heat in the depths of his own body, and for the space of a breath he wrestled with the idea of silencing her full, plum-ripe mouth with his own. A sharp kick against his shinbone jarred him back to reality. This woman had every reason to hate him. Married or not, he had no business kissing her.

Steeling himself, he kept his hold on her. "I'm well aware of who and what I am," he said, spitting out the words syllable by syllable, "and right now all I'm trying to do is keep you from freezing."

For an instant longer he felt her straining in his arms. Then she muttered something under her breath and sagged wearily against his chest. It was a victory of sorts, but as he held her Malachi realized he had no idea what he'd won.

The dark hollow beneath the rock had grown disturbingly quiet. He could hear the steady drizzle of rain pouring off the edge of the outcrop and the low gurgle of the mule's gut as the animal shifted in the shadows. He could hear the wind soughing down the canyon and feel, where his hand cradled Anna's ribs, the low, rapid beating of her heart, like the tick of a tiny watch against his palm.

She had ceased all effort to move or speak. Her stillness only heightened Malachi's awareness of his aching groin. He had told her, none too gently, that she had nothing to fear from him. Too late, he realized how wrong he had been. Anna had as much to fear from him as from any man, and the fact that she was his legal wife only made matters worse.

Had she told him the truth about her reason for coming here, he wondered, or was she lying to him just as she'd admitted lying to Stuart? Only a fool would trust such a creature, and life had long since kicked all the foolishness out of him. So why was he suddenly overcome by the urge to keep her safe, to protect her and fight off her fears? His emotions were making no sense, least of all to himself.

He leaned back against the rock, her wet hair drizzling down the front of his shirt. She smelled of rain and lilacs and sweet, clean woman. The subtle aroma swam in Malachi's senses, fueling the blaze that her voluptuous little body had ignited in his vitals. He bit back a groan as she stirred against him. Lord, didn't she know she was tormenting his body and soul? Hellfire, of course she did. Anna was the kind of woman who would know exactly how to trigger a man's desire. She was probably playing with him, laughing inside as she drove him to a slow frenzy.

And, heaven help him, he didn't want her to stop.

"Who are you really, Anna?" His voice came out thick and muzzy, as if he had just been roused from sleep. "Where did you come from and what the blazes are you doing here?"

"Does it matter?" Her voice carried an edge of weariness. "Would you believe me even if I told you?"

Malachi sighed, knowing he needed the distraction of talk. "Maybe not. But I could use a good story."

She hesitated, then laughed huskily, low in her throat. "In that case, I'm the missing heir to the throne of Montenegro. My father the king—a good sort, but desperate for aid against the Turks—was forced to pledge my hand to the evil and repulsive Prince of Transylvania. On the eve of the wedding, I

stole the crown jewels and fled westward with a band
of roving gypsies. The prince's agents are everywhere, and if they catch me, I'll be forced to wed
their warty master. The next day, after a hellish wedding night, my bleeding head will be impaled on a
pole outside the palace gates.'' Anna had spoken so
rapidly that when she paused for breath, the sharp
inhalation pressed her ripe, lovely bosom into Malachi's chest. "There, are you satisfied?" she asked.

Malachi groaned.

"You told me you wanted a story."

"I'd have preferred the truth."

"I told you the truth earlier. See where it got me."
Her voice rasped with exhaustion. She sagged in his
arms for the space of a heartbeat, then seemed to
rally. "What about you? What black secrets lie behind that great, stony face of yours?"

Malachi shifted his back against the lumpy rock.
"What did my cousin tell you?"

"That you were a widower…and an upright, God-
fearing man. Are you?"

Malachi laughed roughly. "A widower? Yes. The
rest is a matter of opinion."

"Could you shed some light on that?" Her small,
square-jawed face tilted upward in the dim light and,
once more, Malachi was seized by the insane urge to
kiss her—kiss her brutally, as she deserved for the
lies that had brought her to his world. He imagined
arching her against him, his free hand ravishing every
luscious curve and hollow of her body, then cupping
her buttocks to grind her softness against his burning
arousal until she whimpered with need. He imagined
flinging her to the ground and taking her right here,

in the cold, muddy darkness, under the legs of the mule. What the hell, in her line of work, she'd likely done that and more. He could even offer to pay—

"Malachi?"

Her voice, and the sudden tension in her body, shocked him back to reality and brought a rush of heat to his face. He remembered that she had asked him a question. But he could not remember for the life of him what that question was.

"Try that again," he said thickly.

"Never mind. I think I'm quite warm enough now." She pulled away from him and this time Malachi let her go. She folded her arms tightly across her chest and turned to stare out at the dwindling rain. "Maybe we should try to go," she said in a cold voice that left little doubt she'd guessed what he was thinking.

"Rain's letting up. Let's give it a few minutes." He moved forward to stand beside her under the lip of the outcrop. Moonlight shone through a break in the clouds, brushing the rain-slicked rocks with a patina of silver. Malachi bit back a curse as self-disgust washed away his desire. He had to get this woman out of here before she brought back all the things he had once been—things that could destroy the peaceful life he had built for himself and his children.

He was staring into the canyon, wondering how big the slide was and how many days of backbreaking labor it would take to build a road over the slippage when he heard it—the faint but unmistakable crunch of heavy footsteps moving across the scree. Something was out there. Something big. And it was coming toward them.

Anna had heard it, too. "What is it?" she whispered.

"Don't know," Malachi muttered, peering into the night. "It's too noisy for a cougar or an Indian." *But not for a white man,* he added silently, remembering too late that he had left his rifle under the wagon seat. There was little to fear from the animals that roamed the canyon. But rumors of gold or the promise of a safe hiding place from the law could, and did, lure vermin of the two-legged sort. This was not a good time to be caught unarmed, with a helpless and beautiful woman to protect.

He saw that Anna had bent to pick up a sharp-edged rock. "Keep back," he cautioned as she edged forward. "Stay behind me, and whatever happens, do exactly what I—"

He never finished the sentence because, at that instant, all hell broke loose. Pandemonium exploded in the small space as a huge, dark shape came hurtling in from the darkness, knocking him to the ground. Something struck his head as he went down. Through the spinning blur of pain he could hear Beelzebub wheezing wildly—which struck him as odd because the wheezer of the two mules was—

Malachi cursed with relief as his vision cleared. Lucifer, caked with mud and bleeding from a gash on his flank, stood quivering beneath the rock. Anna was clinging to the mule's neck, fussing and crooning over the miserable beast as if she'd just recovered a long-lost relative.

They rode double to spare the injured Lucifer on the way down to the ferry. Anna clung to Malachi's back in wretched silence. She was cold and hungry, and the hostility that radiated from his tense body did nothing at all to warm her. She knew what he thought of her, and she knew it would be a waste of time to try to set him straight. There was no chance of resolution here for either of them. The sooner she got out of this place, the better it would be for them both.

The storm had passed as swiftly as it had begun, leaving a wake of wispy clouds that trailed across the moon. Stars, as cold as they were beautiful, glittered like spilled diamonds across a black velvet sky.

She had felt Malachi's desire when he'd held her. And she had felt the hot flame of her own response— the throbbing deep in her loins, the moisture that had trickled between her thighs, betraying her readiness for his thrust. How long had it been since a man's touch had made her ache like that? How many nights? How many years?

Too many, Anna lashed herself. This was no time to be dwelling on what she had once had, and lost. The past was dead and buried, and a new life awaited her in California, as soon as she could find the means to get there. She would be a fool not to look ahead, to hope for better times.

The darkness around her quivered with sound— clicks, croaks and squeaks from a myriad of tiny creatures displaced by the storm. The small cries of life filled Anna with a melancholy so deep that it threatened to burst her heart. Desperate to ease it, she spoke into the sullen void of Malachi's silence.

"How much farther?" she asked, knowing she sounded like an impatient child.

"Not far. Another mile or so." His tone was flat

and impersonal, as if he were reading some stranger's obituary in the newspaper. "Why? Do you need to stop?"

Anna chose to ignore the question. "You must be anxious to get back to your children," she said, pressing against the barricade of his reserve. "Can you tell me more about them?"

He sighed wearily. "Not that much to tell. Young Joshua's a typical boy. Likes to ride and fish and help with the stock. Carrie…" he paused, as if conjuring the girl up in his mind. "She does a fine job of running the house. She's getting tall. Going to be a pretty woman one day, like her mother."

Anna felt the tremor in his chest as he swallowed. She could not doubt that Malachi's drowned wife had been beautiful, nor that he still loved her deeply.

"What do you do about their schooling?" she asked, shifting the talk to safer ground.

"They school themselves—with help from me when the ferry traffic's slow. We're not as uncivilized as you might think. There are plenty of books at the ferry—Shakespeare, Dickens, Plutarch. There's even a piano that I bought off a Mormon family in Kanab and hauled down to the house. Carrie plays a little— but only by ear. Can't read the one music book we've got."

"I could teach her—" Anna gulped back the rest of the offer. There would be no time for piano lessons. As soon as Malachi could clear the road and repair the buckboard she would be gone.

"It sounds as if you've done a fine job of raising them."

"Credit their mother for that. It's been a struggle

for me just to keep them fed and schooled this past year, let alone dress them decently and teach them proper manners. They need the touch of a good woman at home.'' He hesitated. ''We all do.''

A good woman, Anna thought, feeling the sting of his words like brine in a razor cut. *But certainly not this woman!*

Suddenly it was all too much. She wanted to wound him, to ravage his pride as he had ravaged hers. ''So, how many others have their been?'' she asked casually.

''What?'' She felt him jerk.

''How many other women has your cousin, Mr. Wilkinson, sent down to you?'' she pressed him. ''How many others, before me, have left because they couldn't measure up to the perfect wife you lost?''

Malachi's body had gone rigid beneath her hands, and Anna knew she had pushed him too far. But then, what did it matter? She had endured the long, punishing ride on the freight wagon, the dust, the flies, the blinding desert sun, only to come face-to-face with a man who'd despised her on sight. A man who'd by turns ignored her, insulted her and treated her like a tramp. She was soaked, frozen, half-starved and so sore she could barely move without wincing. If he didn't like her question, the high-minded Mr. Malachi Stone could go skin himself with a rusty hatchet!

''How many do you think?'' She could almost hear his teeth grinding as he bit back his irritation.

''I asked you,'' she shot back. ''You certainly can't expect me to guess about such a delicate matter.''

He growled something Anna couldn't understand. "Blast it, you know you're the first, don't you?"

"The very first?" Anna feigned shock. "But surely not the last! Do you plan to try again and hope for better luck?"

"Not until I've wrung Stuart Wilkinson's neck and hired myself a new matchmaker."

"Why not give me that job?" Anna needled him. "I could find you the ideal wife! All I'd have to do is look for a woman the exact opposite of me—as big as a barn door, as strong as a lumberjack and as proper as a nun! Now that would be worth the fare to San Francisco, wouldn't it?"

Malachi swore under his breath, probably thinking that he would cheerfully pay her passage to hell and back if she would just leave him alone. Surely a railroad ticket to California wouldn't be too much to ask of him.

Anna was about to push her request once more when a glimmer of light, far below the road, caught her eye. She strained outward, peering down into the darkness of the canyon. Malachi, sensing her excitement, said quietly, "It's the ferry. They've hung out the lantern."

Both of them fell silent as they wound their way into the depths of the great chasm. Anna could hear the hissing rush of the swollen Colorado. She could feel the air warming around her, growing as damp and heavy as a muggy New Orleans night.

The mules, in their eagerness to be home, had broken into yet another bone-jarring trot. This time Malachi made no effort to hold them back. Anna clung grimly to his waist, her jaw clenched against the agony of her strained hip joints and raw thighs. Drugged by exhaustion, she forced herself to stay awake, to think of the hot coffee and clean bed that would surely be waiting for her at the end of the ride. She would strip off her wet clothes, crawl between the sheets and sleep for hours—maybe for days. Malachi Stone had already declared their contract null and void. She was under no obligation to clean his house, cook his meals or wash his clothes. She could take her leisure while he repaired the road and the wagon. Then she could put this awful experience behind her once and for all.

The floor of the canyon had leveled out now, and the sound of the river was very close. Eight-foot clumps of spring willow and feathery tamarisk lined the road, obscuring whatever lay ahead. Minutes crawled by, each one an eternity, before Anna caught the flare of lamplight through the brush. An instant later her view opened wide, revealing a log fence with a lantern hung from a nail on one post. Beyond the fence, the light revealed shadowed glimpses of a barn, a corral, an open ramada and a rambling adobe house with a roof of Mexican tile.

As the mules clattered through the gate, the door of the house burst open, casting a long rectangle of light on the sandy ground. Silhouetted by that same light, two figures, one small and wiry, the other taller, willow-slim, stood framed by the doorway.

As they started forward, the smaller one bounding toward the gate like a terrier, the taller one—the girl—hesitant, hanging back, Anna's heart shrank in her chest. She had done her best to put this first confrontation out of her thoughts. But that was no longer possible. Ready or not, she was about to meet Malachi's children.

Chapter Four

Anna saw that the girl was holding a lantern. She raised it high as her father pulled Beelzebub to a halt, but she made no move to come closer. As Malachi had mentioned, she was tall, nearly as tall as Anna herself. But she was as thin as a willow wand, her eleven-year-old figure just short of budding into womanhood. Her hair was braided into frizzy black pigtails, and the pale flannel nightgown she wore barely reached her knees.

"Papa?" The uncertain voice was thin and musical. "Papa, is that you?"

Anna heard Malachi's low breath of relief as his body slackened. Only then did she realize how worried he had been about leaving his children alone—and how important it had been to find them a mother.

As the girl hesitated, lantern raised high, a smaller form shot past her like a Pawnee arrow. "Pa!" Only Malachi's carefully extended boot kept the boy from running headlong into the mule's legs. "Is she here? Did you bring her?"

Anna's spirit shrank from the eagerness in his

young voice. She tried to avoid looking directly down at the boy, who appeared to be wearing nothing but one of his father's old work shirts cut off at the sleeves. The long tails hung nearly to his small bare ankles.

"I brought her." Malachi's reply was flat and weary as he swung a leg forward over the mule's neck and eased himself down the animal's shoulder. Anna was left sitting alone on Beelzebub's back with her skirts hiked above her knees. "Josh," Malachi said without looking up at her, "this is Anna."

The round, upturned eyes were dark brown and as friendly as a puppy's. "Pleased to meet you, ma'am," Josh piped, ignoring Anna's bedraggled hair and mud-soaked clothes. "Can I call you Ma yet?"

Anna's mouth had gone chalky. She clung to the mule's rain-slicked back, wishing she could melt into the darkness and disappear. She knew the boy was waiting for an answer, but for the life of her she could not speak the hurtful words.

In the awkward silence, the boy turned to his father. "Pa, can I call her—"

"Ma'am will do," Malachi said gruffly. "She doesn't plan on sticking around long enough to warrant being called Ma." He turned and reached up to help Anna down from the mule. The hands he offered her were cool and rigid. His eyes were like silver flints in the lamplit darkness.

The boy edged backward as Anna slid wearily to the ground. She gazed straight ahead, trying not to look down at the small, dejected face, the drooping shoulders. Guilt gnawed at her. She willed herself to ignore it. The boy's disappointment was Malachi's problem, not hers. All she wanted right now was a hot tub, some dry clothes and a good night's sleep.

Malachi's daughter had remained on the stoop, her shy gaze darting up, down, anywhere but directly at Anna. Only now, as she caught sight of Lucifer's gashed flank, did she react. With a little cry she ran across the yard to the injured mule. She pressed close to the big, muddy animal, her long, white fingers probing the gashed flank. "What happened to him, Papa?" she demanded. "Is he badly hurt? Wait—I'll get some salve."

"I'll see to the mules," Malachi said curtly. "You show Anna inside, Carrie. Get her something to eat and show her to the privy if she needs it. Is her room ready?"

"Yes, Papa." Carrie turned reluctantly from the mule and strode past Anna, head high, in the direction of the house. Anna followed the flash of white nightgown across the yard, her own legs raw and rubbery from the long ride. Clearly the girl did not want her here. But hostility was easier to handle than Josh's puppyish need for affection, Anna reminded herself. She would not be here long. The less she entangled herself with Malachi's children, the better for all concerned.

Dragging her tired feet, she crossed the low porch and stumbled over the threshold. One muddy hand groped the door frame as she staggered into the house, eyes blinking in the sudden brightness of a brass lantern that hung from the low ceiling. The house opened into a long common room, furnished with a heavy pine table in its center. One end was occupied by a cluttered kitchen, the other by a massive stone fireplace, three well-worn armchairs, a tall set of shelves overflowing with books, and the piano Malachi had mentioned on the way down the trail. Three doorways opened along the far wall leading, Anna presumed, to the bedrooms. There would be one for Carrie, one for Joshua, and one—

Anna's throat closed in an audible hiccup as the possibilities struck her. But no, the contract had specified that she would not be expected to share Malachi's bed. Her sudden attack of stomach flutters was quite unwarranted.

"Are you hungry? There's a pot of beans on the stove." Carrie's voice was strained, her posture tense. The full light showed magnolia skin and huge dark eyes that dominated her heart-shaped face. The girl would be a beauty one day, Anna mused, especially if she could outgrow the shyness that caused her to shrink into herself like a cornered animal.

"I'm too tired to be hungry," Anna replied. "But some hot coffee might taste good."

"I can make some." Carrie turned hastily away and began rattling pans and utensils, making far more noise than necessary. Anna was on the verge of telling her not to bother with the coffee, but she held her tongue. The girl had lost her mother less than a year ago. It stood to reason that she would not take kindly to another woman in the house.

"You don't have to worry about my taking your mother's place, Carrie," Anna said, warmed by impulse. "Your father and I have already agreed that this arrangement isn't going to work. I'll be leaving as soon as the road is cleared."

Carrie did not answer. Her elbows jerked as she pumped water into an enameled coffeepot. Her pretty mouth was set in a grim scowl that made her look startlingly like Malachi. Brooding, Anna surmised, seemed to run in the Stone family.

"Your father said something about a privy." Anna did not really need one right now, but any excuse was better than standing here in the kitchen making polite, one-sided conversation with this sour child.

"Out the door and to your left. You won't need a light. Just follow the path around the back of the shed."

"Thank you." Anna made a hasty exit, closing the screen door behind her. The yard lay muddy and trampled, silent beneath the moon, with no sign of Malachi, the boy or the mules. Welcoming the night-time solitude she stepped off the porch and veered to the left.

Her steps slowed as she found the path and followed it through a stand of willows. Cricket songs filled the warm darkness. Anna could hear the rush of the river and smell the sweetness of rain-soaked earth. Above her, on all sides, the walls of the canyon rose like a towering fortress. Anna's breath eased out in a long, ragged sigh. Her arms dropped to her sides, tension flowing out of her fingers. Here, for the first time in months she felt safe.

How long would it take Malachi to clear the wagon road? she wondered. How long before the chase began again, the haunted nights spent listening for the creak of a floorboard, the terror every time she walked down a public street, heart pounding with the fear that someone would recognize her? The sketch on the Wanted poster was taken from her performance picture—Anna DeCarlo in low-cut satin, her hair piled high on her head, her face artfully painted, her rhinestone earbobs sparkling with light. Her present, sub-

dued appearance had fooled Stuart Wilkinson. But it
would not fool a seasoned bounty hunter. One chance
encounter, one careless slip, and she would be hauled
back to St. Joseph in irons to face Louis Caswell's
own brand of justice—and Anna's instincts told her
she would never live to tell her story in a court of
law.

She had spent long hours speculating why Harry
had been murdered. Caswell had all the earmarks of
a lawman in the protection business. Had Harry
threatened to expose him with evidence? Was that
why the safe had been rifled? Had Caswell found
what he was looking for?

Anna ran a hand through the muddy tangle of her
hair, pushing it back from her face. She was tired of
questions, long since sick of fear and uncertainty. But
even here, in this deep, isolated canyon, there could
be no refuge. Her time here would be nothing more
than an all too brief respite from terror.

The path meandered through the willows, then
curved back behind the barn. Lamplight danced and
flickered through the open chinks between the boards.
Anna heard murmur of voices and the low, wheezing
snort of a mule. This, she swiftly realized, was where
Malachi had taken Lucifer to dress his wounded side.

"Well, I don't care what Carrie thinks. I say she's
pretty and I like her." Joshua's voice piped through
the wall with bell-like clarity. "Why do you want her
to leave, Pa?"

"I didn't say I wanted her to leave." Malachi's
shadow moved, blocking the light as he worked. "I
said we talked it over and came to an agreement.
Anna's not the kind of woman who'd be happy in a
place like this."

"How did you know? Did she tell you?"

"She didn't have to tell me." Malachi muttered a curse as some unseen object clattered to the floor. "Blast it, Josh, she's not what I expected, let alone what I wanted for you and Carrie. And I'd wager I'm not what she wanted, either. The only thing I can do now is clear the road, drive her back to Kanab and put her on the stage."

The silence that followed Malachi's outburst was broken only by the low, wet breathing of the mule. Anna stood frozen to the spot, knowing she should leave at once, but strangely unable to move.

"Well, why don't you sleep with her for a while before you decide?" Josh's voice cut through the stillness like the sound of a tin whistle.

Malachi first response was a half-strangled groan. Then, finding his voice, he demanded, "Who the devil put that idea into your head?"

"Eddie Johnson's pa. When he was here this spring I heard him tell you that the only way to really get to know a woman was to sleep with her."

"You've got big ears," Malachi growled, "almost as big as Sam Johnson's mouth."

"But what about it?" Josh persisted with maddening innocence. "You slept with Ma. And Anna's your wife now. What's your bedroll doing laid out here in the tack room?"

Was Malachi grinding his teeth or had Anna only imagined hearing the sound? She bit her cheeks to hold back her amusement as she imagined Josh's earnest eyes and Malachi's reddening face.

"Pa?"

She heard the exasperated hiss of Malachi's breath and waited tensely for the explosion that was bound to follow. Instead, Malachi's shadow moved lower against the light, as if he had dropped to his son's eye level. When he spoke his voice was so low that she had to press close against the wall to hear him.

"Son, it isn't that simple," he said, stumbling over the words. "When a man and woman share the same bed it's supposed to mean something."

"Like what?"

"Like—" Malachi cleared his throat. "It's like a promise, that they'll always love each other and stay together. It means they want to be a family—"

"I slept with Cousin Katie when I was six and we went to her house," Josh interjected. "I didn't know it meant any of them things, or I'd have climbed out and slept on the floor."

"Those things." Malachi pounced on the grammar mistake like a drowning man clutching a life preserver. "It's those things, not them things."

"Those things," Josh corrected himself. "But anyway, I don't see what all the fuss is about sleeping with somebody."

"You will when you're older." Malachi's voice rasped with unease. "Anna and I aren't much more than strangers. Even if she did plan to stay, I wouldn't be sleeping with her anytime soon. I'd give her some time to get used to me."

"Oh." Josh sounded crestfallen. "But what you say can't be true all the time. Eddie Johnson says there are ladies in Kanab who'll sleep with anybody who pays them enough money. You don't even have to—"

"That's enough!" Malachi cut in irritably. "Hand me that big tin of salve, and stop asking so many questions."

"But, Pa, how will I ever—"

"I said that's enough. Go and see if Carrie needs any help with supper. Go on."

Anna heard the boy moving away. Then he seemed to hesitate. "I didn't mean any harm by it, Pa, saying you ought to sleep with her."

"I know you didn't son. Run along, now." Tenderness muted Malachi's voice. Anna pushed herself reluctantly away from the wall. She'd done enough eavesdropping for one night. It was time she found her way back inside before she stumbled into quicksand, got bitten by a snake or carried off by marauding bandits. Some women took wild, dangerous places in stride. Unfortunately, she was not one of them.

Malachi's tender, stumbling words echoed in her memory as she picked her way through the mud. Would she ever meet a man to whom lovemaking was a promise, a vow to stay together forever and build a family? Not likely, Anna reminded herself. Such blessings came to women who deserved them, not women who'd made the kinds of mistakes she'd made—and certainly not women who were wanted for murder.

Had she taken a wrong turn? Anna gasped in sudden surprise as she stumbled into a muddy hole and felt water seeping into her fragile kidskin boots. The swollen river had spread into the willows here, rousing myriads of small creatures that squeaked and splashed in the darkness. To her left, the massive trunk of a dead tree, its roots likely drowned in some long-ago flood, rose against the sky like a gnarled and twisted hand. She would have remembered such a tree if she'd come this way before. Clearly, she had stumbled onto the wrong path.

As she turned to go back the other way, she heard, on the wind, the now familiar call of a coyote. Faint though it was, the sheer lonesomeness of it prickled the skin on the back of her neck. It was only an animal sound, she knew, but that long, haunting wail seemed to contain all the sorrows of the world. It seemed to rise from the very depths of her own battered, frightened heart.

She listened, her throat tightening as the sound faded away. Then, lifting the sodden remnant of her skirt, she began trudging back along the path. The smell of coffee drifted to her nostrils on the night wind. Giddy with relief, Anna sucked the rich aroma into her senses. Yes, this was the way back. Minutes from now she would be sitting in the warm, cluttered kitchen, holding a hot mug and laughing at her own foolishness.

And yes, by heaven, she would survive this experience. As soon as the road was open she would be gone. She would put this place and this great, brooding hulk of a man behind her and she would never look back. California lay ahead of her with its glittering promise of fame, fortune and freedom. All that and more—maybe even happiness.

She squared her shoulders and began to sing.

"Love, oh, love, oh careless love. Love, oh—"

The song died in her throat as a shaggy, wolf-like form parted the willows ahead of her and glided into the open.

What was it?

Panic rose in Anna's throat as the creature lowered its head and padded toward her, snarling as it came.

She forced her leaden limbs to move, to turn her body and propel it back along the path to her only known chance of safety—the tree.

She ran, gasping with terror and effort, her boots splashing water, her arms stretching, her muscles tensing for one last, desperate leap.

As Joshua's footsteps faded into the night, Malachi sagged against the workbench. His stomach felt knotted and his knees were as wobbly as a newborn calf's. The conversation with his son had undone him in a way that he could never have imagined. What business did Sam Johnson and his tobacco-chewing teenage son have, putting such ideas into the head of an innocent boy like Joshua? Josh was only eight, barely out of diapers, or so it seemed. What had happened to the years? Where had they gone?

With an impatient sigh, he jammed the cap onto the tin of Hoskins' Salve and began gathering up the bloodstained rags he'd used to clean Lucifer's wound. The mule's wet coat steamed in the darkness, filling the barn with the odors of blood and animal heat. A bead of sweat broke and trickled down the hollow of Malachi's neck. He could smell his own sweat, rank beneath his filthy clothes.

Hellfire, had he really meant what he'd told Josh about sleeping with a woman? Or had his words been nothing but self-righteous, hypocritical drivel? Back there on the trail, when he'd held Anna in his arms and felt his flesh rise and harden against her, he'd wanted nothing more than to take her then and there, to fling her on her back, part her thighs and bury himself to the hilt in the moist satin depths of her. Even now, as he thought of her, Malachi felt his body respond, making lies of all his high-sounding words. Even now he wanted her—wanted those slim, pale legs wrapping around his hips while he drowned himself in her sweet hot honey with no thought of promises, tomorrows or honorable intentions.

He would not do it, of course. He was seeking a mother for his children, not a fast, easy roll in the hay. And any entanglement with Anna, or whatever her real name was, would be a sure recipe for regret. The woman was nothing but a tawny-haired, curvaceous bundle of trouble. For his children's sake and his own, the sooner he sent her packing, the better.

The mule snorted and rubbed its head against a timber, sending down a shower of loose bark. Malachi blew out the lantern and let the animal into the corral with the other stock. Only as he was turning back toward the house did he realize that the dog, who usually hung close at his heels, was nowhere in sight.

"Doubtful?" He whistled softly, the sound blending with the shrill night music of frogs and crickets. "Doubtful? Here, boy!"

There was no answering yelp from the big wolf-shepherd cross he'd bought as a half-starved pup from band of wandering Paiutes. Maybe Doubtful had taken off after a gray fox or a rabbit. Or maybe he'd simply followed Josh to the house and was waiting on the porch. Doubtful was a one-man dog, but he tolerated the children and took it as his duty to protect them. Malachi encouraged that protectiveness, knowing it might well save their lives one day.

"Doubtful?" He whistled again, his instincts stirring cautiously. If the dog had been close by, he would be here by now. Something had drawn him away.

Malachi took a moment to fetch the loaded Winchester rifle from the shed. Then, with the weapon cocked and ready, he slipped through the willows and onto the path that meandered down toward the flooded river.

Anna was still not sure how she'd managed to clamber up the dead tree. She was even less sure how long the dry limb from which she hung, gripping with both arms and legs, would hold her before it snapped under her weight, sending her plummeting down into the jaws of the beast that paced the ground below. As long as she kept still, the wolfish animal remained quiet and calm. But every time she stirred in an effort to ease the strain on her limbs, the awful creature would lunge upward, snarling and snapping, its fangs tearing at the hem of her skirt. She knew she should scream for help, but her throat was so constricted with fear that she could manage little more than a whimper. Even if she were able to shout, Anna realized, the sound of her voice would likely be lost amid the rush and tumble of the Colorado.

The creature glared up at her, its pale eyes reflecting miniature moons in the darkness. Was it a wolf, a very large coyote or some hellish denizen of the canyon, unknown to the outside world? Anna had no wish to find out. She only knew that her hands were bleeding and her arms were getting weaker by the minute. It would only be a matter of time before she lost her grip and fell.

"Doubtful!" Malachi's low voice came from somewhere beyond the willows, barely rising above the sound of the river. Anna's pulse leaped. Clutching the limb, she filled her lungs with air and poured her remaining strength into one desperate cry.

"Malachi!"

She could hear his boots splattering water as he ran toward her. For an instant she glimpsed the flash of moonlight on metal. Relief gushed through her body, leaving her weak. Malachi was coming. He had a gun. He would shoot the monster and she would be safe.

The willows rustled as Malachi burst into sight, then stopped in his tracks. The next sound Anna heard was the deep rumble of his laughter.

"Doubtful, you old rascal, what have you treed here? Is it a fox, or maybe a wildcat?"

The creature that had been threatening Anna's life turned and bounded toward him, tail wagging. Anna was so astounded she almost let go of the limb. The slavering beast was a dog—a blasted pet!

Malachi walked to the foot of the tree and stood scowling up at her. "It's a mite dark for tree climbing, wouldn't you say?"

"This isn't funny!" Anna gripped the rough bark, her nails jagged and broken, her palms bleeding. "Your shaggy friend there tried to attack me!"

"Doubtful's just doing his job. He'd have done the same to any stranger he caught sneaking around in the dark. You should've stayed close to the house. What were you doing out here, anyway?"

"That," Anna snapped, "is no question to ask a lady! But then, you've never thought of me as a lady, have you?"

Malachi ignored her question. He stood scratching the wretched dog's ears, as if to show her how gentle the beast really was—but only with people worthy of trust. "If you're talking about the privy, that path branches off twenty yards back,'' he said. ''This is the path to the bathing place.''

''The bathing place?'' Anna blinked in disbelief, almost losing her hold. ''You're saying you don't even have a bathtub in this miserable place?''

''We've got the biggest tub in these parts—the Colorado River. But it'll be no good for bathing till the flood goes down. Too muddy. If you want to wash, you'll have to do it at the pump.'' He gazed thoughtfully up at her, his fingers working the thick fur at the crest of the dog's neck. ''So, do you plan on spending the night in that tree? I'd be happy to fetch you a quilt.''

Anna clenched her teeth, biting back a hot retort. She was at his mercy. He knew it, and he was toying with her, making a game of her humiliation. As soon as she got her feet on the ground Malachi Stone would pay. He would pay for every taunting, sarcastic word!

''Well?'' he asked, waiting.

''I can't get down,'' she muttered.

''What's that? I couldn't quite make it out.''

''Damn it, look at me!'' Anna exploded despite her resolve to hold her tongue. ''I'm hanging from this branch like a blasted possum, and there's nothing else for me to grab! If I try to climb down, I'll fall!''

''Then fall, Anna.'' Malachi spoke so softly that she could barely hear him above the sound of the river. Out of the corner of her eye she saw that he had lowered the rifle to the ground and was holding out his arms beneath her. ''Let go,'' he said. ''I'll catch you.''

Anna clung stubbornly to the branch, her pain-numbed fingers weakening by the second. ''No,'' she said, grinding out the words. "You're still teasing me! You'll let me fall. I'll land in the mud, and even if I don't break my neck, I'll be at the mercy of that snarling monster you call Doubtful!"

Malachi exhaled wearily. "You," he said, "are the most mule-headed woman I ever met in my life! Just let go. Do it now."

Anna willed herself to disobey him, but her fingers had grown so slippery and sore that they could no longer hold her weight beneath the branch. Little by little she felt her grip weakening. At last, with a furious little cry, she lost her hold altogether. The moon spun in her head as she plummeted down, down into the uncertain darkness below.

She felt the shock as he caught her, and for a moment she could only lie still, gasping for breath. His chest was as hard as an anvil, and the musky, sensual man scent of his body made her head swim. True to his word, Malachi had not let her fall. Here in his arms she was as safe as she had ever been in her rough, tumultuous life.

So why did she suddenly feel so vulnerable? Why was she shaking like a newborn calf, her eyes blinking back hysterical tears?

She reminded herself how he had taunted her while she clung to the tree, how she had vowed to make him pay for everything he said. Where was her anger now? Why wasn't she clawing the wretched man's eyes out?

Her hand lay lightly on his chest. Beneath her palm Anna could feel the steady drumming of his heart like the cadence of an army marching to battle. Her own pulse leaped and skittered erratically. She felt like a child in his arms, he was so large, so powerful.

"Are you all right?" he murmured thickly.

"I—think so." She groped for the simplest words, struggling to reconnect the link between her mind and her tongue. "Just shaken, I think."

"I can put you down."

"Yes," Anna said. "Yes, I know."

The coyote's mournful call rose again from a distant mesa, the sound echoing down the moonlit hollow of the canyon. Anna fought its melancholy spell, fought its power to tug at her heart. She needed no one, she reminded herself, least of all this man who held her as if she'd been dipped in snake venom. He had insulted her, humiliated her, dragged her through rain, mud and danger to a place fit for nothing but lizards, coyotes and vultures. All of this for a one-way ticket back to Salt Lake City.

Yes, she would hurt him. She would make Malachi Stone curse the day of his birth. And she would start now, by doing the very thing he feared most.

Driven by cold rage—and a simmering desire that even she could not deny—Anna slid her hand up Malachi's chest to his shoulder, then, with a quick motion, hooked the back of his neck and jerked his head down toward her face. Before he could react, her moist, yielding lips had captured his mouth in a kiss calculated to melt granite.

She felt the resistance in him, the rigid lips, the straining muscles. Then, as she'd hoped, need overcame pride. With a low moan he crushed her in his arms. His hot, hungry mouth opened to hers, demanding, devouring, awakening responses that surged through her body like rivers of heat. Fighting for self-control, Anna willed the tip of her tongue to invade his mouth in tiny, darting licks, like a bee seeking moisture. Once again he moaned. His arms tightened around her, molding her to his chest as he claimed that tongue, drawing it deeper, meeting its thrust with his own.

Anna felt the seething heat in her body, and she realized, with a shock of dismay, that she was no longer the one in charge. Malachi was master now, and, heaven save her, she needed this man. He was her lawful husband, and her whole being ached for what he alone could give her.

Her hands raked his hair, pulling him deeper, demanding more. His breath rasped as his hand skimmed her thigh. Then, as if sensing he had gone too far, he stiffened against her. She felt his resistance return, felt the pride and self-righteousness that would not let him cross the line he had drawn between them. She felt his loathing as, with a single rough gesture, he tore her away from him and set her firmly on the ground.

Anna swayed dizzily, the darkness surrounding her like a clammy blanket. Frog and cricket calls shrilled in her head, an irritating blur of sound. She looked up to find Malachi glaring down at her, his eyes as hard as flints.

"How many men have you kissed like that, Anna?" he said in a flat, cold voice. "And how much did they pay you for more?"

Chapter Five

The sting of Malachi's words was as sharp and raw as if he'd slashed her across the face with a razor.

Reeling with shock, Anna stared up at him. Her throat moved in an effort to form words, but no sound emerged from her mouth. She was choking on her own pain and rage. What if she were to tell him the truth about herself? Would he believe her, or would he simply hog-tie her like an animal and haul her off to the nearest lawman to claim the reward?

Malachi's eyes glittered with contempt beneath the jutting crags of his brows. "You haven't answered my question," he said, slurring the words as if he had just awakened from a deep sleep. His lips were still wet and swollen from their soul-searing kiss. "How much did they pay you, Anna? If I get desperate enough I may make you an offer—strictly business, you understand."

She struck him then. The slap resounded like the blow of an ax on a hickory log, stinging her hand as smartly as it stung his the side of his face. Malachi showed no more response than a granite pillar. He stood without moving, one restraining hand on the dog's neck, as Anna pushed furiously past him and fled back up the path.

The house would be enemy territory as well, she knew. But at least, for the children's sake, there would be a veneer of civility. Malachi would not say such terrible things in front of his son and daughter.

The lamplight glowed yellow through the hot blur of her tears. She stumbled onto the porch and bent briefly to unlace and remove her mud-caked boots. The aromas of beans, onions and coffee wafted through the open doorway, but Anna's stomach was a clenched knot. The very thought of eating made her feel ill.

She stepped into the kitchen, conscious of her blazing face, her wantonly bruised lips. Would Malachi's children guess what had happened when they saw her? Would they say anything?

Carrie glanced up from washing dishes. "Coffee's ready," she said, turning swiftly back to her task. "There's a cup and saucer on the table."

"Thank you, but I'm not feeling well," Anna murmured, keeping to the far side of the kitchen in hope that the girl would not notice her appearance. "If you'll point out my room, I'll just go on to bed."

"It's the one nearest to the fireplace." Josh spoke up from the table where he was hunched over a page of arithmetic problems, working them laboriously on his slate. "Carrie laid out one of Pa's clean nightshirts for you, since you don't appear to have brought along any clothes. Wherever you came from, you must be pretty hard up. But Pa won't mind that. He says he's not looking for a wife with money."

"My trunk is in the wagon." Anna would have laughed under happier circumstances. "Your father will be bringing it down tomorrow. But the nightshirt will do for now, thank you kindly." She slunk along the wall, wanting only to reach the bedroom before Malachi came into the house. Her spirits sank when Josh pushed his chair away from the table and stood up.

"I'll show you the way," he said. "You're a guest, and we have to be polite to you. That's what Pa said."

"He also said you were to finish your schoolwork before bedtime," Carrie put in sharply. "You've dawdled over it too long already."

"I'll only be a minute." Josh came bounding over to Anna wearing a friendly grin that drove a barb of guilt into her heart. The boy was her only ally in this place, she knew. But right now she would have gladly traded him for a bevy of backstabbing enemies.

"This way, ma'am." He ushered her toward a wide, hand-hewn pine door with iron hinges and a handle made from a section of curving tree root. The door swung open to reveal a simple, almost monkish room from which every trace of femininity had been stripped. The single high window was bare of curtains and shuttered against the night. The tall mirrored wardrobe was missing a door on one side and appeared to be empty. The massive double bed was made from skillfully joined pine logs which had been stripped of their bark and polished to the sheen and hue of wild honey. Someone had once lavished time and attention on that bed. Had it been Malachi?

The quilt that served as a coverlet was, in contrast, a dark piecing of squares cut from what looked to be old winter coats. It lay slightly askew on the bed, as if the person who'd laid it there had not cared enough to straighten it. Carrie, perhaps?

A long flannel nightshirt, stiff from washing and faded to the color of river mud, lay across the foot of the bed. At least it looked clean, as did the pewter pitcher and matching basin that sat on the washstand with a folded cloth beside it. Beside the basin sat the only touch of color in the room—a wilting bouquet of crimson wildflowers arranged in an empty bitters bottle.

"I picked them myself," Joshua said, "for you."

The cold barb of guilt twisted deeper into Anna's heart. Tears scalded her eyes. She blinked them swiftly away before the boy could see. Why had she come to this place, to stumble so ineptly into the lives of these people? She'd have been better off taking her chances with the bounty hunters!

"There's clean pump water in the pitcher so you can wash up," Joshua said. "If you need anything else, just call me. Pa won't be able to hear you, since he's sleeping outside. But I will. My room's just through that wall."

Anna swallowed the bitter lump in her throat. Why couldn't this love-hungry little boy have gotten the mother he needed? Someone warm and open and competent, instead of a jaded saloon singer on the run from the law? "Thank you," she said, choking slightly on the words. "I'll remember that."

"Joshua Stone, you get in here and finish your take-aways, or you know what Papa will say!" Carrie's strained, young voice called from the kitchen. Anna struggled to ignore a jab of pity. Malachi's daughter had too much responsibility for her tender age. A girl like Carrie needed fun and pretty dresses and the laughter of friends. She needed time to enjoy her growing-up years, instead of being shoved into adulthood as Anna herself had been. What would become of her if no one cared enough to ease her way?

"Joshua—" Carrie's voice carried an implied threat.

"Coming!" The boy scampered out of the room, leaving Anna to latch the door and sink wearily down on the edge of the bed. No, she admonished herself, she could not allow herself to get involved with these appealing youngsters. She could not allow herself to look at their father and wonder what he really needed in a woman. Tomorrow, or surely the day after, she would be gone from this miserable place. She could not afford to leave any part of herself behind—least of all her heart.

Aching with weariness, she stood up, stripped off her muddy gown and petticoat and let them drop in a sodden circle around her feet. Long thorn scratches and itchy red mosquito bites covered her arms. She wet the washcloth and, starting with her face and neck, began to scrub away the worst of the mess. Once, turning, she caught a glimpse of herself in the mirrored door of the wardrobe. The face of a wild-woman stared back at her, eyes laced with red and sunk into dark pools of exhaustion, hair plastered to her skull except for a few mud-stiffened locks that stood straight out from her head.

Anna jumped back with a startled gasp. Then, as she recognized herself, she broke into silent, half-hysterical laughter. What a mess she was! She'd probably scared Malachi Stone half to death when she'd kissed him. Well, so much the better!

Her hand still stung from the vehement slap she'd delivered to his face. Malachi had deserved that slap and more. If she could apologize, it would only be for not having hit him harder.

Anna shuddered, remembering those contemptuous eyes and the words that had sent her reeling. No, she could not leave this place too soon. Coming here had been just one more mistake in a life filled with mistakes. Another bad dream in a life filled with nightmares.

Gingerly she peeled her underclothes and stockings off her bruised body. Her feet, skin puckered from the dampness, were so sensitive that she winced when they came in contact with the plank floor.

Malachi's flannel nightshirt was rough against her bare skin, but Anna was too tired to care. She used the washcloth to sponge as much mud as she could from her hair. Then she blew out the lamp, crawled between the worn sheets and closed her eyes. Through the gathering fog of sleep, she heard the heavy tread of Malachi's boots in the kitchen and his deep voice speaking to the children. Then the darkness swirled around her and she sank gratefully into it.

The crow of a rooster woke Anna from a slumber so heavy that her memory of the night seemed no longer than a breath. She jerked awake, eyes wide-open, muscles tensed for flight. Only as she remembered where she was did she allow herself to sink back onto the pillow and ease into the morning.

The bedroom was dim, but bright sunlight filtering through a crack between the shutters told her the morning was well along. Where were Malachi and the children? Why hadn't anyone awakened her?

She sat up groggily, her hair spilling over the shoulders of Malachi's old nightshirt. The garment all but drowned her petite body, neck askew, sleeves hanging over her hands. Impatiently she pushed the cuffs up to her elbows and flung back the coverlet. Ready or not, it was time she got up and faced the day.

Her sore muscles screamed as she swung her legs over the side of the bed and stood up. So much for riding bareback astride a mule. Likely as not she'd be hobbling around like an old woman all day.

Grimacing, she groped for her clothes, only to discover that her dress and underthings were gone. Only a damp spot on the plank floor marked the spot where she'd left them. Someone, it appeared, had stolen into the room and gathered them up to be laundered. Carrie, Anna surmised, since she could not imagine either Malachi or the boy doing such a thing. It was an embarrassing act of kindness, proving as it did, her own utter uselessness. But the least she could do was go outside and express her thanks.

Steeling herself for the next encounter with Malachi, Anna squared her shoulders, padded stiffly through the empty kitchen, hobbled out onto the porch and stopped short, stunned by what she saw.

Nothing could have prepared her for the sight of the canyon in full daylight. Rocky walls rose upward on all sides to crest in towering buttes and pinnacles in shades of fawn, gray, mauve and terra cotta. Their size dwarfed the house to the proportion of a toy, the people and animals to the size of ants. Even the river was no more than a chocolate ribbon, trailing through the narrow lowland, cutting ever deeper on its slow journey into the depths of the earth.

High above, billowing white clouds drifted in a sky of pure turquoise. Their moving shadows cast a kaleidoscope of subtly changing color on the rocks—lavenders deepening to umber, browns brightening to gold. A pair of ravens, inky black etchings against the brightness, spiraled on updrafts of warm air.

A low growl jerked Anna's attention back to earth. Malachi's big wolf dog crouched in the dooryard a dozen paces away, its teeth bared and its ears laid flat against its massive head.

Anna's throat had gone dry, but she willed herself not to back away. The beast was tame, she reminded herself. She had seen Malachi scratching its ears. Last night she had panicked, but no common cur was going to make a fool of her a second time.

Looking into the wild, pale eyes, she reached to one side and picked up a stick of firewood from a stack on the porch. Not that she planned to use it as a weapon—Anna had a higher regard for animals than she did for most people. But she did want the dog to know that she was through being intimidated.

"Easy boy," she coaxed, stepping off the porch. "Let's make a truce. You don't growl at me, and I won't run when you come around. What do you say?"

She took a tentative step forward, the firewood held lightly at her side. "It's all right," she soothed. "I'm not asking for love. Just a bit of civility."

The dog lowered its head. A warning growl rumbled in its throat. Then, suddenly, it lunged, snapping and snarling with such fury that Anna dropped the firewood and staggered backward, stumbling against the edge of the porch.

"Doubtful! Shame on you!" Carrie came out of the willows carrying a basket of wet laundry. The dog broke off his attack and bounded to her side, romping like an overgrown pup.

"Please tell your dog I'm not a prowler," Anna said. "He still doesn't seem to know that."

"You shouldn't have threatened him." Carrie scowled down at the fallen chunk of wood. "Doubtful doesn't like being challenged."

"I wasn't threatening him last night." Anna struggled to her feet, hot-faced and irritated.

"But you were sneaking around in the dark. Papa told me all about it."

All? Anna wondered, deciding she wouldn't lay bets on that likelihood. "Where's your father now?" she asked, rubbing a bruised hip through the long nightshirt.

"Papa went up the road at first light to get the wagon." Carrie shifted the laundry basket to one hip. "He took Josh along to help with the mules—not that Josh is all that much help. But at least, without him around to pester me, I can get some work done." She adjusted the basket once more, then turned and strode around the corner of the house, the dog frisking ahead of her.

"Let me help you!" Anna burst out impulsively. She had planned to keep her distance from the children, but suddenly the last thing she wanted to do was sit idle until Malachi returned with the wagon.

The sharp rocks bruised her bare feet as she sprinted around the house. Catching up with Carrie, she snatched the basket from the girl's awkward grasp. "I'll take this," she said. "It's too heavy for you."

"I carry it all the time," Carrie retorted. "And I don't need any help."

"Maybe not, but I could use some company. Where's the clothesline?"

"Over there, between those two trees." Carrie pointed indifferently. "But you don't have to work. You're a guest."

"I know. But even as a guest, I like to pull my own weight." Anna flinched as her heel came down on the tip of a cactus spine. The dog had circled back to sniff her legs and growl.

"That's enough, Doubtful." Carrie spoke sharply and the dog veered away. "If he was going to bite you, he'd have done it by now," she said. "He's probably just curious."

Anna shifted the basket, which was so heavy. Too heavy for a girl as young as Carrie, she thought. "Why do you call him Doubtful?" she asked.

"Mama named him. When Papa brought him home as a scruffy little pup, she took one look and declared that it was doubtful he'd ever amount to anything. The name stuck."

"You must miss your mother," Anna said.

Carrie twisted one black pigtail, her clear, dark eyes staring at the ground. "I don't know why Papa thinks he has to find us a new mother," she said. "We manage just fine on our own."

Anna set the basket down next to the clothesline and picked up a set of Joshua's overalls. "I haven't seen you do anything but work since I got here," she said. "Don't you ever have any fun, Carrie?"

The girl gazed at her for an instant before she bent down, picked up a wet dishcloth and fastened it to the line with a wooden clothespin. Everything in the wash was tinted with the rusty brown of river water— lending new meaning to Joshua's earlier mention of "pump water." Water from the well was evidently too precious to be used for bathing and laundry.

Carrie reached for a dark cotton work shirt so large that it could only be Malachi's. Anna caught herself gazing at the shirt, imagining his rangy, muscular frame filling the body, the loose, soft collar, the frayed sleeves.

"Fun isn't everything." Carrie grasped the shirt's hem and shook out the creases, sprinkling water on the dry ground. "Work's more important, that's what Papa says. It takes all of us working, even Josh, to keep this place running as it ought to."

"But don't you have any friends?" Anna persisted. "Don't you ever go visiting or attend parties?"

"No parties around here. And even if there were, I wouldn't have the proper clothes to wear. But sometimes a family passing through on the ferry will stop for the night. Sometimes, if they have a girl near my age, we'll visit for a while, and later on maybe I'll even get a letter. I guess that's about as good as having friends."

"But don't you ever get away from this place? Not

even for a visit?'' Anna's gaze traced the girl's finely drawn profile. Yes, Carrie would be a ravishing beauty in a few years. Then heaven help her—and her father.

''We used to go to Kanab sometimes when Mama was alive. And once we even went to visit her family in New Mexico. But now Papa doesn't have time to take us much of anyplace. He needs to be here to run the ranch and the ferry.''

She lifted a small, brownish shirt out of the basket and began pinning it to the clothesline. The dog had stretched out on a patch of warm red sand. He lay with his nose on his paws, watching them.

Anna reached into the basket and came up with a large cotton union suit, still heavy with water. The garment was so faded and stained by river mud that there was no way to tell its original color, and so long that even when she grasped the shoulders and lifted her arms as high as she could, the legs trailed on the ground. A smile teased at her chapped lips. Wrong-headed, stubborn and irritating he might be, but by any woman's measure, Malachi Stone was a lot of man.

Beyond the high willows, where the river ran, she could see the tall poles, rigged with cables for securing the ferry in its path across the rushing Colorado. She imagined Malachi erecting the timbers, stringing the cable—the backbreaking work of it all.

''We're all right here, the three of us.'' Carrie took the heavy union suit from Anna, doubled it smartly at the waist and hung it over the clothesline. ''We manage fine, and we don't need a new mother to help us.''

"You do manage well." Anna squeezed the excess water out of the sleeves and legs, relieved that her own position had already been made clear. "But surely you don't plan to spend your life in this place. What's going to happen when you and your brother are grown?"

"Josh will go to college," Carrie said. "Papa's already saving the money for it. Me?" She shrugged. "Papa can't afford to send us both. But I'll get by. Anyway, as Mama used to say, it's no skin off your nose."

"True." Anna studied the girl's thin, work-worn hands. Her calico dress might once have been pretty, but now it was worn and mud-stained from too many washings in the river. Worse, the dress was so small that the cuffed sleeves ended halfway between Carrie's elbow and her bony wrists. No wonder Malachi had been so desperate to find a mother for his children. What a shame he hadn't had better luck.

Anna's own clothes lay at the bottom of the basket, brown and soggy from their baptism in the Colorado. To be sure, the girl would have given them a good scrubbing, but they would never be presentable again.

She sighed as she shook the wet creases out of her dress. The lavender voile had been the prettiest gown she owned, and she had worn it to impress Malachi on their first meeting. If only she'd known what lay ahead…

"I tried to get your things clean," Carrie said a bit defensively. "But they were pretty muddy to start with, and there's only so much you can do when you're out of soap. I tried making some soap last week from lye and drippings, the way Mama used to, but I couldn't find her recipe. All I did was make a mess.''

Anna draped the once lovely voile over the clothesline. The skirt was so tattered that even if the mud and the washing hadn't ruined it, the dress would have been unwearable. Likewise the petticoat, drawers and camisole. The corset would be mud-stained forever, but she would have to salvage it because it was all she had. "It's all right," Anna soothed. "I think I noticed a case of soap in your father's wagon. And since he'll also be bringing my trunk I'll have plenty of other clothes to wear."

Carrie turned away and began pinning up the ragged petticoat. "Might as well have them clean anyway," she said, then glanced back at Anna as if remembering her manners. "I'll bet you could use some breakfast. Soon as I gather the eggs, I'll go inside and fix you something."

"Please don't bother," Anna said quickly. "You have enough work without having to wait on me. I'll just go inside and rustle up something for myself, maybe some bread and jam."

The corners of Carrie's mouth twitched wryly. "We ran out of Mama's jam this spring. But there's bread and a little milk. Help yourself." She tossed Anna's drawers and corset over the line and secured them with the last of the pins. Then she gathered up the wash basket and strode off, clearly anxious to end what had become a strained conversation. The dog stood up and, with a baleful glance at Anna, followed his young mistress in the direction of the chicken coop.

Anna picked her way back to the house, avoiding

the rock chips and cactus spines that littered the door-yard. Everything in this place seemed to have sharp points and cutting edges, even the people.

The morning air shimmered with heat. Anna brushed back a lock of sweaty hair, feeling hot, dirty and plain miserable. She had no bathwater, no proper clothes, not even a brush to run through her tangled locks. Right now, she groused, if a bounty hunter were show up and offer her a warm bubble bath and a fresh gown in exchange for her freedom, she would bloody well be tempted to take him up on it!

Her discarded boots lay on the porch, dried, now, into grotesquely shriveled shapes. One of them looked as if the dog had chewed on the leather laces. Anna sighed, then gathered the boots up and whacked them against the side of the house to loosen the dried mud. She would be wise to take better care of them, she reminded herself. She had nothing else to wear on her feet.

In the kitchen she hesitated, then decided to clean herself up and put on her shoes before having break-fast. She couldn't do much about the baggy flannel nightshirt, but at least she could wash her face and get the tangles out of her hair. Carrie was bound to have a brush or comb she could borrow.

Josh had mentioned last night that his bedroom was next to her own. Carrie's, then, would be the third room, the one just off the kitchen, its door invitingly ajar. Hoping the girl wouldn't mind, Anna opened the door and stepped gingerly over the threshold.

Someone, at least, had tried to make the small, neat room look pretty. Sun-faded calico curtains hung at the window and the patchwork quilt that covered the bed was worn, but still colorful. A braided rag rug covered the bare planking between the dresser and the big pine chest that stood against the far wall.

Anna was glancing around for a hairbrush when she noticed the photograph—a small oval portrait in a silver frame whose fineness seemed out of place amid the room's shabby furnishings.

Drawn by curiosity, she picked up the frame and studied the face in the portrait—the wide, dark eyes, the abundantly curling ebony hair and pale, perfect oval face. No question as to who it was. Elise Stone had passed her striking features on to her children. Carrie would look a good deal like her one day.

Anna knew she should put the portrait down, find the hairbrush and leave. But something held her gaze to the high cheekbones, the elegant neck, the delicately arched brows and deep, compelling eyes. Malachi had loved this woman. He had courted her, wed her and brought her here, to this desolate place. She had given him a son and daughter. Now she was gone, claimed by the onrushing river.

And no one, Anna realized, could ever truly take her place. A second wife would mother Malachi's children, share his fortunes and, in time, even warm his bed. But no mere mortal could measure up to the memory of this haunting face. Malachi's wife, his true wife, was the most beautiful woman Anna had ever seen.

Chapter Six

Malachi arrived home late that afternoon, hot and muddy and in such a black mood that even the dog, after trotting out to meet him, slunk behind the house without so much as wagging its tail.

Damn the luck! Damn the dirty, rotten luck!

At the corral he swung off Beelzebub's back, unlooped the wire that secured the gate and waited for Josh to ride the other mule inside. "Get them some water and oats, son," he said. "I'll be in the house."

Carrie had come out onto the porch, her hands coated with flour. She stared, perplexed, at the two mules in the corral. "What happened, Papa?" she asked. "Where's the wagon?"

"Floating down the river in pieces, if it's not buried under twenty feet of landslide." Malachi stomped the mud off his boots. "The wagon's gone, along with everything in it."

"Oh, Papa!" Carrie's hands twisted a corner of her apron. Hell of a life he'd given the girl, Malachi thought. She was pretty and smart, and she was stuck at the end of nowhere working her fingers to the bone. Just like Elise.

"Where's Anna?" he said. "She'll need to know what happened to her trunk."

"She wandered off about an hour ago. Said something about finding a place to bathe so she could be clean when she got her good clothes back."

"The river's too muddy for bathing." Out of habit, Malachi lifted the lid on the pot of stew that simmered on the stove. It smelled good, but today he had no appetite. The wagon would be expensive and, unless there was one to be had in Kanab or on one of the ranches, ordering a new one could take weeks. The very prospect made him feel tired. And even that was pleasant compared to the thought of telling Anna what had happened to her trunk.

"What did she do all day, lie in bed?" he asked.

"Not really." Carrie rolled the biscuit dough out on the floured bread board, then set about cutting biscuits with the edge of a tin cup. "She helped me hang the wash, and she cleaned up the kitchen. Later on, when I needed wild onion for the stew she went out and found some for me. She's not too bad to have around—but maybe that's because she doesn't plan on staying." Carrie shot him a wary glance. "She *isn't* planning to stay is she?"

Malachi shook his head, then ran a hand through his dusty hair. "Did she tell you much about herself?"

"No, Papa. The little talking we did was about me."

"And you say she went to bathe?"

Carrie's long, nimble fingers arranged the biscuits

in a greased baking pan. "I told her the river was too muddy, but she said she'd manage. If you ask me, she's got a stubborn streak almost as wide as yours."

Malachi hesitated, sighed, then turned back toward the door. "Your brother hasn't eaten since noon," he said. "See that he's fed when he comes in."

Anna's trail wasn't hard to follow. Her little pointed boots left distinct prints that led down among the willows and emerged on the path where he had found her last night. The place brought back the memory of it with the force of a slap—her slap—which he had justly deserved. He had said things to her that no man should say to a woman. Any woman.

Why in hell's name had she kissed him? What had possessed her to do the one thing that would lay him open like an ax blow, exposing everything he had tried so hard to hide? Malachi thrust his hands into his pockets and began to walk, the line of delicate footprints drawing him on.

Where the water seeped into the sand, forming treacherous, sucking pools, she had taken off her boots and gone barefoot. He worried for a moment, then felt the lightness of relief at the sight of her wet tracks emerging on a long sand bar.

The river boiled between its banks, still thick and brown with runoff from the storm. Anna would not have tried to bathe here. But there were springs around the next bend, trickling down the cliffs that rose above the river. If she'd made it far enough to see them, that was the way she would go.

Malachi strode now along the path made by her narrow, almost childlike feet. Why was he following her? he lashed himself. The last thing he needed in his present state of mind was to catch a glimpse of Anna undressed. As for seeing to her safety... He cursed under his breath. Let the fool woman stumble off a cliff or get struck by a rattler. The way things stood right now, that seemed to be the only way he was going to get rid of her.

Ahead, and high to the right, he could see the ledges where crystal pure water wept down the coppery rock, leaving bluish-black streaks in its wake. Clumps of brilliant green foliage festooned the cliff-side like a hanging garden. Yes, the spot would draw Anna like a magnet. She would be somewhere nearby. If he had any sense he would sit down right here and wait for her, or, better yet, go back to the house and eat. Perversely, Malachi did neither. Anna's footprints led him like a golden strand from a siren's net, on a path he had no conscious wish to follow—a path to his own damnation.

The water was deliciously cold. Anna gasped as it soaked her hair and trickled in icy streamlets down her bare back. She willed herself to endure it. Cold didn't matter. Clean did.

She had no soap, of course. That would have been asking too much. But at least the water was clear of mud. And this hollow below the overhanging rocky ledges, lush with maidenhair fern and exquisite clumps of white-and-yellow flowers, was a miniature paradise amid the harshness of the canyon. As the mud and grime flowed away beneath her bare feet, Anna's spirits began to rise. Everything would be all right, she reminded herself. Before sundown Malachi would be back with her trunk. She could look forward to putting on decent clothes, pinning up her hair and looking like her old self again. Maybe then she could work on persuading him to give her the fare to California.

A little tune stirred in her throat. She began to hum. Then, because it felt so good, she began to sing.

> "Come all you fair and tender ladies,
> Be careful how you court young men,
> They're like a star of a summer's morning,
> They'll first appear, and then they're gone."

Malachi was mounting the long slope below the ledges when the sound of Anna's voice stopped him in his tracks. He stood transfixed for the space of a long breath, listening to the velvety timbre of her rich, husky voice, the way it played with words and melody, lingering on each note and syllable. Even he, with his unschooled ears, could tell this was no amateur performance he was hearing.

Who the devil was this woman?

At a slower pace now, he moved upward through the thick clumps of tamarisk, Anna's voice still floating in his ears. One thing was certain. If this woman was a whore, she was no ordinary whore. Nothing about her, in fact, was ordinary. But if she wasn't a prostitute, who—or what—could she be? What would a woman with Anna's looks and talent be doing at the bottom of the biggest hole in the country, married by proxy to a stranger?

The more Malachi thought about the answers to those questions, the less he liked them.

"I wish I was a little sparrow,
That I had wings, could fly so high,
I'd fly away to my false lover,
And when he's talkin' I'd be by."

Her voice was a seductive purr that stirred his
senses like the touch of silk on bare skin. Malachi felt
the honeyed heat of desire, felt his own arousal as he
imagined her standing naked among the ferns, water
trickling over her ivory breasts and down her belly....

The woman had lied from beginning to end, he
reminded himself harshly. She had lied to Stuart, she
had lied to him, and, given the chance, she would lie
to his children as well. But the time for lying was
over. He would get the truth if he had to shake it out
of her.

"If I'd a-known before I courted,
I never would have—"

"Anna!" Malachi's shout startled a flock of roost-
ing quail. They exploded from a mesquite thicket,
shattering the peaceful spell Anna's song had cast
over the canyon. "Blast it, what are you doing up
there?"

"What do you think I'm doing?" A small thread
of panic ran through her defiant answer. "Where are
you? You've no business coming up on me like
that!"

"At least I had the decency to yell," Malachi
snapped. "Get yourself dressed if you're not. We
need to talk."

He heard the light crunch of bare feet on gravel,

then the sound of her hands sluicing water from her body. Malachi struggled to ignore the sweet, forbidden images that swam in his mind. "Shake your boots good before you put them on," he said. "Scorpions and tarantulas like crawling into dark places."

He heard the whack of leather against stone. "Ha! No scorpions. Not even a baby one. You were just trying to scare me, weren't you?"

"No, just giving you a sensible warning. You're not in Salt Lake City anymore."

"You needn't remind me!" The feathery pink tamarisk branches stirred and she stepped into sight, wearing nothing but her boots and the old nightshirt that Carrie had found for her. It clung to her damp curves, just closely enough to reveal that she had nothing on underneath. Her wet hair lay flat against her elegant little head, and drops of water glittered like jewels on her face and throat. For the first time he noticed the pearl studs, gleaming like miniature moons against the golden skin of her earlobes—the sort of baubles a man with taste and money would give such a woman.

She stood glaring up at him, her chin thrust out in defiance. "Tell me you brought my trunk down and I'll be getting out of here soon," she said. "After last night, those are the only words I want to hear from you, Malachi Stone."

Malachi steeled himself like a man about to be shot. "Your trunk's gone," he said flatly. "The wagon with it. Carried away by the slide."

"What?" Her eyes widened in disbelief. "I don't believe you! This is just another one of your cruel jokes!"

"I didn't realize I was in the habit of playing jokes," he said. "Even so, I wouldn't do it now. Your things are gone, Anna. And you won't be leaving anytime soon. Not unless you want to ride into Kanab astride a mule, wearing nothing but that flannel nightshirt."

He saw her expression change, saw her features collapse as if she'd just been kicked in the stomach. Her body sagged, and for a moment Malachi expected her to faint, or at least burst into tears.

But Anna did neither. Malachi saw the anger simmering in her eyes, saw it heat and boil, giving off little amber sparks of rage. It was a damned good thing she didn't have a gun, he thought. She would blow a hole through his chest without so much as a flicker of regret.

"Just about everything I owned was in that trunk," she said, the words as cold and dead as a January dawn. "Last night, when we had to leave the wagon, I begged you to take it along. But no, you couldn't be bothered. You actually threatened to make me walk if I so much as—"

"Now wait just a minute, lady!" Malachi cut her off, his own temper rising. "If I'd taken the time to get your trunk off the wagon, the slide would have gotten us, too. Be grateful for small favors. At least you're alive!"

"And with little more than a pair of muddy boots to call my own!" The fury building in her was evident in her seething eyes, her rigid neck and her small, clenched fists. Malachi remembered the hot sting of her slap on his face. He was not about to let slapping him become one of her regular habits.

"Just simmer down!" He reached out and pinioned her arms against the sides of her body, holding her like a doll between his big hands. It was a move of self-protection, with no thought of tenderness or intimacy. All the same, as he held her, desire forked through Malachi's body with the force of a lightning bolt. That in itself was not surprising, given the thoughts he'd battled as she dressed. But the surge of tenderness that followed caught him completely off balance.

He found himself wanting to catch her in his arms and cradle her close, to stroke her with his hands and press his lips against the wet sleekness of her hair while he murmured little phrases of comfort. He wanted to take the wretched events of the past two days and force them to come out right. Against all reason, he wanted to protect her, to make her happy.

"Let me go!" Anna's words were breathy with suppressed rage. Her eyes were amber pools of fury. Malachi fought for his very soul as he held her at arm's length, reminding himself of the way this voluptuous little golden-haired angel had lied to him.

"Who are you, Anna?" he demanded.

"Why should it matter now?"

"It shouldn't—didn't, in fact. Not until I heard you singing. A voice like that wouldn't belong to a common whore."

"Oh? What about an uncommon whore, then?" Her sarcasm cut like a blade dipped in acid.

"Don't, Anna." He loosened his painful grip, but still did not let her go. "In the two days since we met, you and I have done each other enough hurt and damage to last halfway to doomsday. Don't you think it's time we declared a truce?''

"What do you want from me?" She glared up at him suspiciously.

"The truth." He let his arms drop to his side, releasing her. "Nothing more, nothing less. And you can start by telling me who you really are."

Anna faced him, her arms tingling where his powerful hands had gripped them so tightly. A ray of late-afternoon sunlight slanted across his light-brown hair, touching the unruly locks with subtle glints of red. His face was smudged with trail dust, his gray eyes bloodshot with weariness. Inexplicably she found herself wanting to reach up and smooth the sweaty hair back from his forehead, then to brush a tentative fingertip along the curve of his wind-burned lips. He was a good man, and so tired…

But that would be foolish, she reminded herself. Malachi had every reason to detest her. If she were to reach out to him, he would be quick to let her know it.

"I'm waiting," he said.

"Why should I waste my breath telling you things you wouldn't believe anyway?" Anna retorted.

His jaw tightened, and for a fleeting moment she thought he was going to be angry again. But then his breath eased out in a weary sigh.

"Walk with me," he said.

When Anna hesitated he took her arm. His touch was light, but forceful enough to convince her against arguing. Together they moved down the rocky slope, through tall clumps of pink-plumed tamarisk and silky spring willows. The sun hung low above the rim of the canyon, casting rainbow patterns of light and shadow on the towering walls. A mourning dove fluttered from the top of a mesquite bush, its wistful call echoing across the canyon.

They had nearly reached the river before Malachi spoke, breaking the silence between them.

"I want to apologize for what I said to you last night," he said. "I was tired, my guard was down— but that's beside the point. No man should speak to a woman like that."

"If you're waiting for me to apologize for the slap, don't hold your breath," Anna said coldly. "You deserved it."

"I understand." He stared at the river for a long moment before he spoke again. "Whatever you might say about my being straitlaced, I'm no saint, Anna. Growing up, I was as wild as any fool kid in the territory. When I was twenty, I spent a year in Yuma Prison for beating a banker's son half senseless in a bar fight. Came out of Yuma ten times worse than when I went in."

He lowered his powerful frame to the flat top of a boulder, eyes gazing out at the river. It didn't take a genius to figure out why he was telling her the story of his life. When he finished, it would be her turn, and Malachi would expect as much as he had given.

"Drinking, gambling, loose women—there was nothing along those lines I wasn't well acquainted with," he said. "I'd find a job herding cattle or busting broncs, and as soon as I got paid, I'd blow most of it on one big night in town. More often than not, I'd get myself fired when I didn't show up for work the next day. Things went on that way for a couple of years. Then, one night in Santa Fe, everything changed.''

Malachi's long, callused fingers picked up a pebble and tossed it into the river. Anna gazed at his craggy profile, trying to picture him as the worthless young drifter he'd described. Only one thing could change a man like that, and Anna knew what it was. Nothing in the rest of his story would come as a surprise to her.

''I'd ducked into a hymn-singing service to avoid a deputy I'd had words with earlier in the week. He'd threatened to lock me up if I came into town again. Anyway, I was sitting there by myself in a back pew, feeling like a fool, when, suddenly there she was.''

''Elise?''

''Elise.'' He spoke the name, Anna thought, like a worshiper invoking the holy virgin. She remembered the photograph in Carrie's room, the haunting eyes, the perfect, porcelain features. How could any man not fall in love with such a woman?

''Her father was the minister, and she was playing the organ,'' Malachi said. ''As soon as I set eyes on her, I knew I couldn't leave without at least knowing her name. I stayed until the service was over, and then—'' He broke off with a rough-edged laugh. ''But there's no point in telling you the whole story, is there? You're old enough to know how those things happen.''

Anna nodded when he glanced at her. She knew. Oh, she knew all too well. But that part of her life was buried, and she wasn't about to dig it up just to satisfy a man's curiosity. She kept her silence and allowed him to go on.

"There's no limit to what a young buck will do for love, and I did it for Elise. By the time we got married, I'd been sober—and celibate—for six months. Her parents still weren't happy about the match, but what could they say? I'd promised to reform, and I'd kept my word."

He fell into silence, and Anna waited, her gaze following the flight of a raven across the canyon. If some man had loved her enough to change, as Malachi had, her own life would have taken a far different turn. But she knew better than to brood on it. Brooding only opened old wounds and let them fester again.

Malachi's expression had darkened. He was staring at the river once more, not at her. "The only problem was, to most folks the change didn't make much difference. When a man's got a reputation as a rounder, it's hard to convince anyone to hire him at a decent wage. We'd have starved those first few years if her parents hadn't helped us."

Anna saw the familiar tightening of his jaw and she knew the shame still burned him. Once more, she battled the urge to reach out and touch him, to lay a hand on his shoulder, to move close and rub the tension out of the taut muscles that bulged beneath his shirt.

"When an old friend offered me a partnership in this ferry—with him putting up the cash and me doing the work—it was like an answer to a prayer, a chance to finally have something of my own. I left Elise with her parents for nearly a year while I bossed the road crew and built the ferry and the house from the ground up. Then I went back for her and the children—Josh had been born while I was away. A few months after that, my partner died and left me his share of the ferry operation. It's mine now—all I have.''

Anna sat still, letting the river's murmur flow through her senses. The water level had begun to drop, leaving a streak of wet, red sand along the bank. ''And was your wife happy here?'' she asked, thinking of the toll such isolation would take on a vibrant young woman.

Malachi tossed another pebble into the river. ''She managed fine,'' he said. ''We all did.''

He fell silent, and Anna knew he was waiting for her to begin her own story. For one long, aching moment she was tempted to tell him everything—to pour out the dark pain, the regrets of her lost years and the fear that had dogged her footsteps in the months since Harry's murder. She wanted to creep into the protective circle of his arms and lose herself there. To feel warm. To feel safe, if only for a fleeting moment.

But Anna knew such a thing could not be. Secrecy was her only protection. Take that away and she would be at his mercy.

He was waiting for her to speak. She could feel his gaze on her, burning through her tough facade, leaving her naked and defenseless. She had to counter now, while she was still able.

''I know this sounds crass,'' she began, ''but you didn't, by chance, save any of your wife's clothes, did you? I could really use something to wear.''

She felt his own defenses go up with suddenness of a slamming door. ''No,'' he said, ''there's nothing. As soon as I'm able, I'll ride one of the mules into town and pick up a dress for you. Until then you'll just have to make do with what you've got.''

"I've got *nothing!*" Yes, it was working. He was becoming so annoyed with her that, any moment now, he would get up and go storming back to the house. "My only dress is ruined! You can't expect me to walk around all day in *this!*" She tugged at the faded flannel nightshirt for dramatic effect. "I demand that you find me something decent to—"

"Pa!" Josh's urgent voice rang out along the riverbank. An instant later the boy burst into sight, out of breath from running.

"What is it?" Malachi had already sprung to his feet.

"There's somebody coming down the road, on two horses!" Josh panted. "Can't tell for sure, but it looks a lot like Eddie Johnson and his pa!"

Malachi muttered something under his breath, turned, and strode off toward the house. Anna stared after him, her pulse suddenly racing. For all the discomforts of this remote canyon, at least she had felt safe here. Now that precious sense of security had vanished.

She fought down rising waves of panic. Why hadn't it occurred to her that there would be visitors? Why hadn't she thought about it beforehand and planned what she would do?

Now it was too late.

Chapter Seven

Anna's stomach churned with apprehension as she rose to her feet, then hesitated, glancing upstream. Maybe she could find some rocky shelter and hide out until the unexpected guests were gone. Or maybe, if she could make it to the bedroom without being seen, she could crawl into the bed, burrow under the quilts and play sick for the duration of the visit. No, Anna decided swiftly, neither plan would work. She might succeed in keeping out of sight, but then she would have to answer to Malachi.

Still uncertain, she gazed at the river, her fingers twisting a loose button on the nightshirt. Judging from what she'd overheard the night before, Sam Johnson was neither a lawman nor a bounty hunter. Perhaps she had no reason to fear him. But there was no way to be sure. The fact that he was Malachi's friend didn't mean he hadn't seen the Wanted poster. It didn't mean he wouldn't turn her in for the reward money.

"Hey, come on!" Josh came bounding back along the trail, waving his straw hat. "We've got company—my friend Eddie and his pa! They'll want to meet you!"

"I'm not exactly dressed for company," she protested, hoping he would leave her alone.

"You look nice and slick, like a wet squirrel! Come on!"

Anna forced herself to follow him, her footsteps heavy with dread and dismay. Unless she wanted to throw herself into the river and drown, there was no way out of this mess. All she could do was hope she would not be recognized.

As they emerged from the willows, Josh seized her hand and tried to tug her forward. "Wait," she insisted, halting behind the house. "Give me a minute to catch my breath."

"You haven't been running."

"Hush." Anna pressed herself against the adobe wall and edged forward. Sam Johnson and his adolescent son were just dismounting from their mud-coated horses. Malachi had opened the corral gate and was leaning lightly against it, one boot resting on the lower rail. Only the twitch of a muscle in his cheek betrayed his unease.

"Had a helluva time getting the horses over that slide!" Sam Johnson had a ruddy, bearded face and a belly that hung over the waistband of his grease-stained pants. "That road's gonna take a heap o' clearin! And what's this I hear topside?" He belched out loud as he swung heavily off his horse. "Hell, man, word has it you've fetched yourself a wife! Bring the little woman out here! I want to meet the female who'd hitch up with the likes of you!"

He guffawed, then took off his hat and wiped his

sweaty face with the back of his sleeve. Where the hat had covered it, his scalp was the color of lard, the sparse hairs long and greasy. His son had come up behind him, a pimply lad whose bony wrists dangled a good eight inches below his cuffs.

"Come on!" Josh was pulling at Anna's hand, threatening to make a spectacle of her if she didn't comply—although she would be spectacle enough in any case, she reminded herself. Especially if Sam Johnson or his son had seen her face plastered on some telegraph pole.

As fear welled up like bile, she felt herself retreating into the playacting game. It was a game she'd invented in the orphanage and played often in the bleak years that followed.

The premise of the game was simple enough. All she had to do was pretend she was an elegant lady in a fine house and behave accordingly. It was a bit like wearing a disguise, and Anna had often used it to put off people who frightened her. She was frightened now. Badly frightened.

Gulping back her terror, she squared her shoulders, fixed a smile on her face, and strode out into the yard. Sam Johnson's jaw dropped as he took in her strange attire. Malachi's face was an expressionless mask.

"Well, Malachi, dear," she bubbled, "aren't you going to introduce me to your friends?"

Malachi flinched as if he'd been stung. "Mr. Samuel Johnson and Eddie," he muttered, gesturing awkwardly toward the pair. "This is Anna...my wife."

Anna forced herself to ignore Sam Johnson's leering eyes. She concentrated on her game, pretending the unkempt father and his shifty-eyed son were

landed gentry who'd ridden over to pay a call.
"We're honored, simply honored to have you visit
our home," she replied, smiling with such gracious-
ness that Malachi shot her a distrustful glance. She
was not fooling him, Anna knew, but it was too late
to retreat.

Flinging him a challenge to join her masquerade,
she crossed the distance between them and looped her
arm through his. "Malachi, dearest." She squeezed
his bicep and felt the muscle harden. "Would you
mind entertaining our guests while I check the
kitchen? Perhaps they'd like to wash or have a little
something to drink."

She released him and glided away without waiting
for a reply. Malachi probably thought she'd lost her
mind. Little did he know that this playacting was the
only thing standing between her and stark panic.

By the time she reached the porch, her legs were
jelly. If Sam Johnson had recognized her, he'd shown
no sign of it. All the same, she would not feel safe
again until he had gone.

The stew was still simmering on the stove, but Carrie was nowhere in sight. Anna's game did not extend
to casting the girl in the role of housemaid, but she
was grateful that the meal was nearly done and that
there was plenty to eat. Finding a set of chipped white
china dishes in the cupboard, she began setting six
places at the table. She had added knives and spoons
and was slicing the bread when Carrie walked out of
her room. Her face was damp from washing and she
had taken off the oversize apron she wore so much
of the time. The taut little nubs of her breasts strained
against the thin fabric of her too small dress.

The child was developing early, Anna noticed, re-membering all too well how it had been in the or-phanage when *she'd* begun to flower—the stares, the lewd jokes, the groping hands that waited for her in dark hallways; the sick, dirty feelings when things happened that she was too innocent to control. Look-ing at Malachi's daughter now, Anna felt a fierce pro-tective surge. She would do anything, she thought, to keep this tender girl from having to grow up too soon, as she had.

Carrie gazed at the table. "Oh," she said, "I could have done that."

"I had time to help," Anna said. "Besides, you made the stew."

"But you're a *guest*." Carrie emphasized the last word as if reassuring herself that Anna was, indeed, just a temporary member of the family.

"Even guests should do their share." Anna fin-ished slicing the bread and arranged the pieces on a blue-glazed platter. "Are the Johnsons close friends of your family?"

The girl shrugged. "Neighbors. I guess that sort of makes them friends. They've got a homestead a few miles north of the rim. When they come this far, it's usually because they're short on money. Papa's too generous to turn down anyone who's in need. But he'll make them work for what they get. That's his way."

"So, how long do they generally stay?" Anna asked, dreading the reply.

"That depends." Carrie toyed with straightening a fork that Anna had laid down too hastily.

"Depends on what?" Anna realized her nerves were screaming.

"Last time they were here, they stayed for two weeks. Came near to eating us out of house and home."

The silence that followed Carrie's revelation was broken by the scrape of boots on the porch. The door swung open and the men came tramping into the kitchen. Malachi brought up the rear, carrying a bundle wrapped in brown paper and twine. His gaze avoided Anna's eyes as he thrust it into her hands.

"Sam happened to mention that he'd been to town and picked up some clothes for Eddie—a pair of denim pants and a couple of work shirts. It struck me that the boy's clothes might fit you, so I talked Sam into selling them."

"At a nice profit, too!" Sam Johnson grinned, showing a wide gap where his two front teeth had been. "Ain't no limit to what a man'll do when he's cuckoo over a pretty little female! Right sorry about your regular duds ma'am, but you won't likely get 'em back. If they ain't buried under the slide, they'll like as not end up down the canyon on some Havasupai squaw!" He guffawed at his own joke. Anna, remembering the game she'd begun earlier, suppressed a groan, then forced herself to glance fondly up at Malachi and smile.

"Why, thank you, Malachi, dear," she cooed. "That's so thoughtful! It *will* be nice to have some clothes I can really work in."

Malachi's eyebrow twitched. Suspicion glittered in his granite eyes, all but shattering Anna's hard-won composure. Before he could speak and finish the job, she turned swiftly toward the boy.

"And Eddie!" she exclaimed. "How unselfish of you to give up your new clothes for me!"

"Can't say as I had much choice." Eddie fingered a ripe pustule on his left cheek, looking unhappy. The kindest response, Anna knew, would be to simply hand the bundle back to the boy, but that would discomfit both Sam and Malachi. And the truth was, she needed those clothes. She needed them even more than poor Eddie did.

She hesitated a moment. Then, remembering something Malachi had said, she loosened the string and slid a finger under the edge of the wrapping. The shirt she tugged loose was made of green-and-red checked cotton twill, stiff with newness. "Here," she said, thrusting it into the boy's hands. "There are two shirts, and I only need one."

"Thanks." He accepted the shirt mechanically, without any show of pleasure or gratitude.

"Eddie and his pa are going to help us clear the road!" Josh came bounding in from the porch, dodging the legs of his elders.

Anna fought back the urge to reach out and smooth back his unruly curls. "Did you wash?" she asked him, startled by the motherly tone of her own voice.

"Uh-huh. Pa made me." Josh slipped into his accustomed chair, his face wet and shining. "Boy, am I hungry!"

"You just ate an hour ago." Carrie ladled the thick stew onto the plates. The stringy-looking meat had a gamy aroma—venison, Anna surmised, not her favorite but far from the worst thing she'd eaten in her day. Carrie had put too much thickening in the gravy, causing the meat, carrots and potatoes to cling together in a gluey brown mass, but no one was picky enough to complain.

After a moment of grace, everyone fell to eating. Sam Johnson and his son picked up their bowls and used hunks of bread to push the thick stew into their open mouths. Malachi's children had obviously been taught better manners. They held their utensils properly, Carrie staring down at her food and taking bird-like nibbles, Josh eating too fast and jabbering between bites until a scowl from his father silenced him.

Malachi sat at the head of the table, eating slowly and saying little. Anna studied him furtively from her place at his right. He had washed his face at the pump and raked his damp hair back with his fingers. It lay against his leonine head, gleaming like wet bronze in the lamplight. A drop of water glistened like a tear on his sunburned cheek. It was not a real tear, of course. A man like Malachi would bury his tears so deeply that no one would ever see them.

But the tears would be there, Anna knew. Only now did it strike her what desperate hopes and dreams must have gone into his sending for a wife. She imagined the anticipation, the fears, the sleepless nights, the putting aside of precious funds to pay her expenses.

What a disappointment she must have been to him—a cheap little bundle of fluff with unskilled hands and dubious morals. What a fraud she was! And what a cruel thing she had done to this family!

Her gaze drifted downward to Malachi's hands—hands so large and strong that the spoon he was holding looked like a child's toy. His big, square nails were scrubbed clean except for the one on his left thumb, which was crushed and blue from some small accident he had not mentioned. Anna imagined picking up that hand, brushing the callused knuckles along the curve of her cheek and skimming the poor, ravaged nail with her lips, as softly as the brush of a feather....

"So what do you think of the canyon, Missus Stone?" Sam Johnson had finished the last morsels of stew and bread. "More to the point, what do you think of Malachi here now that you're wed?"

"The canyon is big," Anna replied quietly, "and so is Mr. Stone."

Sam stared at her, then chuckled. "I say, Malachi, you got yourself quite a prize there. And I'll wager she's as good lyin' down as settin' up!"

Silence fell over the table as Malachi glanced up from his meal. "That's enough, Sam." His voice had scarcely risen above a whisper, but its tone was as menacing as the snarl of a cougar. "When you're gone from here you can say whatever you please, but under my roof, you'll speak respectfully in front of my wife and children."

Sam's face paled for an instant. Then he grinned and licked a drop of gravy off his mustache. "Shucks, Malachi, I was only funnin'. Didn't mean no harm by it." His little pig eyes glittered as he turned toward Anna. "Right sorry, ma'am. No offense intended."

"Apology accepted," Anna murmured, hoping someone else would change the subject. The last thing she wanted was to call more attention to herself. Glancing around the table, she saw that Josh was taking in every word of the strained conversation, his eyes bright with interest. Carrie was staring intently at the bottom of her bowl, looking as if she wanted to sink into the floor. As for Eddie—

Something dark and ugly turned in the pit of Anna's stomach as she looked across the table. Eddie was leaning back in his chair, a slow grin playing around the corners of his mouth. Beneath half-lowered lids, his eyes were clearly fixed on Carrie's budding young breasts.

Anna lay awake in the darkness listening to the night sounds that drifted through the quiet house. She had cleaned up the kitchen while Josh and Carrie labored over their books, then sent the children off to slumber. Not long after that, she had crawled into bed herself. She was exhausted, but now her churning mind would not release her body to sleep.

Restlessly she turned onto her back and lay staring at a patch of moonlight on the whitewashed wall. From somewhere outside, she could hear the snort of a mule and the sharp cry of some small animal that had fallen pray to claws or fangs in the darkness.

Protective rage welled in Anna's body as she remembered the way Eddie had looked at Carrie across the supper table. She had weighed the wisdom of telling Malachi what she had seen, then decided against it. He had enough worries on his mind. But she would guard the girl, Anna resolved, and if the young lout so much as breathed on Carrie, she would have his hide.

Malachi had gone outside after supper and had not come back. Was he talking with Sam, telling him about his new wife's mysterious background and singing talent? Was he, with no ill intent, passing on the details that would put every lawman in the territory back on her trail? Anna turned over again and punched the pillow hard. What would she do if they came here looking for her? Where could she go? How could she get out of the canyon by herself?

As she pondered her dilemma she could almost feel the towering cliffs closing around her like a trap. Why had she come here? Surely she could have found other places, other ways to escape....

The creak of the kitchen door shattered her thoughts. Anna went rigid in the bed as all the old, well-honed instincts sprang to life. Fear shot through her body. Her muscles tensed as she forced herself to lie still. Then she heard the now familiar tread of heavy boots across the floor, and she realized that it was only Malachi.

Only Malachi.

For a moment she almost convinced herself that he had come inside to check on his sleeping children—indeed, his footsteps did pause at each of their doors, but only for the space of a breath. Those footsteps were coming closer now, slowing hesitantly as they neared her door.

Her pulse exploded as she heard the latch lift. Then the door swung quietly open and Malachi stepped into the room.

Anna lifted her face from the pillow. She could see him clearly in the moonlight that shone through the window on the far wall. He had removed his work shirt, but was still wearing his trousers and his long johns beneath. For a moment he slumped against the

wall, looking frustrated and tired. Then he straightened and cleared his throat.

"What do you think you're doing?" Anna raised
up on her forearms, taking the offensive before he
could speak. "You have no business sneaking in here
like that, scaring me half to—"

"Be quiet, Anna," he interrupted in a raw-edged
whisper. "Believe me, I've no intention of touching
you, let alone harming you."

"Then maybe you should tell me why you're
here," she challenged him, sitting straight up.

"Why the blazes do you think I'm here?"

Anna sat back on her heels, gazing at him in the
moonlit darkness of the bedroom. Her eyes traced the
shadows that fell across his chagrined face. Then, as
the answer suddenly came to her, she burst into giddy,
ironic laughter.

"Shhh!" Malachi hissed. "You'll wake up the
children!" Then, when Anna continued to laugh, he
added, "Anyway, I don't know what you think is so
damned funny."

"You are!" Anna hugged her ribs, struggling to
contain herself. "Sam Johnson doesn't know about
our sleeping arrangement, and you, bless your big,
manly heart, have too much pride to explain it to
him!"

"It's not a matter of pride!" Malachi growled.
"Anything Sam knows will be spread over half the
territory in a week's time. Whatever happens—or
doesn't happen—in this so-called marriage is between
us, Anna. It's nobody else's business."

Anna shook her head and wiped a mirthful tear
from the corner of her eye. Malachi, she realized was

at her mercy. If she were to make a fuss and send
him away, he would be humiliated to the core of his
manhood.

She remembered the things he had said to her the
night before. For the space of a breath she was
tempted to take her revenge—but no, even she could
not find it in her heart to be so mean-spirited. She sat
back in the bed and clasped her arms around her
knees. "Well, Malachi," she said, "at least you
might have knocked before you came stumbling in
here and scared me out of my wits."

He stared down at his shadow on the floor, then
met her gaze again. "I was hoping you'd be asleep,"
he said. "That way I could've just stretched out on
the rug and slept until first light—which is still what
I intend to do, if you'll be quiet and leave me in
peace."

Without waiting for her response, he lowered his
lanky frame to the braided rug that lay alongside the
bed. Anna heard the scrape of his boot heels against
the floor as he stretched out to his full length and
settled into silence.

She burrowed into the quilts once more and laid
her head on the pillow, but it was no use trying to
sleep. If anything, she was even more agitated than
before. Malachi had made it clear that he didn't want
to be disturbed, but his presence was no easier to
ignore than if a great bull buffalo had wandered into
her room and lay down beside her bed.

"Malachi?" she whispered into the darkness.

"What?"

"How long are Sam and his boy going to be
here?"

She heard him sigh as he turned over, trying to accommodate his broad shoulders to the hard floor. "Depends on how long it takes us to clear the wagon road. Four or five days by my reckoning."

"And then?"

"Then I'll take the mules to Kanab, buy a wagon or order one, if there's none to be had." His belt buckle scraped through the rug as he turned over again, stoically trying to get comfortable. Anna stared at the moon shadows on the ceiling, her mind weighing the thing that lay between them, the thing Malachi had not mentioned. When the road was open and the wagon procured, she would be leaving his world for good. Their brief sham marriage would be over. Finished.

He was lying still now, frustration and discomfort evident in every labored breath. He had not asked for a blanket or a pillow. It was going to be a long, miserable night.

"Malachi?" Anna could feel her heart pounding as she spoke.

"What now?"

"This is a very big bed."

He groaned. "Are you out of your mind, Anna?"

The sharpness in his tone hurt her. "I think your virtue would be safe if you were to lie down on top of the covers," she retorted, hiding the sting. "Of course, I'm not strong enough to force you...."

She heard a muttered curse and, a moment later, he stood up, looming over the bed. "Is this part of the little wifely act you were putting on earlier?" he asked.

"No." Anna sighed wearily and shifted to the far

side of the bed, smoothing the covers for him. "It's just simple practicality. With you down there suffering on the hard floor, neither one of us is going to get any sleep. Now take off your muddy boots and lie down before I change my mind and throw you out of here!"

The bed creaked beneath his weight as he sat down on a corner of the mattress and tugged off his work boots, being careful not to drop them and make a noise that would alert his children. That done, he stood up and unfastened his belt, then hesitated.

"Don't worry, you're not going to shock me," Anna said. "I'm no stranger to men's underclothes."

"Don't remind me." He dropped his trousers and stepped out of them. The faded union suit beneath was buttoned and revealed little more than the outline of the muscular body beneath.

Without another word he lay down on top of the quilt. The night air was cool, but if he felt it he did not complain.

Turning onto her back, Anna aligned herself with the far edge of the bed, pulled the quilt up to her chin, closed her eyes and willed sleep to come. But, if anything, she was even more restless than before. The masculine aroma of Malachi's body invaded her senses, awakening a myriad of sensation—tugs and tingles she had no right to feel. She battled the urge to move closer, to curl against his side and lose herself in his protective warmth. Maybe then she would feel safe enough to sleep.

But Malachi would not welcome her touch, she knew. This bed was a shrine. He had shared it with the beautiful Elise, made love to her between these very sheets. He was probably thinking about her now, wishing she was the one beside him.

It was a good thing she was leaving soon, Anna lashed herself. No new wife could hope to replace Elise in Malachi's heart, let alone in his bed.

And heaven help any woman who let herself fall in love with him!

What had Elise been like, to make a man love her so much? Anna thought of asking, but Malachi's breathing had already fallen into the steady cadence of slumber. And, incredibly, she could feel herself slipping away as well, spiraling outward and downward into darkness.

This had been a bad idea. A very bad idea. Malachi lay with his eyes closed, feigning sleep and struggling to ignore the hot bolts of desire that forked through his vitals like chain lightning, raising a spar that thrust against the crotch of his long johns. He could only be grateful that Anna wasn't awake to see his condition. It would not be like her to blush, avert her eyes and hold her tongue.

With a silent curse, he eased onto his belly, burying the beacon of lust against the quilt. Beside him, Anna slumbered like a baby, the rhythmic little wheeze of her breath giving evidence that she wasn't playing possum. Good thing. If she'd had any idea how much he wanted her, she would probably beat him senseless with the pitcher on the washstand. This was a brand-new definition of *hell,* Malachi reflected—being married to a beautiful woman he had given his word not to touch.

The night air was chilly through the back vent of

his long johns. Malachi felt a prickly wave of goose bumps creep over his skin. Tomorrow would be a hard day and he needed rest. But he was, he realized, too damn-blasted cold to sleep.

With a sigh, he rolled off the bed and stood looking down at Anna. She lay sound asleep, her hair a spill of tawny silk across the pillow. He ached to gather her in his arms and love her. But it would not happen. He would not violate her trust. And he would not risk the calamity of sending her away with his child in her body.

It would be all right, he assured himself as he folded back the covers and slipped between the worn flannel sheets. His loins might be throbbing with need, but he was a rational man. His mind was in full control of his actions.

The bed was deliciously warm. Malachi eased onto his back, steeling his senses against Anna's fragrant, silken warmth. It seemed strange lying next to a woman again—especially a woman who was nothing like Elise. But it was not a bad strangeness. Not at all.

Anna stirred, whimpered, then curled onto her side like a contented cat. Her warm little buttocks pushed across the bed to nestle against Malachi's flank. The sweetness of that simple contact almost brought tears to his eyes. He lay there in the darkness, afraid to move, fearful that he would awaken her, ending the bliss of having her so close.

Would she stay? he wondered sleepily. After all that had happened between them, could he think of asking her?

Malachi was still turning the question over in his mind when he drifted into sleep.

Chapter Eight

The narrow corridor was so dark that Anna could barely see her way. She drifted like a swimmer between walls of black stone, her feet just skimming the rough slate floor. All around her, she felt the cold, leaden presence of fear. Her instincts shrilled that she should turn around and go back, but she knew that she could not. There was something at the end of the dark passageway. Something she had to find.

She forced herself forward, faster and faster, but the end of the passageway was no nearer than before. It twisted and turned, branching off one way, then another, into labyrinths of darkness.

The wind was cold on her face. It moaned through the narrow space, the sound echoing off the walls like the cry of a child in pain. Anna rushed on through the terrible maze, drawn by that cry—a cry that tore its way into her heart.

The blackness deepened. The walls of the corridor narrowed and shrank, the ceiling becoming so low that she had to crawl on her hands and knees. She clawed her way toward the cry, feeling it quiver in-

side her, filling her ears, her body. Far ahead, she could see a ghostly light—a chamber, carved into the end of the passageway. Anna's pulse raced as she clambered forward, the cry clear and close. And now she could see that the only object in the chamber was a small wooden cradle.

At last...

The room opened above her and she struggled to her feet. Only then did Anna realize that the crying had stopped. She was looking down, not into a cradle but into a tiny pine coffin. Inside, a doll-like figure lay deathly still, ice-gray in its muslin shroud....

Malachi awoke to the sound of weeping—not just petulant female tears, but racking sobs, so heartfelt that they seemed torn from the very depths of grief. As he came fully awake, he realized that Anna lay huddled against his back her body jerking with anguish.

"Anna—" He rolled over and, not knowing what else to do, gathered her into his arms. She clung to his chest, her face wet, her ribs heaving.

"Anna, it's all right. You're safe." He cradled her close, rocking her as he might rock a crying child. She was so small and warm, so frightened. "Wake up, woman," he murmured. "You're having a bad dream, that's all." He pulled her closer, feeling the hourglass curves of her body beneath the threadbare flannel. Her arms slid around his neck, gripping him as if she were drowning in the depths and he was her only anchor to life.

"Anna..." His lips brushed her damp hairline, her closed, quivering eyelids. His throat tightened as he felt her satiny legs tangling with his own and the fullness of her firm breasts, the nipples ruby hard against his chest. "Anna, don't, we mustn't..."

But it was the feeblest of protests. His body was burning with need, the pressure in his loins sweet and hot, all but unbearable.

"Malachi—" Her choked utterance of his name went through him with a poignant jolt. "Hold me," she whispered. "Please hold me. I'm so cold...."

He kissed her wet mouth, tasting the salt of her tears. Caution shrilled that he should stop, at least long enough to find out what was wrong. But the hunger in him was a forest fire blazing out of control. His hands slid upward, over her taut little buttocks and along the smooth curve of her back, pushing away the crude flannel until he found his fingers brushing naked skin.

Anna moaned low in her throat. Her fingers raked his hair as he kissed her salty mouth and throat, blazing a trail downward until he was nuzzling the soft, white flesh of her breasts. Her nipples were like summer raspberries, sweet and firm. He slid one into his mouth, his tongue stroking and circling the puckered tip until she whimpered with need. Her hands pressed his head in against her as he sucked. Her hips writhed and twisted against the tingling ache of his arousal, setting off rocket bursts of sensation. Was he awake or dreaming? Was this woman really his wife? Did he care?

"Anna...oh, Anna..." His hand moved between her thighs and slid upward to brush the crisp golden nest that lay at their apex. She gasped as he touched

her, then pressed herself eagerly into the cup of his
fingers—so moist, so warm—

At that instant all pandemonium broke loose.

The wild cacophony of barks, yowls and screeches
came from the far end of the yard. Malachi was out
of bed like a shot. "Damned bobcat," he muttered
by way of explanation to the startled Anna. "After
the hens again."

He jerked on his boots and, not bothering with trousers or apologies, bolted out of the house.

Anna sprawled across the rumpled bed, stunned by
what had nearly happened. Her nightshirt lay open in
front, its long tails rucked around her ribs, exposing
everything but her arms. As she jerked the flannel
across her bare body she could hear Malachi's furious
shouts from the yard, interspersed with the sounds of
barking.

What had she done—or nearly done? She remembered the awful blackness of the dream, the terrible
certainty of what she had known in her heart all
along. She remembered her despair, the explosion of
grief and then the tender comfort of Malachi's arms.
She had needed him—wanted him, ached to feel his
hands on her skin, his powerful thrust filling her, his
love healing her, making her whole at last.

Dear heaven, what had possessed her?

As she lay still, struggling to understand her own
mind, she heard a whimper from Josh's room. The
uproar in the yard must have awakened the boy. He
could be frightened and needing comfort.

Fumbling with the buttons on her nightshirt, she
swung her legs over the side of the bed and pushed

herself to her feet. The core of her body still ached
and quivered, but her head, at least, was beginning to
clear. For that, she had a marauding bobcat to thank.
She could only hope the blessed beast had made a
clean getaway.

Josh was sitting up in bed, rubbing his eyes and
whimpering softly. Anna sank onto the edge of his
bed and, acting on instinct, gathered the boy into her
arms.

He clung to her, his curls soft and damp against
her cheek. "What—was all that—noise?" he asked,
hiccuping between the words. "It scared me. I want
my pa."

"Shhh," Anna soothed, her fingers massaging the
small, trembling back. "Your pa said there was a bobcat after the hens. He went outside to scare it off."

The boy fell silent. Anna could almost feel him
thinking, pondering what he'd just heard. "Was Pa
sleeping in the house?"

"Yes." She felt the sharp rise of color in her
cheeks.

"With you?"

"Yes."

"Oh." He settled against her with a little sigh. "I
was dreaming about my ma," he said.

Anna felt her heart contract. "Was it a good
dream?" she asked softly, and felt his head nod
against her breast.

"She was in heaven," he said, "and she was smiling at me."

Anna brushed her lips over a curl of dark hair that
spilled onto his forehead, thinking how difficult it was
not to love this little boy. "Tell me about your

mother," she said. "I saw her picture. She was very pretty, wasn't she?"

"Uh-huh." Josh yawned and snuggled closer. "She used to sing to us and dance with Pa. She taught us to read, too, and made us practice sums and take-aways."

"You miss her a lot, don't you?"

"Uh-huh."

"And I'll bet your pa misses her, too, doesn't he?"

Malachi's son did not respond. He had fallen asleep with his head nestled against Anna's shoulder.

Very gently she lowered him to the pillow. He was beautiful in the moonlight—as beautiful as his mother must have been. Anna tucked the quilt around him, then rose to her feet and, lingering a moment, gazed down at his sleeping face.

What would it be like to tuck in a child of her own? she wondered, then swiftly dismissed the question. A family was not in the cards for her, not now, not ever. She was a hunted woman. She had to be free to run at a moment's notice, to change her name and alter her appearance, to lie, to cheat, to do whatever it took to go on living.

As she stole out of the room, closing the door behind her, the memory of her dream, still raw, closed around her like the grip of an icy hand. She felt the leaden weight of it, the awful, cold blackness of grief.

The bed would be warm, but she knew she would find no comfort under the quilts where Malachi had once made love to his beautiful wife. She had no right to any part of that bed, or to Malachi's love.

Wearily she filled the coffeepot, put it on the stove and added a few kindling sticks to the embers beneath. Then she sank down next to the table, where the children's books and slates still lay, and buried her face in her hands.

Malachi used the dog to track the bobcat into the brush, but the trail ended where the crafty beast had leaped into the rocks. A quick inspection of the chicken coop revealed a broken board and a missing hen—one of the good layers he'd bought at a neighboring ranch.

He walked slowly across the yard, rubbing the back of his neck and feeling as cross as a wounded bear. If the cat came back, and it would, he'd have no choice except to set a trap for it. Elise had hated traps, and he wasn't all that fond of them himself. But there was nothing else to be done. His family needed the hens and the precious eggs they laid.

In the east, the sky above the canyon had paled to the steely hue of a shotgun barrel. In an hour it would be light enough to wake Sam and his boy, grab some breakfast and head back up the trail to the slide. No use going back to bed—especially when all the temptations of purgatory lay between those soft flannel sheets.

It wouldn't have been a smart thing, making love to Anna. He knew that now, with his ardor cooled to a low simmer. She was the wrong kind of woman for him and for his children. Even now, his mouth went dry with need at the thought of having her. But no, a taste of paradise wasn't worth a lifetime of regret.

He stood gazing up at the fading stars, pondering what to do next. The wisest course would be to avoid the house altogether. Unfortunately, he had left his pants on the bedroom floor. He had no choice except to go inside and get them. Malachi sighed and turned toward the house. Maybe Anna would be asleep. Maybe he wouldn't have to face her.

The dog trailed behind him as he mounted the porch. He reached down and scratched the massive head. "Don't worry, old boy, we'll get that cat next time," he murmured. Doubtful growled agreeably, turned around twice and settled onto the muddy rug as Malachi opened the door.

The aroma of fresh, hot coffee filled the kitchen. Anna was sitting at the table in the semidarkness, a lock of pale-gold hair tumbling over her face. Her hands cradled a white china mug. She looked tired, he thought, and sad.

When she did not speak, Malachi poured himself some coffee and took a seat across the table. "Are you all right?" he asked.

She hesitated, then shook her head.

"Should I apologize again?" he asked, knowing the words would stick in his throat. Holding her in his arms was something he would never truly regret. More to the point, what had happened in the bedroom had been as much her doing as his, and she had no right to pout and cast blame.

He was about to tell her as much when she shook her head again. Her eyes, red-lined from weeping, stared into the steaming cup.

"The dream, then?" he asked, less harshly than before.

Anna exhaled raggedly. When she looked up at him, pain was etched in every line of her beautiful face. "I never knew my father and barely remember my mother,'' she said. ''I was raised in an orphanage, an evil place. To be a young girl there—''

She lowered her gaze. A shudder passed through her body. Malachi half rose, seized by the urge to go to her side and comfort her. Then she looked up at him again, her eyes so cold that he sank back onto his chair.

''The girls were preyed upon by the men who worked there—and by the older boys. One day when I was fifteen, a gang of them caught me in a dark hallway....'' Her voice wavered and nearly broke.

''Anna, you don't need to—''

''No. I have to finish this. I've never told this story to anyone. Maybe if I do, the truth will be easier for me to live with.'' She laced her fingers around the cup and closed her eyes for a long moment, inhaling the redolent steam. Malachi waited, feeling the dark weight of what he was about to hear.

''When the matron discovered I was with child, she called me a wicked girl and locked me in an attic room. I stayed there the whole time, eating the bread and gruel she sent up and doing huge baskets of sewing. I became very good at sewing.'' Her gaze flickered away, then came to rest on Malachi again.

''All those months alone, with no company except my baby—you might think it strange, Malachi, but I grew to love that poor, innocent little mite as I'd never loved anything in my life. It was mine—all mine, all I had. I would sing to it while I sewed and tell it little stories about what the world was like. Silly little stories—'' Anna closed her eyes, the memory passing like a shadow across her face.

''When my time came, the matron sent for the midwife, an old witch of a woman. It was a painful birth, I was so young and so small.'' A sad little smile flickered around the corners of her mouth. ''But all women have pain, don't they? I was no different. But I tell you, I wanted that baby. I wanted to raise it, make a home for it somehow.''

Her throat worked convulsively and Malachi thought she might break at last, but her jaw tightened determinedly, and she continued.

''They'd given me laudanum—I was barely awake when the baby came. But I heard it cry. A strong, healthy cry, and I heard someone say it was a girl. Then the women took it away and told me to sleep. When I woke up—'' Anna stifled a little choking sound ''—they told me the baby had died. I begged them to let me see it, but they refused.''

Anna tossed the loose hair back from her face. Her hands shifted restlessly sloshing a few drops of coffee onto the open page of Josh's arithmetic book.

''As soon as I was strong enough to walk, I ran away from that place,'' she said. ''And I've made my own way in the world ever since. I started by hiring myself out as a seamstress. Then, as I came of age, I discovered I could make more money singing—and not in churches or concert halls.'' Her eyes glared into Malachi's across the table. ''I'm not a whore, Malachi Stone. But I sing in saloons. And if the atmosphere of the places where I've earned an honest living has rubbed off on me, I'm not going to apologize to anybody!''

Malachi studied her across the table, struck by the courage that blazed in that small, voluptuous body. Her hair hung in damp strings around her tear-streaked face. Her eyes were bloodshot. She looked awful, he conceded. But what a feisty little figure of a woman.

"And the dream?" he asked, remembering after a moment.

She seemed to wilt a little. Her throat rippled as she swallowed a mouthful of coffee. "For years I pretended that those women in the orphanage had lied to me," she said. "I pretended my baby had been given away to some fine family, that she was growing up somewhere, safe and happy. But deep down I knew better." She stood up and walked to the window, where the sky was just beginning to pale above the towering ledges. "I saw my baby in the dream, Malachi. She was lying there dead—just as I've always known she was. Those evil old witches killed her."

Malachi sat holding his coffee cup, stunned and sickened by what he had heard. His gaze traced the rigid line of Anna's back, only to lose itself in the wild mass of tawny hair that tumbled over her shoulders. At that moment he wanted nothing more than to walk up behind her, slide his hands around her waist and hold her against him, comforting her in the circle of his arms. He wanted to protect her, to shield her from the forces that had so scarred her young life.

He was about to move when a rooster crowed outside and the first beam of sunlight slanted through the window. Anna turned back toward him, her face a serene mask. "Isn't it time we were starting the day?" she asked with forced cheerfulness. "Go put your pants on, Malachi. I'll wake your children and start breakfast."

* * *

Had she told him too much?

That question haunted Anna as she went about the morning chores, doing her best to take some burden off Carrie's young shoulders. Early that morning she had watched as Malachi rode up the trail on the lead mule with Joshua clinging on behind him. Her worried gaze had followed him until he disappeared around the first bend.

What would the men talk about as they labored to clear the slide? Would Malachi tell Sam that his new wife had been a saloon singer, thus setting up one more link to the wanted Anna de Carlo? Would he tell Sam the story about her baby—the story that had laid her soul bare to him that very morning? There was nothing to prevent him from doing so, Anna realized, her spirits darkening. The very thought of her private agony being bandied about like a joke made her stomach clench.

Why had she lowered her guard with Malachi? Why had she opened herself and her poor baby up to gossip and ridicule? What had made her think she could trust him? He was a man, no better or worse than any other.

Forcing the worries from her mind, Anna picked up the egg basket and strode across the yard toward the chicken coop. The pants and green plaid cotton shirt that Malachi had bought off Eddie Johnson fit her remarkably well, and she was pleasantly surprised at the freedom of movement the new clothes gave her. She had brushed back her hair and tied it with a faded bandanna she'd found in one of the drawers. Not exactly elegant. But it was far better than flapping around in Malachi's old flannel nightshirt.

Most of the hens, she noticed, were outside foraging. There would be little danger of getting pecked—something that had happened often when she'd gathered eggs at the orphanage. Pushing that memory aside, she ducked into the coop and began reaching into the nests, slipping each warm, brown egg into the wire basket. One big red-speckled hen was brooding a clutch of a dozen eggs. Anna left her in peace, knowing those eggs were meant for hatching.

By the time she had checked the last nest, there were eleven eggs in the basket. Eleven eggs for two hungry men, two children and a near-grown boy who would probably eat more than all the rest of them combined. She would be wise to mix up a fresh batch of bread when she got back to the kitchen, and maybe have Carrie check the root cellar for more potatoes.

Before leaving, Anna paused to scan the shadows for any nests she might have missed. There in the darkness, the sudden memory of last night washed over her in a flood of sensation—Malachi's body, iron hard beneath the worn underclothes, his rough, hungry mouth on her breasts, the urgent pressure of his hand between her thighs... Her knees melted as she considered what had nearly happened, and where it might lead if he came to her bed again tonight.

Would she have the will to resist him, or would she make a complete fool of herself, as she seemed to do whenever Malachi touched her? It was a question she could not even afford to ask. Not when the last thing she wanted was to bind herself to this man, these children, and this isolated place.

Pushing her concerns aside, she glanced around the coop one last time. Only then did she hear the throaty growl behind her. Anna's heart dropped as she turned and saw the big wolf-dog crouched in the doorway, its black-lipped muzzle drawn back to show gleaming, yellow fangs.

Fear congealed in the pit of her stomach as her predicament sank home. She moved the basket in front of her, though it offered scant protection. If the beast chose to attack her, she would be at its mercy.

"Hey, Doubtful," she said, speaking softly. "It's all right, boy. I know you think I'm stealing eggs, but you're wrong. I'm doing my job, just as you are." She gripped basket so hard that the wire handle dug into the flesh of her fingers. When she edged forward, the dog's lip curled in response.

"It's all right," she murmured again. "Run along, Doubtful, and catch that bobcat. He's the real thief, not me."

The dog snarled and lunged toward her—only a threat, but the suddenness of it startled Anna and sent her stumbling backward. Her foot came down on a round stick that was lying on the floor. The basket went flying as she lost her balance and toppled backward to land hard on her rump.

Her eyes were level with the dog's now, and as she stared into the gold-flecked orbs, Anna felt her courage shrink and wither. The beast could kill her if it chose to. She would end her hard-fought life right here. Hours from now, perhaps, someone would find her sprawled on the floor of the coop, her throat ripped open, her blood mingling with earth and chicken droppings.

As the dog growled again, her groping hand closed on the stick that had made her stumble. It was thick and solid, of a size that Josh might have used for a stick horse or a pretend rifle. She lifted it and swung it toward her tormentor.

Doubtful was intelligent enough to recognize a weapon when he saw one. He sprang back out of reach and began to bark furiously.

The explosion of sound echoed off the canyon walls, startling the chickens and sending a flock of crows into squawking flight. Amid the bedlam, Anna could hear Carrie's voice shouting across the yard.

"Doubtful? What is it, boy? Have you caught the bobcat?"

An instant later she burst into sight, her willowy young body framed by the open doorway. Her face fell as she saw Anna sprawled on the ground, surrounded by broken eggs and chicken litter.

"Doubtful! Shame on you!" she scolded. "Go on, get out of here!" The dog lowered his tail and slunk around the corner of the coop. Anna scrambled sheepishly to her feet, dismayed at the sight of so many broken eggs.

"Guess it'll be biscuits and gravy for breakfast tomorrow morning," Carrie said. "Did Doubtful hurt you?"

Anna shook her head. "He was just trying to do his job," she said, brushing dried chicken manure off the seat of her pants. "Your mother knew what she was talking about when she named that beast. I've got my own doubts about his worth."

"Oh, but my mother changed her mind later on." Carrie bent to pick up the basket and retrieve the two eggs that were still unbroken, wiping them carefully on her apron. "She and Doubtful became the best of friends. He followed her almost everywhere."

Anna sighed, beginning to understand. "So he was *her* dog?"

"As much as he was anyone's dog." Carrie checked the nests for any eggs Anna might have missed. Unfortunately there were none. "For the first few weeks after she died, he used to howl at night," she said. "But he stopped after a while. I suppose he's forgotten about her by now. Papa says animals are like that."

"But not people." Anna trailed her out of the coop, keeping pace with the girl's coltish strides. "Not you or Josh or your father."

"No," Carrie said in a taut little voice. "We all needed her, especially Papa. She was the love of his life, and I don't suppose he'll ever get over her."

Of course not. Anna ignored a jab of dismay. She would be wise to close the subject and walk away, she knew. But she had to understand what had happened here—had to understand how it had affected Malachi and his children.

"Where's your mother buried?" she asked. "I don't recall seeing a grave."

Carrie hesitated. "There's…not one. I mean, there used to be a grave, but not anymore." A nervous little laugh caught in her throat. "I guess I should explain—"

Even now Anna was tempted to spare the girl. But something in her needed to know more about what had happened. She held her tongue.

"Mama disappeared while Papa was away," Carrie

said. "When he came home, he took the dory down-river with Doubtful to help him search. A few hours later he came back with her body wrapped in a piece of canvas. I...remember wanting to see her, but he wouldn't let me. He nailed some boards together to make a coffin, and we buried her up there." Her gaze drifted to a low bluff that overlooked the ranch and the ferry. "There's a stone up there that Papa carved her name on. But she isn't there, not anymore."

"You're saying she's in heaven?"

"No." Carrie scuffed at the ground with the toe of one worn-out boot. "I mean, that's not what I'm talking about. Two months after Mama died, her parents came with a couple of workmen. They dug up Mama's coffin, put it on a wagon and took it back to Santa Fe. They said they wanted to bury her with her people, in the graveyard next to their church.

"And your father just let them take her?" Anna asked, her throat dry.

"Not without a lot of arguing. He gave in, finally, when Grandma broke down and cried. But when they said they wanted to take me and Josh, too, he wouldn't stand for it. He threatened to get his gun and drive them off the place. They left without us, but they haven't given up." Carrie's dark eyes narrowed. "Two months ago Papa got a letter from Santa Fe. I found where he'd hidden it and sneaked a look while he was out running the ferry. It was from a lawyer that my Grandpa and Grandma had hired. They've filed papers with the court—" She blinked back furious tears. "They claim that Papa can't give us proper care, and they're asking the judge to take us away from him."

138 Bride on the Run

"Oh, Carrie—" Anna restrained the impulse to gather the girl into her arms, fearing it might only make her more emotional.

"Sometime before the end of the month, two ladies from the Children's Aid Society are coming here to check on us," Carrie said. "If Papa can't prove we're being well cared for, we'll be taken back to Santa Fe. For good."

Chapter Nine

Anna picked her way along the bank of the river, gathering chunks of sand-scoured wood that had been left by the receding flood. The water had gone down fast, leaving a broad, wet ribbon of sediment in its wake. As soon as the road was clear, Malachi would be opening the ferry to wagon traffic again. Strangers would be passing this way, some of them enemies. Anna could feel the danger closing in, tightening around her like a noose.

Carrie's revelation churned in her mind like fallen leaves in an eddy. Only now did she understand the desperate measures that had driven Malachi to take on a mail-order bride. And only now did she realize how sadly she had failed him.

He had needed a respectable mother for his children, one whose fitness would withstand the scrutiny of any court. Instead, he had gotten Anna de Carlo, a saloon floozy and accused murderess whose face was posted in five states. If Elise's parents got wind of the truth, Carrie and Joshua would be snatched from this place in a twinkling, and Malachi would never see his children again.

The sand lay in delicate ridges where the water had rippled along the bank. Down toward the bend, two ravens were tearing at some small dead animal the flood had left behind. Was that how Malachi had found his wife, by seeing the ravens? Anna wrenched the thought from her mind as she retrieved one last precious stick of firewood, dropped it into the basket she carried and struck out for the house.

She had every right to be furious with Malachi for hiding the truth. But then again, she had been far from honest herself. They were two strangers, each using the other for their own desperate ends—a conclusion that gave her no comfort at all.

As she neared the house Anna heard the dog barking. Her instincts shrilled an alarm. Her pulse jumped, and her muscles tensed. Someone was coming. Maybe a lawman or bounty hunter. Maybe a traveler who would remember seeing her face. Hide—yes, that would be the smart thing to do. Disappear into the canyon until the coast was clear.

She was slipping back into the tamarisk when she remembered that Carrie was alone in the yard.

She froze, deliberating for only an instant before she turned once more and raced back toward the house. Whatever the danger, she could not slip off and leave the girl. If anything were to happen to Malachi's precious daughter she would never forgive herself.

She was out of breath by the time she reached the dooryard. But it was no stranger she saw. It was only

Eddie Johnson, unsaddling his bony horse at the corral gate. A dozen paces away, Carrie stood watching him, her nervous fingers twisting one long, black pigtail. The dog, no longer barking, crouched at her feet.

"I got a bellyache," Eddie explained before Anna could question him. "Pa said I could go back to the house and lay down for a spell." His low-lidded gaze flickered over Carrie, who blushed and twisted a lock of hair around her finger. Anna's protective instincts seethed. Carrie was only a child. This insolent boy had no right to look at her in such a manner.

"You can rest in the shed until the men come back," she said coldly. "And since you have a bellyache, I don't suppose we should plan on you for supper."

Eddie's Adam's apple bobbed up and down in his skinny throat as he swallowed. "Don't count me out right yet, ma'am. With a little shut-eye, I should be feelin' fine by the time supper's on."

"We'll see." Anna turned away, not bothering to hide her distrust of his motives. "Come along now, Carrie, we have work to do."

The pinto beans, seasoned with molasses and wild onion, simmered on the back of the stove, their pungent aroma floating through the warm kitchen. Crisp, brown loaves of bread, fresh from the oven, lay cooling on the counter, ready to be sliced and spread with the butter Carrie had churned. The table was set, the garden weeded, the laundry washed and hung and the chickens locked safely in their coop.

At last Anna had a moment to catch her breath. She stood now, gazing out at the play of fading

light on the walls of the canyon—the long, moving
fingers of shadow, the subtle deepening of colors from
gold to sienna, tan to umber, that she was already
coming to love.

Carrie had gone off to what she called the bathing
place to swim and wash her hair before the men came
back. Anna had worried about her going alone, but
the girl had insisted that she always bathed by herself
and would be fine. "I always take Doubtful with
me," she'd added, tossing her braids. "Nothing
would dare to bother me when he's around—except
maybe a few mosquitoes."

At last Anna had relented and let her go. She was
being overprotective of the girl, she had chided herself. Carrie would be fine. All the same, she had taken
a moment to tiptoe out to the shed and check on
Eddie. She had found the youth spread-eagled in the
hay, snoring soundly and dead to the world.

Maybe she had misjudged him. It was only natural,
after all, for an adolescent boy to be curious about
girls, even girls as young as Carrie. But there was
something about the way he looked at her that stirred
Anna's memories of those boys in the orphanage, and
she knew she would not relax until Eddie and his
father were gone from the canyon.

How much did Carrie know about men and
women? She had surely seen animals mate, Anna reminded herself. But no, for all that, Malachi's daughter was as innocent as a drop of pure spring water.
Her mother would have died too soon to tell the girl
anything about life. And as for her father... Anna
shook her head as she imagined big, taciturn Malachi

trying to explain the facts of life to his young daughter.

Turning away from the window, she dried her hands on Elise's old calico apron and walked past the table, down along the whitewashed wall to the open door of the bedroom. Malachi would be home soon. Her pulse skipped irrationally at the thought of him riding into the yard, swinging down from the mule and striding onto the porch. She pictured his powerful frame filling the doorway, blocking out the sunset's red glow for an instant before he lumbered inside, hot, thirsty and coated with dust. She imagined his steel gray eyes devouring her, as if he had been thinking of her all the way down the trail....

The daydream burst like a soap bubble as Anna turned and glimpsed herself in the mirror. The face that stared back at her was dusted with flour, smeared with soot across one cheek and framed by strings of sweat-matted hair. She forced herself to laugh. Anna de Carlo had come a long way from the glittering vixen who had posed on the edge of the stage and charmed every male in hearing range with her sultry songs of love gone wrong.

She filled the washbasin, humming a little tune as she wrung out a cloth and wiped the dirt from her face. The bed, its coverlet carefully smoothed, seemed to mock her with its silent presence, challenging her to come to terms with what had happened last night. Damn it, she knew what had happened—or nearly happened. She had wanted that big, rough man with all her soul—wanted his hands on her body, his weight bearing down on her, his manly lust filling her, warming all the cold, lonesome places deep inside.

Only the ruckus with the bobcat had stopped her from making a complete fool of herself.

What would stop her tonight, if Malachi came to her bed again? Would she have the willpower to resist him? Anna jerked the kerchief off her hair, snatched up the brush and began working out the tangles in swift, agitated strokes. What was the matter with her? She knew she couldn't spend another night next to Malachi. If he took her in his arms again, she would be lost. She would fall in love with him, causing her to stay too long and ruin the lives of these dear, innocent people. Worse, even—''

''Oh!'' Anna gasped with dismay as the brush caught on one pearl earring and tore it out of her ear. She heard the subtle click as the pearl struck the floor, then bounced and rolled under the bed.

Anna dropped the brush as her fingers flew to her earlobe. No blood, thank goodness. It was the gold fastener that had given way. The mangled wire still hung from her earlobe but the pearl was gone. She could only hope it had not rolled into a crack and vanished beneath the floorboards.

Dropping to a crouch, she groped under the edge of the bed, her wrist skimming the hem of the coverlet. She found a thin layer of dust and a shirt button that she judged to be Malachi's, but no pearl.

With an impatient sigh, she flattened herself on the floor and thrust her arm as far under the bed as she could reach. Her fingertip brushed something small and hard, nudging it farther away. Yes, it had been the pearl. She stretched, trying to capture it once more, but she was too late. The precious bauble had rolled out of reach.

Muttering a curse, she flipped up the edge of the coverlet to let in more light and shoved her way forward beneath the frame. Motes of dust swam in the dim light, and she could make out a large spiderweb suspended between the rails. Clearly no one had cleaned under the bed since Elise's death. Perhaps tomorrow she would do the job herself.

Anna's attention was riveted by a glint of reflected light. Yes, there was her pearl. It had rolled into a wide crack and lodged there between two boards. Sliding forward she struggled to free it with her finger. The pearl seemed tightly wedged—but strangely enough, one of the boards seemed loose. When Anna pushed against it, the crack widened and the pearl dropped out of sight.

Edging closer, she worked a forefinger into the crack and pried the loose board upward. It came out easily, and Anna found herself looking down into a shallow hole, hollowed into the sandy earth beneath the floor joists. Her pearl glimmered whitely in the half light. When she reached for it, her fingers brushed against something else—something soft and smooth. Only when she touched it again did Anna realize that it was the worn leather cover of a book.

Anna tucked the pearl into her left fist, then reached gingerly into the hole, slid her right hand carefully around the book and lifted it out. It was small in size, the embossed cover soft from handling and mildewed from the dampness beneath the floor. A journal, Anna guessed; and as she brought it into the light, she saw that she'd been right.

She dropped the pearl into her shirt pocket for safe-keeping. Then, still on the floor, she sat leafing slowly through the mildewed pages, her eyes skimming the delicate, unmistakably feminine script. This was wrong, she chastised herself. She had no right to be reading the private thoughts of a woman who had clearly meant these pages for no eyes except her own.

But Anna could no more put away the journal than she could stop breathing. She had taken up the thread of Elise Stone's life. She had slept in Elise's bed, fussed over her children, embraced her husband. The urge to know this woman's thoughts was too strong to dismiss in the name of propriety.

Perhaps she would even learn why Malachi had loved Elise so much.

Anna shifted her position on the floor. Then, unable to wait any longer, she opened the little volume to a random page and began to read in earnest.

February 10, 1888

Today I looked into the glass and saw a woman growing old. The signs of it are already etched across my face—the deepening lines, the fading color in my cheeks, the first strands of gray hair, which I swiftly pulled out. I am barely thirty. These things should not be happening so soon.

It is this place, I know, that is draining the life out of me. The heat, the burning sun, the loneliness. Dear heaven, the loneliness! Malachi does nothing but work from dawn to dusk. He expects me to do the same and be content with it. But oh, I am not. What I wouldn't give to put on a pretty gown and go out to the theatre, or even to a church social!

Last night, yet again, I begged Malachi to sell this wretched ferry business and move our family back to Santa Fe. Wasted words! He would not even discuss the matter. This place is his own piece of the earth. Aside from the river and these monstrous canyon walls, he built everything that is here. In this canyon, he is king of all he surveys and he can do and be whatever he chooses. Clearly, that fact means more to him than my love and respect!

Anna stared down at the mildewed page, the handwriting on it so fine and regular that when she allowed her eyes to blur it took on the appearance of delicate Belgian lace. But the things that writing contained— even now the revelation stunned her. Beautiful, perfect Elise Stone had been miserable in this lonely canyon. This journal had been her only friend, her only confidante. Its pages contained the private outpourings of her heart.

Anna closed the book, hesitated, then slipped it beneath the foot of the mattress. A wiser woman, perhaps, would have left well enough alone and consigned the book to rot away in the hole beneath the floor, with the board nailed firmly in place. But wisdom had never been Anna's strong suit. She would not rest, she knew, until she had read every page of the journal. Perhaps, if it contained nothing hurtful, she would even give it to Carrie—

Carrie.

The silence in the house struck Anna like a sudden blow. Her gaze darted frantically to the small clock on the dresser. Time had seemed to stop when she'd found the journal. But no, it was all right. The girl had been gone less than half an hour.

So why did she have this terrible feeling that something was wrong?

Goaded by a fear too awful to name, Anna scrambled to her feet and raced outside. Nothing. The dooryard was empty except for a few chickens scratching around the coop and Eddie's horse swishing flies in the corral. The slanting sunlight gilded the massive stone towers and cast long shadows that pooled in the hollows of the canyon. High overhead, a golden eagle drifted on its vast, silent wings.

The place was too quiet, Anna thought. Too peaceful. She plunged across the yard to the shed where Eddie had been sprawled asleep not twenty minutes before. A moan of dismay escaped her lips as she peered through the fading light and saw his bedroll lying on the hay, rumpled and empty.

Raw panic shot through Anna's body as she sprinted toward the river, where the trail led off through the willows toward the bathing spot. Where Carrie's long, narrow feet had pressed the sand, the tracks were filled with seeping water, as were the rounded pawprints of the dog. The larger boot tracks, however, leading off in the same direction, were still empty. Eddie had passed that way no more than a few minutes ago.

White-hot fury, fueled by the horror of her own early years, exploded in Anna's mind. She snatched up a broken limb that the flood had washed onto the riverbank. Then, gripping the makeshift weapon, she charged wildly down the path.

* * *

Malachi sat lightly in the saddle, bracing his feet in the stirrups so that the mule's rocking gait would not disturb his sleeping son. Cradled against his chest, Josh made little wheezing sounds as he breathed. The boy had started the homeward journey on Lucifer, but when he had dozed and nearly toppled off the edge of the trail, Malachi had paused, lifted his son onto his own mount and settled him in his arms.

Malachi had always loved holding his children. But Carrie had long since grown too old for it, and soon Josh would be too old as well. He would miss the sweetness of a small head drooping against his shoulder. For years he had wanted more children, but Elise had not shared that desire, and now it was too late. He could only savor this moment of cradling his sleeping child, knowing that this time would be short and infinitely precious.

Lord, what if he lost his children when the visitors from the Children's Aid Society came? The very thought of it almost strangled him with pain. He felt as if he were drowning in a cold, black pit, reaching out, struggling to keep a grip on everything he had every loved.

Would the children be better off in Santa Fe? The question had kept him awake for more nights than he cared to count. True, they would live in a nicer home and be able to attend school. They would be taken to church every Sunday, and Carrie's clothes, if not colorful and pretty, would at least be presentable. But the thought of his children being raised by Elise's somber, unloving, ramrod-straight parents chilled his blood. They had caused enough damage to their daughter. He would die before he let them do the same to their grandchildren.

A hush lay over the canyon, broken only by the plodding footsteps of the mules and the call of a wild quail from a nearby ridge. Malachi had used his sleeping son as an excuse to let Sam ride on ahead—a blessed relief from the man's constant stream of crude conversation. Far down the trail, through the twilight haze, he caught occasional glimpses of Sam on his big piebald horse. He was jogging down the trail with the haste of a hungry man headed to supper.

Malachi could feel the smoldering of his own hunger, like the hot, red core beneath a layer of banked coals. It was a hunger that had had nothing to do with food. The sight of Anna that morning, striding across the yard in those tight-fitting denim pants, her breasts straining the buttons of that boyish plaid shirt, had tormented him all day.

He had long since made up his mind to send her packing—a wise decision he would carry out as soon as he could clear the road and get a wagon in. When it came to satisfying the Children's Aid people, a woman as alluring as Anna would be far worse than no woman at all. But meanwhile, how was he going to keep his hands off her? How was he going to keep his mind above his belt when the barest glimpse of her quickened his pulse and jerked a noose of desire around his throat?

The warm, humid air of the lower canyon closed around him as the road wound downward. From below, Malachi could hear the rushing murmur of the Colorado. The air smelled pleasantly of wood smoke from the kitchen stove. Anna would be waiting below, at the end of the road. Heaven help him.

The mules, anticipating food and rest, had picked up speed on their own. Bracing Josh with one arm, Malachi slackened the reins and gave Beelzebub his head. Lucifer, he knew, would follow along and keep up.

Awakened by the increased bouncing, Josh stirred and opened his eyes. "Where are we, Pa?" he asked, blinking.

"Starting down the slope before the last bend," Malachi said. "We'll be home in a few minutes."

The small body relaxed against Malachi's chest, then suddenly tensed. "I hear something," Josh said.

Malachi held his breath, ears straining. "I don't—"

"No, listen!" Joshua whispered. "It sounds like Doubtful!"

Malachi did hear it then, the faint but furious barking of the dog, echoing up the canyon to mingle with the sounds of awakening night.

"Maybe he's treed that old bobcat," Josh said. "D'you think so, Pa?"

"Maybe." Malachi weighed the notion but it didn't feel right. Doubtful tended to bay when he had an animal cornered. The frantic barking would more likely mean something else. Trouble.

"Hang on!" Malachi tightened his clasp around his son's waist and caught the reins with his free hand. Then he jabbed the mule's flanks with his boot heels. Beelzebub snorted and burst into an explosive sprint, with Lucifer wheezing along behind. Two faces flashed through Malachi's mind as he leaned forward in the saddle. One was Carrie's; the other was Anna's.

The wild ride down the rest of the trail took only a couple of minutes. Sam had reached the yard ahead of them, but there was no sign of the dog or anyone else. The house stood dark in the gathering twilight, the door swinging open and shut on its hinges in the light breeze. Malachi felt dread tighten like a fist around his heart. "Down there," he said as his ears caught the sound of barking once more. "The river."

Lowering Josh swiftly to the ground, he swung out of the saddle, whipped the rifle out of its leather scabbard and bolted town the path.

Seconds later he burst out of the willows and onto the riverbank. There he stopped cold, stunned and bewildered by the sight that met his eyes.

Eddie Johnson was cowering at the base of the massive dead tree, his face as red as a hot branding iron. A stone's throw away, Doubtful circled wolf-fashion, alternately growling, barking and lunging. Carrie stood at the river's edge, fumbling with the buttons of her dress, her wet hair streaming over her shoulders.

"Papa!" She ran to Malachi's side with a little cry. "Oh, do something, Papa! I think she's going to kill him!"

But Malachi scarcely heard his daughter's words. His attention was riveted on Anna. She stood over the sprawling Eddie, both hands gripping a tree limb that was nearly as big as she was. Her eyes flashed as she caught sight of Malachi. The branch quivered in her hands but she kept it high, as if daring the boy to move so much as an eyelash. Only then did Malachi notice the swelling bruise across Eddie's cheek.

"What in hell's name's going on?" Sam burst out of the willows, cursing under his breath.

"I'll tell you what's going on, Mr. Johnson." Anna spoke for the first time, her voice taut and trembling. "I caught your son lying down in those willows over there. He was spying on Carrie and doing—" Her eyes darted toward the girl, then back to Sam. "Well, never mind, I'll just let you guess!" She glowered at the boy, her small frame vibrating with a fury that only Malachi fully understood.

"That true, son?" Sam did not sound unduly concerned.

The boy's eyes rolled. "Aw, shoot, Pa, I was only lookin'," he whined. "I didn't mean no harm. She wouldn't'a even knowed about it if this blond bitch hadn't snuck up behind me and clobbered me with that damned tree limb—" He tried to edge toward his father, but Doubtful lunged at him, growling and snapping, and Eddie shrank back against the tree trunk.

Malachi's own anger had risen to a murderous pitch. He clenched his fists to hold it in, to keep himself from grabbing the boy with his bare hands and breaking him like a twig. He had taught his children to forsake violence. He could not be a bad example to them now.

He glanced at his wide-eyed daughter—so beautiful and so innocent that it almost broke his heart. "Are you all right, Carrie?"

"Yes, Papa," she whispered.

"He didn't hurt you?"

"Hurt her!" Eddie interrupted. "Hell, I never touched her. You don't pluck a cherry afore it's ripe, that's what Pa always says. An that little cherry, I can tell you, she's got a long ways to go!"

Again, the rage that surged up in Malachi was so powerful that it almost made him nauseous. "Go on back to the house, Carrie," he said softly, holding himself in check. "Take Josh with you."

Carrie obeyed him without a word, pausing only to catch her brother's arm as she passed him. The dog hesitated, then trotted off behind her, into the willows. Eddie slumped on the ground, his Adam's apple working furiously. Malachi battled the urge to jerk him up by the scruff of his collar and give him the thrashing he deserved.

"I want that boy gone, Sam," he said forcing each word through clenched teeth. "You, too. By first light tomorrow morning."

Sam looked pained. "Aw, Malachi, the boy didn't do nothin'. Just exercisin' his natural curiosity, that's all. Boys'll be boys. You know that."

"I'll pay you what I owe you," Malachi continued as if he hadn't heard. "And I'll bring your supper out to the shed. But I won't have that boy under the same roof as my daughter. And if he so much as looks at her again, so help me, I'll horsewhip him within an inch of his life!"

Malachi could feel the blood pounding in his head. He was dizzy with anger, not only at the boy but at Sam, who failed to find any fault in his son's loutish behavior.

Anna had lowered the tree limb so that the end of it rested on the sand. Her face was pale, her eyes wide and dark in the deepening twilight. Her beauty sapped the strength from Malachi's knees, just as it had the first time he'd set eyes on her. Had the rush of anger heightened other emotions as well? Malachi was at a loss to understand it, but he knew suddenly that, right or wrong, this was a woman he could love.

Her gaze hardened as she turned toward Sam and Eddie. "Mr. Johnson, if you won't tell your boy what he needs to hear, then I will," she said in a voice that defied anyone to silence her. "Eddie, you think it's all right to look at a young girl's body. What will you be thinking next? That it's all right to touch her? All right to force her against her will? All right to hurt her so badly that her life will never be the same again?" The last few words came choking out of her. She closed her eyes for an instant, trembling as she fought for self-control. "I hope somebody teaches you right from wrong, young man. And I hope you take the lesson to heart or next time it may be too late!"

Sam's eyes had narrowed to angry, porcine slits. "You watch your mouth, lady," he growled. "I won't have nobody tellin' me how to raise my boy or makin' him out to be some kind of criminal when all he done is a little harmless peekin'. I seen a lot of women, and I know your type! You put on airs and make yourself out to be so high and priss-perfect. But underneath those fancy manners you ain't no different from any common slut—"

"That's enough, Sam!" Malachi snapped, battling the urge to punch the man's face to a bloody pulp. "Nobody talks that way to my wife! Take your boy and your money and get out of here now. You can camp on the road if you have to. All I ever want to see of you two again is your backsides headed up the road!''

Sam's upper lip curled as if readying a surly retort, but, in the face of Malachi's size and anger, the words remained unspoken. ''Come on, boy!'' He jerked Eddie to his feet. ''The sooner we put these highfalutin' folk behind us, the sooner we can get back to town and wash off the stink of sanctity!'' He swung back toward the front yard and lumbered into the willows, dragging Eddie behind him.

Malachi's whole body ached with tension. He exhaled forcibly, feeling the slow ebb of it. Anna watched him in silence. Although the end of the tree limb rested on the sand, her fingers still gripped the base as if her flesh had grown around the wood.

Words warred in Malachi's mind, forming themselves into thoughts, then dissolving into nothing. He did not know what to say to her.

He could feel the slow beating of his heart as their eyes met through the gathering darkness. Her lips trembled, and in the first light of the rising moon he caught the glimmer of a tear on her cheek.

''It was too close,'' she said, her shoulders sagging as she dropped the limb. ''All those memories—I went a little crazy. If I drove your friends away—''

''Don't, Anna.'' Malachi ached to gather her into his arms, but he feared the emotional avalanche the contact would trigger. ''Some friends aren't worth keeping—if they could've been called friends to begin with. I'm beholden to you for Carrie's sake.''

''I didn't do it for you.'' She raked a nervous hand through the loose golden mane of her hair. ''Heaven help me, I don't know if I even did it for Carrie. When I swung the limb at that young fool, I wasn't defending your daughter. I was doing what I wished I could have done so many years ago—''

Her voice broke. She pressed her lips together hard, shoulders quivering as she battled the rush of memory.

"Anna—" He took a step toward her, overcome by the need to take her in his arms and hold her. Just hold her.

"No." Her eyes blazed in the moonlight. "Don't come any closer, Malachi. No matter what you think, I'm not staying. I answered your cousin's advertisement because I was desperate and needed a refuge. But I never meant this to last more than a few months. I came to you under false pretenses, and the sooner you can get me out of here, the better!"

She spun away from him and fled into the darkness.

Chapter Ten

Anna lay alone in the warmth of the bed, watching the moon creep toward the top of the window. Malachi had long since taken his rifle and gone outside, announcing to all who could hear that he was going to sit in the rocks above the chicken coop and watch for the marauding bobcat. It was a handy excuse. But she did not even have to think twice about his real motives.

Turning over, she punched the flattened pillow to plumpness. Then, still restless, she curled onto her side. Exhaustion was a leaden weight that seemed to fill every bone, muscle and nerve in her body. But she could not sleep. Not when all the alarms in her mind were shrilling at her to run. Now. Before it was too late.

She had made a dangerous enemy in Sam Johnson. The man was petty and unforgiving, and it would be only a matter of time before he saw a poster with her face on it—before he made the connection between the wanted Anna de Carlo and the woman who had humiliated his son.

She sat up and swung her legs over the side of the bed, her hands clasping in agitation. Could she wait for the road to be cleared? Or would it be wiser to get out now, any way she could, before the lawmen and bounty hunters descended on the canyon?

Raking back her hair, Anna stood up, walked to the window and stared out at the waning moon. She could leave right now, she thought, clutching at the possibility. She could stuff a pillowcase with food and a water jug, steal one of Malachi's precious mules and ride out of the canyon this very night. If need be, she could even set out on foot and hope for the best.

But what was she thinking? It would be suicidal, trying to walk out of this place and find her way back to civilization. And in any case, Malachi would be outside ostensibly watching for the bobcat. If she tried to take a mule, he would be sure to see her.

Anna sank down on the edge of the bed, feeling like a trapped animal. There was no way out for her. Not unless she could persuade Malachi to take her back to Kanab at once by muleback—but no, that idea was useless as well. Once Sam Johnson recognized her, she would not be safe anywhere outside the canyon. For the present, at least, she had no choice except to stay here.

The moon gleamed brightly through the open window, illuminating a rectangle of light on the patchwork quilt. Anna sprang to her feet once more, pacing one direction, then the other. She was no better than a prisoner in this place, surrounded by these towering sandstone walls.

Was this the way Elise had felt?

On sudden impulse she paused, fumbled beneath

the foot of the mattress and brought out the slim leather journal. The frailty of the little volume recalled the woman whose writing filled its pages. The worn leather cover was as soft as human skin, the mildewed pages so damp and delicate that it was all Anna could do to separate one from another without tearing the fine paper.

Carefully she laid the open book in the bright moonlight. With effort, she began to read.

The first few entries were mundane accounts of washing, gardening, cooking and schooling the children. Then, as Anna turned to the next page, a longer section caught her eye.

March 7, 1888

Last night Malachi spoke to me yet again about having another baby. Oh, why does he keep bringing this up? I've told him time and again that I have no wish to bear another child and raise it in this godforsaken place. In truth, I am terrified of giving birth alone here, with no doctor to attend me. What if something were to go wrong? A breech, perhaps? And what about the baby—if it were to sicken and die here for want of some medicine easily bought in a town, my heart would shatter into a thousand pieces. Once more, I made my terms clear to him—I will only consider having another child if he sells this wretched ferry operation and takes us all back to Santa Fe. Until then, he is not to come near me....

Anna was startled by the sudden sound of Malachi's footsteps and his light knock on the bedroom door.

"Anna?" His rough whisper made her pulse leap. "Anna, are you awake?"

"Just a minute—" She closed the journal and, fumbling with haste, stuffed it back under the mattress. What would happen, she wondered guiltily, if he were to barge in and discover she'd been prying into the most intimate corners of his life?

"Anna?" His voice had become more insistent, though still very low to avoid waking the children. She scrambled to her feet, pattered across the rug and opened the bedroom door. Last night she had nearly given him what his wife had withheld. Was that why he had returned?

His massive frame loomed above her in the darkness. "We need to talk," he said.

Anna's heart fluttered, then dropped like a wounded bird. "Yes, I suppose we do." She slipped out of the room and closed the door softly behind her. She knew all too well what would happen if they tried to have a conversation in bed. And the subtle tightening of his jaw told her that he knew it, too.

"Did you give up on the bobcat?" she asked as he followed her across the kitchen and out onto the moonlit porch.

"Wasn't the bobcat I was worried about." Malachi closed the door and lowered his long body to the edge of the porch. "After the scare Doubtful gave him, I don't think he'll bother us for a while. But now that Sam's riled I wouldn't put it past him to sneak back down the trail and carry off a thing or two. I've seen how he treats people he doesn't like."

His words tightened the knot of fear in Anna's stomach, but she chose to ignore it for now. "I thought maybe it was me you were avoiding," she said lightly, settling herself a few inches away and drawing her knees up under the loose flannel body of the nightshirt.

Malachi's breath caught. "Let's not even get into that," he rumbled. "You're leaving. As far as I'm concerned that cancels all contracts between us. So you've no call to wonder about my claiming my husbandly rights. It's not going to happen."

"Of course it isn't." She glanced at him, remembering Elise's disturbing journal entry. How could any woman refuse this big, strong, stubborn, tender man? she wondered. If she had been in Elise's place, the house would be overflowing with children by now.

"You said you came here under false pretenses." His words cut into her reverie. "Since I paid your way here, I think the least you owe me is an explanation."

"You weren't exactly honest yourself," she parried. "Carrie told me about how her grandparents were trying to take her and Josh away from you. That's something I should have learned from you."

He stiffened beside her. "How the devil did she—" He broke off, his shoulder's sagging as he exhaled. "Never mind. She's a smart little girl. And no, I didn't tell you. Seemed to be no point in it after we met, and I realized you weren't the woman I expected, let alone the woman I needed to convince those starch-shirted vultures my children were getting proper care."

"I see." Anna stared into the darkness, struggling to ignore the sting of his honest words. The late-night breeze was cool on her hot face, the moon now low above the western towers of the canyon. Bats darted and dipped above the willows, hunting the insects that swarmed along the riverbank.

"So when will the people from the Children's Aid Society be showing up?" she asked.

"Any day now. You know how uncertain travel can be in this country."

"So there's not time for you to bring in a more, uh, *respectable* wife? One who doesn't look like she spends the night hours singing in saloons or maybe worse?"

"Damn it, I didn't say that. Worst thing is, I don't know if it would make any difference. Whoever the court sends from Santa Fe is bound to be prejudiced in favor of Elise's parents. There's not a snowball's chance in hell they'll find in my favor."

"So what are you going to do?" Anna asked, aching for him.

"I don't know." His throat moved as he swallowed. "Lord help me, Anna, I don't know. My whole reason for living will be gone if I lose those two youngsters."

He hunched his shoulders and fell into a long silence. Anna could sense the pain in him, the gnawing, desperate anxiety. What had she done to this man and to his children? Maybe if she hadn't answered the advertisement and charmed the socks of Stuart Wilkinson, the lawyer would have chosen another woman—the right woman—to make this journey and become Malachi's wife.

She had to help him now. After what she had done, she owed him that much.

Her hand stole upward and settled gently on his shoulder. She felt him shudder beneath her touch, like a wild stallion flinching at human contact. "There's got to be a way," she said. "We just have to find it."

"We?" His eyes sparked like flints in the darkness. "Since when did my children and I become your concern?"

"That's not a fair question." Her hand slid off his shoulder and dropped to her lap. A cloud had slipped over the moon, leaving the canyon cloaked in deep-black shadows.

"I thought we'd agreed that you were leaving," he said.

"I thought so, too. But I'm here, Malachi, and I care enough about your children to want what's best for them."

Malachi sat as still and as silent as one of the massive stone pillars that rose out of the canyon floor. An eternity seemed to pass before he coughed slightly, then spoke.

"One thing I grant you," he said. "You've got an unholy talent for turning any conversation away from yourself!"

"Is that a compliment?" She feigned a lighthearted little laugh.

"Take it any way you want. But I'm wise to you, Anna, and you're not getting away with it again. I want to know who you are, where you came from and what you're doing here." His iron-hard hand shot out and locked around her wrist. "And you're not going anywhere until I have my answers."

* * *

Malachi watched her, gauging her response to his demand. Her features, like cast pewter in the cloud-veiled moonlight, had not altered their expression at all. Even the sinewy flesh of her wrist, where his hand gripped it, remained taut and cool. He had held this woman in his arms and felt her turn to molten flame at his touch, Malachi reminded himself. But now she was ice.

"Well?" he asked, probing impatiently.

"What difference could it make?" She gazed toward the river, deliberately avoiding his eyes. "I'll be gone one of these days, and suddenly nothing we did or talked about will be important anymore. In time, you won't even be able to picture my face. I've already told you more than you need to know. Why should I bare more of my dark little secrets?"

"Because you're my wife," Malachi said quietly.

"Your wife!" She swung around to face him then, eyes blazing. "I'm not your wife, Malachi Stone! We may have signed a legal contract, but that doesn't make us truly married! I'm no more wife to you than one of those mules out there in the corral!"

She strained upward and might have sprung to her feet and gone storming into the house if he had not kept his grip on her arm. "We could change that," he said huskily, feeling the heat of desire seeping through his body from the point of contact. "It would be all too easy, you know that as well as I do."

She glared at him—a mental slap. Then her gaze dropped and her shoulders sagged in dejection. "What is it you really want from me?" she asked.

"The truth. You lied your way into this mess. It's

going to take you more than lies to get you out of it.''

She tightened her jaw, pressing her lips together. In the silence, Malachi was aware of the dog slipping up beside him, nosing his free hand. The moon had emerged from the cloud, bathing the canyon in silver.

''So, what are you going to do if I won't tell you anything,'' she challenged him, ''twist my arm off?''

Malachi released her wrist. ''You're the stubbornest damned women I ever met!'' he exploded.

Anna laughed softly, sensually, in the darkness. ''Thank you. I do believe that's the nicest thing you've ever said to me, Malachi. You're not very free with compliments, you know.''

''Take it any way you like,'' he muttered, thrown by the sudden change in her demeanor.

''Truce?''

He blinked, still reeling, then forced himself to shrug. ''What the hell. All right, truce it is.''

''Done!'' She edged a little closer to him, her loose hair brushing his shoulder. ''We've no time to lose,'' she said in a conspiratorial whisper. ''As I see it, if you want to keep your children, you've got two choices. You can hustle me out of here now, and take your chances alone, *or* you can swallow your manly pride and allow me to stay here and help you.''

''Help me?'' He stared at her gloomily, feeling as if he were about to step over the edge of a precipice. ''And how do you propose to do that?''

''By putting on a performance that will rival anything on the New York stage!'' Her eyes danced in the moonlight. Malachi willed his own responses to slow to the pace of cold tar on a winter morning. He could not afford to let himself get caught up in a frenzy of false hope—especially over any scheme that involved Anna.

"Well?" She was gazing openly at him, her head cocked like a curious little bird's.

He allowed himself time to breathe. "You are a devil of an actress," he said. "Having seen you perform, I'll grant you that."

"I've had to be. It's a matter of survival." Her features dropped into shadow for a moment, but when she looked up, the bright mask was in place once more. "Now, how long can you get away with keeping the road blocked?"

"That's hardly a matter of choice. My livelihood depends on keeping the ferry open. If it's closed for any length of time, word will get around, and the people who would have crossed here will go around by way of Lee's." He scowled, his own thoughts racing. "Working alone, it'll take me at least another week to clear the slide. But there's no guarantee it would keep the Children's Aid people out. In a buckboard, yes, but not if they came on horseback."

"That's a chance we'll have to take." Her eyes were alive again, glittering with vitality. "Your children are well behaved and well schooled," she said. "That much, at least, we won't have to stage. As for the rest…"

She glanced around at the moonlit yard and the corral, the barn and coop, the ramada and the garden, and finally back at the house. Malachi could guess what she must be thinking. The place had gone to rack and ruin since Elise's death. It had been all he could do to run the ferry and the ranch, maintain the road and keep his children fed and schooled. There'd been no time to worry about how things might look to outsiders.

"You've got your work cut out," he said. "And it goes without saying, you won't have much to work with."

She nodded slowly, lost in thought. "Malachi, what happened to your wife's clothes?"

"They're gone."

"But where?"

He shook his head, willing the memory away. "It's a long story. Don't ask."

"Help me. Did she have any cloth? Any scissors or needles? Did she sew?" Anna leaned forward, moonlight flooding the shadows that deepened the *V* of her unbuttoned collar, revealing a glimpse of satiny breast. In spite of his resolve, Malachi felt the stirring deep in his body. The night was warm, and she was tantalizingly close.

"She did a little mending, I remember." He spoke with effort, his mind elsewhere. "But that was all. Last year a peddler came through and paid for his crossing with a half dozen bolts of cloth. Elise put them away—I don't remember where—and never used them. Most of her clothes, and the children's, were ordered from Santa Fe with her mother's help. Needless to say…" He left the rest of the words unspoken. Aside from their efforts to take them, Elise's parents had shown little interest in Josh and Carrie. No letters or cards. No gifts, not even on their birthdays.

"But the cloth—" Anna's fingers caught his arm, the light contact igniting him like a match dropped on dry tinder. "I can sew like a wizard, Malachi! I could work miracles with that cloth—"

Flinging caution to the devil, he kissed her.

Even Malachi was startled by the suddenness of it as he seized her waist, jerked her close and captured her unwary mouth. Caught off guard, she resisted for an instant. Then her ripe lips softened. Her body melted into him, warm and yielding and fragrant with her woman musk. The sweetness of it! Malachi drank her in, devoured the feel and scent and taste of her like a man starving in the desert would wolf a pomegranate. His tongue invaded her mouth, probing and licking, feeling the heat of her response. She moaned as his hand slid upward to cup her unfettered breast through the worn flannel, pushing the fullness upward so that it bulged over the open collar.

Dizzy with need, he bent lower and buried his lips in that buttery softness. She arched against him, demanding more. Her breath came in sharp little gasps as he freed her nipple and circled the soft mauve aureole with the tip of his tongue. Her head dropped forward, veiling him in the silky curtain of her hair as she held him, her frenzied fingers pressing him hard against her breast.

His free hand found the hem of the flannel nightshirt and, after an instant's fumbling, the naked satin legs beneath. *Enough of this madness,* a voice in his head urged. *She's your wife. Take her now. Just pick her up, carry her into the bedroom and end this game playing once and for all!*

Drawn by hungers he had no more will to resist, Malachi let his hand move between her thighs toward the sweet, moist heaven at their joining—the heaven where he knew, at last, he belonged.

Anna whimpered as his fingers brushed her exquisitely sensitive flesh, their work-roughened tips sending rivulets of fire surging upward through her body. Need was a cry in her, an aching hollow that his love could warm and fill. *Just this once,* her heart whispered. *It doesn't have to be forever, as long as it's now....*

She pressed herself into the hollow of his hand, letting him claim her, feel her moistness, her urgent heat.

No! The word exploded like a gunshot in her head. What was she thinking? Malachi didn't love her. True, he was lonesome and woman-hungry, but his heart belonged to a memory. Anything that happened between them tonight would be a mockery of that early, all-consuming love.

And she was a hunted woman. She could not bind herself to this man, not even for a single night. She could not leave any part of herself in this place. And she could not carry anything, even a memory, away with her when the time came to run.

With the last of her remaining strength she wrenched herself away from him. "Malachi, stop—" she murmured, her words slurring with desire, her lips wet and swollen.

"Why?" He reached for her again and pulled her back toward him. "We're married, Anna. Give me one good reason why we should—"

"We have a business arrangement!" she gasped, twisting away and staggering to her feat. "And for my own private reasons, I have to keep it that way!"

His eyes had gone cold in the moonlight, and Anna knew she had hurt him. How she ached to fling herself into his arms again, to lose herself in his loving until she forgot the sight of Harry's murdered body, the blood smearing her hands and clothes, the terror of Louis Caswell and his hideous companion passing her on the stairs. It would be so easy, so tempting. But in the end, it would be no good. If she gave herself to Malachi, they would both pay a heavy price in pain and regret.

He had risen to stand beside her, as cold and remote now as the face of the moon. "All right, business it is," he said curtly. "If you stay long enough to help me keep my children, you'll no doubt want something in return."

"Yes, of course." So things had come full circle, back to this. Anna willed her emotions to freeze before she spoke again. "Here's my proposition," she said. "I'll do everything I can to help you. If we fail, you can take me to Kanab, put me on the stage, and send me back to Salt Lake City."

"And if we succeed?" he asked cautiously.

"You give me stage fare to Salt Lake and train fare all the way from there to San Francisco. Either way, I'll be out of your life for good."

"Sounds fair enough." He thrust his hands into his pocket and stood gazing up at the river of stars that glittered above the towering canyon walls. "And now, if you'll excuse me, I'll get back to watching for that bobcat."

"You said it wouldn't come tonight."

"I've been wrong before." He turned away, his jaw set in a grim line.

Anna watched him stride across the yard with the dog trailing at his heels. There would be no bobcat, she knew. And most likely, at this late hour, Sam Johnson and his son would be sleeping somewhere along the trail. The only reason for Malachi to stay outside was the one she had just given him.

Malachi Stone was a proud, stubborn man. He would keep the bargain they had made. Anna knew he had come to her bed for the last time.

Chapter Eleven

By the time Anna awoke the next morning, aching and weary after a fitful night, Malachi and the mules were gone. She stumbled into the kitchen to find Josh seated at the table, having a leisurely breakfast of bread and milk.

"Pa told me I was to stay here and help with chores," he said. "See, I've already gathered the eggs."

"That's right fine." Anna managed a tired smile. "Where's Carrie?" she asked, noticing that the girl's bedroom door was open, the bed empty.

"Gone to milk Patches." The boy studied her earnestly, his round spaniel eyes following Anna's movements as she wandered to the stove, rummaged for a mug and poured herself some coffee. Mornings had never been her strong suit. Especially with talkative children around.

A used plate, mug and knife sat on the counter. Malachi's she surmised. And he had probably made the coffee as well, all very stealthily, to avoid waking her up and having to face what had happened last night. The coward.

"Do you love my pa?" Joshua's piping voice caught her off guard. Anna raked her hair back from her face and struggled to compose herself as she took a gulp of the thick, black coffee. It was strong to the point of bitterness and only lukewarm. Grimacing, she put the mug down on the counter.

"What kind of question is that?" she sputtered.

"It's *my* kind of question," Josh persisted. "*Do you love him?*"

Anna sighed. "Josh, at this point, it doesn't make much difference whether I love your father or not."

"Then you *do* love him!" Josh grinned and bounced in his chair, sloshing the milk in his spoon.

"Did I say that?" Anna weighed the idea of going back into her room, crawling back into bed and starting the whole day over in an hour or so.

"You didn't have to. You let him sleep with you. And Pa told me that when a man and lady sleep together, it means—"

"I know what he told you!" Anna turned away to hide the rush of hot crimson to her face. The boy must have heard Malachi in her room the night before last. Sweet heaven, what else had he heard?

"It wasn't what you think," she said, feeling as if she had just stepped into a quagmire. "Your father was tired, that was all. He needed a place to lie down and rest."

"Uh-huh. And you let him." Josh was gazing at her in wide-eyed innocence. "And that means you want to be with him forever and make a family."

Anna stifled a groan. "Josh," she said, "someday

your father will find the woman he really wants. Then you'll have a real mother and be a real family. In the meantime—''

''Patches is out!'' Carrie burst into the kitchen, wild-eyed and out of breath. ''I tracked her down to the river! She's stuck in some mud—looks like it might be quicksand!''

Anna raced after the children. There was no time to dress, no time even to pull on her boots. She ran full out, ignoring the pain of sharp rocks and stickers. From the direction of the river she could hear Doubtful barking frantically and, as she came within earshot, the pained and exhausted lowing of the cow. Had Sam Johnson unlatched the barn door out of pure meanness as he was leaving last night, or had it been a simple oversight on someone's part—the children's or even her own? No matter. The cow was a friend and provider for Malachi's children. The family could not afford to lose her.

Anna's heart sank as she burst out of the willows and saw the brown-spotted cow. Patches stood belly deep in a spot about fifty yards downstream from the ferry, where the eddying current had left a swirl of treacherous, sandy mud. She could not have been there long, or Malachi would have discovered her, but she looked as if her strength was already spent. As Anna watched, the trapped animal bawled piteously and tried to lunge forward. The effort only caused her to sink deeper into the dark, sucking mud.

''Get a rope!'' Anna shouted to the children. She had no idea how she would get a rope around the poor cow, let alone pull it out, but they had to do something.

Frantically she glanced around. A half dozen yards from the riverbank was a dead cottonwood, not as massive as the one upstream near the bathing spot, but it would have to do. Anna ran to it, kicked it, shook it, testing its strength. It felt solid enough to use as an anchor. But she could not be sure. The cow was so big and so horribly mired.

Through the willows she could hear the shouts of the children. Seconds later they burst onto the bank, Carrie staggering under a massive coil of rope. Both of them had been crying.

"Is Patches going to drown?" Josh asked, choking back tears.

"Certainly not!" Anna answered too quickly. "We won't let that happen. See, we've got a good, strong rope and three good minds to figure out what we're going to do!"

"But we aren't strong enough to pull her out!" Carrie argued. "Patches weighs more than all of us put together!"

"Just give me the rope." Anna seized the heavy coils, masking her own fear with action. "We'll just make a loop, like this, toss it around her neck, and—"

"No, you'll choke her that way!" Carrie objected. "Rope her horns. That's what Pa would do."

"Yes…I know." Anna's hands shook as she opened the loop and waded into the edge of the current. Years ago, in Kansas City, some friendly cowboys had shown her how to throw a lasso. She could only pray the memory would serve her now.

The sandy mud sucked at her feet as she approached the terrified Patches. The cow's eyes bulged, showing bloodshot white around the rims. Anna could feel the mud sucking at her own feet, but she knew she would need to get as close as possible or the rope would miss. She would be all right as long as she kept moving, she reassured herself. Yes, that was the secret of walking on quicksand. Don't let your weight settle, and don't stay too long in one place. It had become her credo for living as well.

For all her caution, she could feel herself sinking as she edged closer. The sandy mud was up to her ankles now, and she had to pause to position the rope. Holding her breath, Anna tossed the loop. It hovered for an instant, like a smoke ring on the air. Then, miraculously, it settled over the top of the cow's head.

"Pull it tight!" Carrie shrieked from the bank. "Hurry, before it slips off!"

Anna jerked the rope hard. The effort sent her staggering backward. As the rope tightened around the base of the long horns, she lost her balance and toppled into the mud.

"Hang on to the rope!" Josh shouted. "We'll wrap our end around the tree! Then you can pull yourself out!"

Anna groped for the rope in the swirling brown water. She was covered with mud by now, and sinking deeper by the second.

"Lie flat and spread out," Carrie shouted. "That's what Papa always tells us. It'll keep you from sinking!"

Anna spread-eagled her arms and legs and found that it was true. The sinking had stopped, and she was able to drag herself hand over hand onto solid ground.

She staggered to her feet, coated in a solid sheet of mud.

"Too bad Patches doesn't have hands," Josh commented sadly. "She could pull herself out, too."

"We'll just have to do that for her," Anna said. But her heart sank as she looked back at the cow. The rope on her horns might keep her head from going under, but no amount of pulling would free her massive body from the quicksand's powerful grip.

"If only Papa was here with the mules!" Carrie sank dejectedly onto a log. "He could get a rope around her, and they could pull her out."

"We've got to get word to him." Anna could feel the mud shrinking and cracking around her in the hot morning sun. For any of them, walking the distance would take hours.

Aching with frustration, she stared out at the wretched cow. The dog whined and sniffed her muddy hand, as if demanding that she do something about this awful situation. Absentmindedly, she scratched the shaggy head.

"I've got it!" Josh shouted, bouncing up and down. "We can tie a message to Doubtful's collar and send him up the road after Pa!"

"Yes!" Carrie was up in a flash. "I'll get a clean dish cloth!" she called over her shoulder. "We can write on it with soot from the stove!"

"But writing will take a long time!" Josh argued, striving to keep up with her on his short legs. "What will you say?"

"Just one word," Carrie answered. *"HELP."*

Anna stood on the riverbank and watched them go. They were wonderful children, she thought. Strong, spirited and resourceful. Malachi was raising them well. The last thing he deserved was to lose them.

The cow was panting, her mud-caked sides fluttering with each shallow breath. Anna pulled the rope taut and wrapped it securely around the tree trunk. Even if Patches didn't drown, how much longer would the poor beast last out there in the brutal sun with big, blue flies swarming around her face? It might be kinder to shoot her now and put her out of her misery. But Malachi would have the rifle, Anna reminded herself. He always took it when he went up to the slide.

"Go, Doubtful! Find Papa!" She could hear the children shouting and cheering as the huge dog raced up the road. Yes, let them hope, Anna thought as she settled herself on the log. Let them believe Malachi would return in time to save Patches from a lingering death. She could not believe it herself. Sad, ugly things happened every day, and there were no miracles to stop them and make everything all right. Malachi's children were too young to know that. But she wasn't.

When the children had quieted down, Anna sent them into the house to finish breakfast and do their lessons while she kept watch on Patches. The sun crawled across the sky, sucking moisture from everything its rays touched. High in the blazing turquoise sky, great black birds—vultures, surely—began to gather and circle.

Anna found a bucket by the pump and used it to fling river water onto the cow's face, cooling her and washing away the flies. Patches continued to sink, slowly but steadily. By now only her head and the top of her back remained clear of the mud.

Anna was scooping water from the shallows when she heard the children shouting. Her ears caught the sound of Doubtful's bark and Lucifer's wheezing bray. Her knees weakened with relief. Malachi had come at last. But she knew he had brought no magic with him. He would spend all his strength for the sake of the children, but in the end...

Anna forced the thought away as she waited for him to appear.

Malachi raced through the willows with the children at his heels. At the river's edge he could see Anna, coated from head to toe with drying, crumbling mud. A stone's toss beyond her, mired to the neck, was the cow.

He swore under his breath, sick at heart. Patches looked like a goner, but he had no choice except to do what he could.

Anna faced him, her eyes red-rimmed holes in the muddy mask of her face. "Carrie found her like this," she said brokenly. "We don't know how she got out. Oh, Malachi, what's the use?"

"Maybe no use at all," he said softly, so the children wouldn't hear. "But Josh and Carrie won't get over it anytime soon if we lose her. They've had enough bad dreams about their mother." He turned away and surveyed the thick rope. "We'll have to get it around her hind quarters, or there'll be no chance at all," he said. "Hold on, I'm going into the river."

Josh and Carrie had emerged from the willows and stood on the bank watching him. Carrie had been cry-

ing again and Josh looked as if he were about to start.
"I'll do what I can," Malachi told them, "but she's
stuck bad. I can't promise—"

He tore his gaze away without finishing the sentence, kicked off his boots and waded into the eddying river. The sandy mud gave way beneath his
weight, pulling at his feet as he plunged forward.
Only speed would keep him from going under. He
lunged toward the cow, his fingers catching the sharp
bony ridge of her spine. Patches shuddered beneath
the familiar touch. Her eyes rolled, showing white as
she lowed piteously. Malachi caught the loop of rope
that encircled her horns. Then he turned and shouted
at the trio on the bank.

"Anna, loosen the rope around the tree and play it
out toward me! Then get ready to catch this end when
I throw it to you! That way I can try to work the
middle part around her rump! Josh, get a couple of
shovels from the shed! Carrie, you bring the mules!"

He rested for a moment, breathing hard, while
Anna freed the rope. Then he drew it toward him,
hand over hand, until he had enough slack to toss the
loop to Anna. She caught it awkwardly, then pulled
it back until the ends were even and Malachi was
holding the middle. "Good!" he shouted above the
sound of the river. "Now hang on to those ends and
give me just a little slack—that's it—"

The cow's hindquarters were imbedded in mud that
had settled and solidified to the consistency of wet
concrete. Malachi stretched his body along her length,
taking care not to add his weight to her own. With
his hands, he began clawing away the mud, flinging
each handful into the current. It was excruciating

work. The mud flowed back into place almost as fast as his hands could scoop it away. His progress could barely be measured in inches.

Time crawled at the pace of slow-dripping blood. Glancing up, he saw that Carrie had brought the mules and that Josh was standing on the bank balancing the two shovels as if uncertain what to do with them. Malachi wanted to call out to his children, but the effort of staying above the cold, sucking mud and trying to work the rope behind the cow had drained his strength. His hands were growing numb, and he had long since lost all feeling in his legs and feet. But he knew he could not give up. Not with so much at stake. If only—

"Give me the rope!" Anna's voice was so close that it startled him. He looked up to see her eyes gazing at him from the other side of the cow.

"For heaven's sake, Malachi, don't be such a proud fool!" she snapped. "You can't do this alone! While you dig away the mud I can work the rope down behind Patches! It's the only way we'll get her out!"

Still numb, Malachi stared at her—this small, determined woman, caked with river muck and glowering at him over the butt end of a cow. She had lied to him, evaded him, inflamed and infuriated him at every turn. He had yet to find out who she was and why she had consented to become his wife. But suddenly none of it mattered. At that instant he knew he loved her—loved her to the depths of his lonesome, miserable soul. And he knew that he would move the whole world, if need be, to make her his.

"The rope—" She reached around the cow and

snatched it out of his grip. Spurred to action, Malachi scraped furiously at the mud. Before each hollow could fill in, Anna shoved the rope lower. She had been right, he conceded. This was far easier than doing the job alone. Even so, it was hard going, especially in the icy current. Anna was already weakening. Her lips were blue, her teeth beginning to chatter. To make matters worse, she was on the downstream side of the cow and had to hang on with one hand to keep from being swept away.

Malachi was scooping the last few handfuls of mud from around the cow's haunches when he heard a little cry. Anna's chilled fingers had lost their grip. The treacherous river had caught her and was sweeping her downstream. "The rope!" he shouted. "Anna, grab the rope!"

He saw the flash of her white hands reaching out, and, an instant later, felt the rope snap tight where it crossed behind the cow's haunches. The loose end, which she had left on the bank, whipped outward, the tension swinging her into the roiling current.

"Hang on!" Malachi shouted, praying she would not lose her grip. He could feel the weight of her body, feel the leaden drag of the water as he pulled her toward him, hand over hand. If he were to lose her now—

His heart stopped as he caught sight of her. By some miracle, the rope had twisted around her hands, but Anna was not holding on. She was floating faceup in the muddy river, her golden hair streaming behind her.

One lunge and he had her by the arms. Her face was as gray as wood ash but her eyes were open.

Dizzy with relief, he caught her close. She coughed, spitting up water. Together they staggered into the shallows, still dragging the rope. "I'm all right," she croaked. "Let's get Patches."

Malachi eased her to the ground. Then, seizing one of the shovels, he began to scoop out a path between the trapped cow and the bank. Anna, still coughing, scrambled to her feet and waded in beside him with the other shovel. Then the children were there as well, scooping out hollows with their small, bare hands. Mud and sand flew, coating all four of them as they dug a water-filled path toward the cow. Patches's front legs were nearly free, but she had long since stopped lowing. Her eyelids drooped; her breathing was shallow and labored.

"Is she going to die?" Josh was covered with mud and close to tears. The boy's question tore at Malachi's heart.

"Not if we can help it. Come on, let's pull her out." Malachi found the mud-soaked rope and tied one end to Lucifer's saddle horn, the other to Beelzebub's pack frame. "Stand between them and keep them pulling evenly," he told Carrie. "Can you do that?"

"Yes, Papa." She stepped into place, dwarfed by the big animals but unafraid. Malachi felt a stab of pride. Lucifer and Beelzebub were headstrong creatures, but his daughter could handle them.

"You be our watcher," he told Josh. "Stand over there on that rock and let us know if you see anything about to go wrong." In truth, Malachi just wanted the boy out of harm's way. But Josh, taking his assignment seriously, clambered onto the boulder and stood at attention with one hand shading his eyes against the glare.

Anna had waded back into the water-filled trench and was half-crouched at Patches's head, stroking the long, bony face and crooning softly. She looked as spent as the poor cow, but Malachi knew better than to order her onto the bank.

Taking his place at the river's edge, he barked a command to the well-trained mules. *"Ha!"* The rope tightened and quivered as they strained forward. Malachi could hear the loosening suction of the mud as the cow's body shifted forward.

"Malachi! She's going down! She'll drown!" Anna's cry pierced his ears, and he turned to see that Patches had fallen to her knees with nothing but her nose and her horns above the water. Anna was shoulder deep in muck, struggling vainly to get her up.

Malachi plunged in and thrust himself beneath the cow's chest, causing her to lurch upward. He felt her stumble forward as the rope cut into her haunches. Then, with a hideous sucking sound, her hindquarters came loose from the mud. Anna held her head, crooning encouragement as she strained forward. One quivering step, then another, until, with eye-bulging effort, Patches lunged up onto the bank, where she stood with her sides heaving and her coat streaming mud.

Anna's knees gave way beneath her. She folded, collapsing like a marionette whose strings had been cut. Just short of the ground, Malachi's powerful hand caught her waist. He had come out of the river just behind her. "It's all right," he murmured, his own voice trembling with exhaustion. "Everything's all right, Anna."

She sagged against him as the children bounded toward them, Josh whooping, Carrie sobbing. They came together and suddenly all four of them were hugging, dancing, laughing and crying. "We did it!" Josh crowed, flinging his arms around Anna's legs. "We saved Patches, all of us together!"

Malachi's arm tightened around Anna's waist. With his free hand he reached down and caught up his son, hefting him to shoulder level. Anna herself reached out and drew Carrie into the circle of arms. She felt the fresh, salty wetness of the girl's tears as she hugged her close.

The dog pressed against Malachi's legs, whimpering and wagging like a puppy. Even Patches was caught up in the spirit of celebration. She snorted, then shook her filthy hide, sending a shower of mud splattering down over them all. Josh and Carrie squealed with laughter.

Anna nestled close to Malachi, savoring the strength of his big, warm, solid body. Was this what it was like? she wondered. Was this how it felt to be a family?

Malachi bent to ease his son's way to the ground. "No more work for the rest of the afternoon," he said. "We'll get Patches cleaned up and resting in the barn. Then we'll pack a quick lunch and take the dory upriver to the Indian Cave. How does that sound to you?"

"Yay!" Josh sprang the rest of the way to the ground, whooping like a little savage as he dashed for the house with Carrie at his heels. Anna knew she should follow them, but Malachi's arm still circled her waist, holding her against him in a powerful grip she had no will to resist.

Arching her back, she looked up into his mud-smeared face. His pale-blue eyes blazed down at her like fire opals, igniting hot little swirls of desire in the core of her body. The need that awakened in her was a deep, throbbing ache, a molten pool of yearning. "You're...all muddy," she whispered inanely.

"Yes." His voice was a thick, velvety rasp. "Yes, I know. So are you." His hands slid around her, their contact so intimate through the wet, clinging flannel of her nightshirt that she might as well have been naked. Anna pressed closer, needing him as she had never needed anyone in her life. She needed his hands, his strong, seeking mouth, the heavenly heat of his skin against her own. But needing was one thing, she reminded herself harshly. Having was something else—something a woman in her circumstances could not dare to dream of.

Aching, Anna pushed herself away from him. "We made a bargain," she said. "And this wasn't part of it."

His features hardened beneath the muddy mask. "So I should remember," he said, the sun glittering in his granite-flecked eyes. "Don't worry, Anna. I won't touch you again."

"Thank you." She mouthed the words as she turned away, hiding her anguish. The shouts of the children echoed down through the willows. Seconds later they burst onto the bank carrying buckets and a scrub brush for washing down the cow. Forcing her face to smile, Anna strode to meet them. They had so few pleasures, these two endearing youngsters. She would not spoil their day.

Taking a bucket from Josh, she waded into the shallows, scooped a pail of water and splashed it over Patches's mud-caked flanks. "We're the ones who need a good scrubbing!" she laughed. "Look at us!"

"We can swim and get clean at the Indian Cave. The water's warm and clear there, and there are old Indian ruins, high up on the cliff." Carrie bent to fill her own bucket. Patches's brown-and-white coat gleamed through the sloughing mud, and the gentle, bovine eyes had begun to show glimmers of life.

Malachi had set off for the corral with the mules, probably glad to be out of her presence, Anna reflected gloomily. Things would be strained between them for the duration of her stay. But maybe that was for the best.

"The Indian Cave was one of Mama's favorite places," Carrie was saying. "We used to have a lot of fun there, but Papa hasn't taken us to the Cave since she died. I guess he was afraid that being there would make him sad."

"But he didn't seem sad today," Josh glanced up from scrubbing Patches's hip with the brush. "Maybe that's because you're here."

Anna squeezed the boy's shoulder, touched by his sensitivity. Her eyes blinked back furtive tears. It didn't matter, she told herself. She would never have to worry about competing with Elise's memory. As soon as she had fulfilled her part of the bargain with Malachi, she would be leaving this godforsaken place. She would begin a new life, hopefully in California;

and she would never see Malachi Stone or his children again.

Resolving to bring up a pleasanter subject, she cleared the tightness out of her throat. "By the way, Carrie," she said, "your father told me that last year, when a peddler came through, he traded ferry service for some cloth and sewing supplies. You don't happen to know where those things are, do you?"

The girl frowned thoughtfully, then brightened. "Why, yes! They're in Mama's old trunk, the one in my room! But I don't know how to sew. Mama wasn't very good at it, either. She was saving the cloth to take to a dressmaker in Kanab, at least that's what she said."

"Well, *I* can sew up a storm!" Anna declared. "And as soon as we get back from the Indian Cave, we're going to open up that trunk and start making some clothes for you and Josh. You can help me— I'll teach you what to do as we go along."

"Really?" Carrie's lovely, mahogany eyes sparkled. "There's a bolt of blue gingham I like—but, Anna, there's so much cloth! We could make some dresses for me and some for you, too!"

"We'll see about that." Anna poured another two gallons of the Colorado over the Patches's muddy neck. "I also play the piano. Not very well, I'm afraid, but if you're interested, I could at least teach you how to read music."

"Oh!" Carrie dropped her bucket and flung her arms around Anna's neck, hugging her exuberantly. "Oh, you can't imagine how much I've wanted to learn! How soon can we—"

The sound that cut off her words shattered the midday calm and startled two ravens into squawking flight. Anna froze, her nerves screaming as the sound echoed down the canyon, ringing off the high, rocky walls.

Someone had just fired a rifle.

Chapter Twelve

"Get down!" Anna seized the children and jerked them flat beside her on the bank. To her surprise, both Josh and Carrie promptly sat up and began to giggle. "What on earth—?" she muttered, spitting out sand.

"Over there!" Josh pointed to a pair of mounted figures on the far side of the river. "Those men need to come across. The shot's a signal for the ferry, that's all."

"I see." Anna clambered to her feet, still uneasy. As far as she was concerned, no visitor should be trusted. But at least this pair of travelers was coming from the south. They would not have encountered Sam Johnson or heard the gossip about the ferryman's blond mail-order bride.

"Come on!" Josh was tugging at her hand, pulling her to her feet. "You've never seen Pa run the ferry. Sometimes he even lets us ride the boat across!"

Anna hesitated, weighing her chance of being recognized against the eagerness of the children. "I look a mess!" she argued, grasping for an excuse to stay out of sight.

"Don't be a goose, we all look the same!" Carrie looped the rope around a stump to keep the cow from wandering, then seized Anna's free hand and pulled her along the bank. The girl was right, Anna conceded. No traveler, seeing her, would ever make the connection between this filthy, bedraggled creature and the glamorous Anna de Carlo. For once, she would be perfectly safe.

Malachi was already at the landing when they arrived. Anna avoided his gaze, focusing her attention on the ingenious system of cables and pulleys he had rigged to guide the large, flat boat across the rushing current. She imagined him leaving his family in Santa Fe for months on end, coming here all alone to build the ferry and the house. She thought of the isolation, the hours of backbreaking work as he strung the cables, hauled the lumber, moved and laid the heavy stones. Malachi had built this place out of nothing but sweat, blood and hope. No wonder he had no desire to leave.

"Pa, can we ride over with you?" Josh bounced with excitement, his brown eyes sparkling. "With just two horses, there'll be plenty of room!"

Malachi scowled at the roiling current. "All right. But you're to stay close to Anna and Carrie and hold on to the side rails. Hear me?"

"Yes, Pa." Josh grinned at his father, then gave a loud whoop as he scampered onto the deck. Even then, Anna might have hung back. But Josh was already aboard, and Malachi had ordered his son to stay close to her. How could she risk letting the boy fall overboard? She followed Carrie, her bare feet stepping carefully on the splintery pine deck, until she stood beside Josh at the rail.

The timbers creaked as the ferry cast off from the landing. Anna gazed down at the water, so thick with silt that it looked like a solid, seething brown mass beneath the boat. An image flashed through her mind—Elise drowning in the darkness, her black hair swirling in the muddy water, her fine, white hands reaching, groping at thin air, then vanishing from sight. How had Malachi managed to find her so soon? she wondered. By rights her body should have been carried far downriver.

Forcing the thought from her mind, she swung her gaze toward Malachi, where he sat manning the long sweeps. His massive shoulders bulged and rippled as he drove the squared-off craft across the sweeping current. The cables and pulleys would serve to stabilize the boat and keep it from being carried downstream, but it was Malachi's strength alone that kept it moving forward.

As they neared the south bank, she could see that the two riders had dismounted and moved onto the landing. They were lean, hawkish creatures, both of them clad in trailworn clothes that had taken on the rusty hue of desert dust. The shorter man held the rifle he had used to signal the ferry. The two would be wearing side arms as well, Anna calculated, her blood running cold in her veins. Such men as these she knew by instinct, as a doe might come to know the sight of wolves. Her throat moved.

"Bounty hunters."

She did not realize she had spoken aloud until Carrie answered her. "Yes, you're right. Those two men come through here once or twice every season, sometimes with a prisoner. But it doesn't look as if they've caught one this time.''

''No...it doesn't.'' Anna swallowed a surge of nauseating terror. What could she do if they recognized her? Where could she go?

Malachi's muscles strained as he pulled the oars, moving the boat across the boiling brown water. Only now did Anna notice that he had slipped a leather vest over his muddy chambray work shirt—a vest that did not quite conceal the outline of the holstered pistol that bulged along his hip. Strapping on the gun would be routine, of course, a precaution against any trouble at the ferry. Malachi would not take any chances with the safety of his family.

But would she want him using the gun to protect *her?* Anna weighed the question, her heart pounding as the boat closed in on the landing. No, she swiftly resolved. There could be no gunplay where Malachi or the children might be caught in the line of fire. If the bounty hunters recognized her, she would have only two choices—surrender peacefully or go into the river.

The end of the boat crunched lightly against the bank, and Malachi strode ashore with the line to secure the craft while he lowered the ramp and collected the required fare. Then he stepped back and allowed the two bounty hunters to lead their mounts onto the flat pine deck.

Anna clung to the side rail, drawing Josh close against her to keep him from getting under the legs of the horses. In truth, she knew the boy could take care of himself. But it was only her grip on the small, bony shoulder that kept her fear from dissolving into utter panic.

Malachi's conversation with the two men was terse, confined to the price of passage and the condition of the road. He was not a talkative man, and neither were the bounty hunters. The two of them stood grimly beside their dusty mounts, steadying the nervous animals as the boat pushed back into the current. Anna studied them with the furtive, frightened gaze of a rabbit watching a pair of coyotes. Could they feel her terror, smell and taste it as she could?

The taller man wore a ragged Mexican serape and a shapeless, moth-eaten felt hat. His mouth was a narrow slit above the greasy black smudge of his beard. His hands, long and thin, like a concert violinist's, toyed with the reins he held, constantly moving, twitching. The shorter man had grizzled hair and a face like the side of an old leather valise. He hawked and spat a yellow stream into the churning water. Neither of them gave Anna more than a cursory glance. She was only the ferryman's woman, barefoot, unkempt and ragged, hardly worth a glance, let alone a one-thousand-dollar reward.

Anna stared down at the mud-spattered deck, keeping her face lowered as her fingers clutched Josh's shoulder. The bounty hunters probably thought she was the boy's real mother. So much the better. She was safe for the moment—but that moment, she knew, would not last. Sooner or later someone would make the connection between the woman at Stone's Ferry and the wanted murderess on the poster. When—not if—that happened, they would come for her, men like these, wolves and vultures in human form who would show her no mercy.

An eternity seemed to pass before the ferry boat nosed up to the landing and Malachi leaped ashore with the rope. He moved with the easy grace of a man who knew exactly who he was and where he belonged, knowing exactly the lay of the deck, the knotting of the ropes, the rise and fall of the water. Whatever had happened to him in the outside world, here he was master.

Anna hung back with the children while the two bounty hunters led their horses down the ramp and mounted up. "You say there'll be no trouble getting over the slide?" the older man asked Malachi.

"Not if you're careful." Malachi bent to tighten one of the lines. "But I'd lead the horses over the worst of it if I were you. No sense taking a chance on one of them breaking a leg or sliding down the scree."

"We'll keep that in mind." The man swung his horse toward the road, his companion following as Anna led the children ashore. Her knees buckled as she watched the pair swing their mounts onto the deeply rutted trail that skirted the yard before joining the road that ascended the canyon. It was all right, she reassured herself. The men had not recognized her, and now they were leaving. But, dear heaven, she had been so afraid—

"Anna, what is it? What's the matter?" Carrie's question pierced the sultry midday silence. Anna's heart dropped as the taller man halted abruptly and turned in the saddle. His hard-eyed gaze caught Anna full-face, and she dared not show her fear by looking away. For the space of a breath he stared at her, as if taking her measure. Then he turned, nudged his mount to a trot and followed his cohort around the bend, behind the willows.

Once more, Anna's legs threatened to collapse beneath her. The man was gone. But he had seen her face and heard her name. An ordinary stranger might forget her, but a man who lived by searching out names and faces would not.

"Anna?" Malachi's daughter touched her arm. "Please say something. Are you all right?"

"Yes." Anna forced herself to stir, to turn and look at the girl. Malachi was watching her with narrowed eyes, his hands resting on the knotted rope. "Yes, I'm fine," she lied. "Just a bit too much sun, that's all."

"Can we go to the Indian Cave now?" Josh tugged at his father's vest. "Can we, Pa? Please?"

Malachi nodded, looking tense and weary. "All right. As soon as the chores are done and the cow's put away and fed."

"I'll make lunch!" Carrie chimed in. "Do you want to help me, Anna?"

"Gladly." Anna followed the girl's darting figure, feeling the weight of the day like a millstone on her shoulders. She would put on a pleasant face for the sake of the children and do her best to enjoy the outing to the cave. But the tension between herself and Malachi had cast a pall over the day. Worse, the encounter with the two bounty hunters had left her with a case of screaming nerves. Bargain or no bargain, she could not risk her freedom or the safety of this family any longer. She would find no peace until she was gone from this place.

"Did you ever hear of Sweet Betsy from Pike,
Who crossed the wide prairies with her lover Ike,
With two yoke of oxen and one spotted hog,
A tall Shanghai rooster and an old yaller dog.
Hoodle dang foldi dyedo, hoodle dang
foldi day..."

Malachi sat on a flat rock, his rifle balanced across his knees. Thirty feet below, at the foot of the ledge, lay the shallow, rock-lined pool where Anna frolicked, laughing and singing, with the children. The lilting melody and nonsensical words that drifted up to him on the afternoon breeze, only served to darken his spirits.

The Indian Cave—named long ago by Carrie—was a complex of hanging gardens above the river, where tiny, sparkling waterfalls cascaded into sun-warmed pools. Clumps of fern, ivy and wild columbine festooned the seeping sandstone walls where swallows dipped and darted in the misty spray.

High above the river, perched like an eyrie near the top of a sheer ledge, was the Indian Cave, a shadowy recess in the rock, walled in by ancient mud bricks. It could be reached only by a dizzying line of footholds that had been chiseled into the stone by long-ago hands. Years ago, during his time alone in the canyon, Malachi had made the ascent and found a store of shriveled maize ears inside, along with some broken shards of pottery. He had left the spirits of the place undisturbed and forbidden his children to make the dangerous climb.

All the same, his entire family had enjoyed the pools. Even Elise had seemed at peace in this mystical place—or so he had thought at the time. But in truth she had never been at peace. Neither here nor any other place.

Willing the memory away, he gazed down into the crystal water below, where Anna and Josh romped like otters while Carrie, already the lady, kept a more sedate distance at the pool's far end. The mud-stained nightshirt Anna had worn all day served, now, as a swimming garment. It floated around her, revealing flashes of leg as she kicked and paddled, ignoring the ravenous gaze from above.

Malachi cursed in burning frustration. At that heart-stopping moment in the river when he'd looked into her muddy face and realized he loved her, someone should have whacked him in the head with a single-tree. How could a woman be so hot one minute and cold the next? And how could a man make such a fool of himself? It was enough to make him swear off the gentler sex for the rest of his life!

But that wasn't the worst of it—not by a long shot. He'd suspected all along that Anna was hiding something, and now he knew it. When that bounty hunter had turned in the saddle to look back at her, the stark terror in her amber eyes had told him all he needed to know.

What was she running from? He could not depend on her to tell him anything resembling the truth. But what difference did it make? If Anna had broken the law, he had to get her out of here before she broke his children's hearts as well.

Even now, it might be too late. Josh was already following her around like an adoring little pup. And Carrie… Malachi sighed as he watched his daughter laughing in the pool, splashing water on her brother.

The girl had unfolded like a blossom since Anna's arrival. The promise of new clothes and music lessons had her glowing with excitement. He had not seen her so happy since the days before her mother died.

How would the girl take it when Anna left? How would Josh? What was he going to tell them, his tender, twice-betrayed young children?

Malachi tore his gaze away from the tawny-hired siren in the pool. He scanned the flawless turquoise sky, his sun-dazzled eyes tracing the high, circling flight of a golden eagle above the vermilion cliffs. The hell of it was, he needed Anna. Without her help, he wouldn't have a prayer of convincing the courts his children had decent motherly care. Even with her help, the odds were so long that it sickened him to think of them.

He looked down at them again, his children, laughing and splashing with Anna in the crystal pool. Josh's wiry young body was as brown as a Paiute's. Carrie's was as pale and delicate as English bone china where she rose from the water in her clinging shift, her arms crossed self-consciously over her swelling young breasts. Malachi ached with the need to shield her from harm. The outside world was such a dangerous place. And now even here, in the canyon, there was no promise of safety.

A vision flashed through his mind—Anna, looming over the supine Eddie, hellfire blazing in her eyes as her shaking hands brandished a limb that was nearly as big as she was. Anna, the destroying angel, the passionate protector of innocence.

The innocence she herself had so brutally lost.

His fingers toyed with the satiny contours of the

rifle stock as he remembered the feel of her in his arms, remembered each lush, ripe curve of her sensuous woman's body and the warm, eager moistness of her mouth. Even now the memory raised the familiar straining tightness against the crotch of his trousers. Even now he was almost crazy with wanting her.

But no more, Malachi vowed, steeling his resolve. He would accept Anna's help with the children. And he would keep his side of the bargain when the time came for her to leave. But leave she would. Her presence in this canyon was a danger to him and to his children. He could not allow her to stay.

Anna was dreaming of blood—Harry's blood... *She was covered in it, her hands, her clothes, her streaming, matted hair. Her bare feet left carmine blotches on the floor as she stumbled forward, groping her way through a serpentine maze of corridors that writhed and moved, separating and joining, changing shape even as she passed.*

Behind her, she could hear them coming, the sinister footfalls echoing off the walls, each step resonating until they seemed to be all around her, filling her ears and head, altering the very rhythm of her heart.

Frantic to escape, she dodged like a frightened animal, one way, then another. Down there—the passage was long and straight. She ran headlong into the tunnel, her feet still leaving blotches of blood. But what she thought was a straight passage only doubled back upon itself, taking her deeper into the labyrinth.

Wild with terror, she plunged off in a new direc-

*tion—only to run headlong into a large, solid lump
of flesh. As she stumbled backward, Sam Johnson's
greasy face leered out of the darkness. He was pointing at her, his face fixed in a drooling grin.*

*His laughter echoed behind her as, wheeling, she
raced down a side passage. She was floating now, her
limbs pumping with laborious grace, as if she were
moving through layers of water. Up ahead—was that
a light? Anna struggled toward it, her heart all but
bursting with effort. Rounding a bend, she stopped
cold. The two bounty hunters stood directly in her
path, their faces as cold as granite slabs. The shorter
man held the Wanted poster, the taller man a hang-
man's noose, which he thrust, sneering, into her face.*

*Again she found herself running—running with
leaden limbs that moved only with the most agonizing
effort. Her pulse was pounding like a steam engine,
threatening to burst her very heart. Her breath came
in wrenching gasps. She had to get away, had to find
a moment of rest or she would die here in this choking, evil blackness.*

*Suddenly, at the far end of a passage she saw Mala-
chi. He stood like an angel in a slanting ray of light,
smiling and holding out his arms to her. With a little
cry Anna ran toward him, floating through the murky
air in a daze of happiness. Malachi, her refuge, her
defender, her love. He was here, wanting her to come
to him, to be his—only his—forever.*

*He caught her in his arms, pulling her close, his
lips devouring her face, her hair, her eager, hungry
mouth. She felt his love washing over her like fresh,
cool water. The awful stain of Harry's blood was
gone. She was clean. She was safe. She was free.*

His kisses awakened wellsprings of joy inside her. She closed her eyes welcoming the freshets of need that surged and quivered in her body. It seemed so natural to love this man, her husband.

"So I have you at last."

The blade-thin voice in her ear was not Malachi's. Anna's eyes shot open. A scream strangled in her throat as she found herself staring into the dark, glittering eyes of Louis Caswell....

She awoke with a jerking spasm of terror. For a long moment she lay still, her heart galloping. The night was silent around her, broken only by the chirp of a cricket and the distant murmur of the river. The cloud-veiled moon glimmered softly through the window, illuminating a dim square of light on the opposite wall.

Turning onto her back, she stared into the darkness, willing her knotted muscles to relax, her breathing to slow. She was safe for the moment. But that moment would not last. The dream had brought that home with a certainty as final as death itself.

How real it had seemed for a moment—Malachi's arms around her, comforting her, protecting her from the terrors that filled her nights. But when the terror became real, she knew, he would not be there to protect her. She would face the danger as she had faced everything else in her life—alone.

But, sweet heaven, how she had wanted him— wanted him from that first moment when she had stepped out of the ranch house and seen him, dusty and sunburned, his silver eyes squinting at her through the glare of sunlight. He was so big and silent and awkward, so tender beneath the layers of strength and stubbornness. Even then she had wondered how his arms would feel, his kisses, the hard, masculine thrust of his body....

Oh, blast! This wasn't helping at all!

Disgusted with herself, Anna sat up and swung her legs over the side of the bed. What she needed right now was a good, cold dose of reality. And her best chance of finding it lay in the words of the one woman who had truly known Malachi Stone—the one woman he had loved.

Dropping her bare feet to the rug, she fumbled for a candle and a match on the nightstand. The flame was small and furtive, and she held it low so that Malachi, if he happened to be prowling the yard, would not notice the light through the window. The flickering flame illuminated the pieces of checked gingham that were piled on the dresser. The previous afternoon she and Carrie had chosen the cloth from among the bolts in the chest, and Anna had measured the excited girl for a new dress and cut the fabric. Since she had no desire to go back to sleep, now would be a good time to begin stitching, Anna reminded herself. But the lure of Elise's journal was too strong. The dress would have to wait.

The slim leather volume lay under the mattress where she had left it earlier. What was she looking for? Anna asked herself as she worked it out of its hiding place and thumbed through the mildew-specked pages. Reading the journal would only make her restless and melancholy. So why torture herself? Was it because the journal was the key to Malachi? A way to know him as Elise had known him?

Dismissing the question, she opened the book and, as if selecting tonight's arrow to her own heart, knelt on the rug and began to read.

The early pages were familiar in their tone and content. The drudgery, the loneliness, the fact that Malachi was always working and steadfastly refusing to take her back to Santa Fe.

Stifling a yawn, Anna turned the page to a new entry, and suddenly the words, hastily scrawled in a surge of excitement, seemed to leap of the page at her.

June 4, 1888

Today I met a man—quite the most fascinating young man I have ever encountered. His name is John Barlow, a photographer by trade, presently working on a collection of Western photographs for exhibit in his hometown of Chicago, Illinois. Oh, but I am getting quite ahead of myself. I must start from the beginning while I can still recall every minute of this wonderful day.

I was hanging out the wash about midmorning when he came riding down the road on a tall roan, leading a pack mule loaded with his equipment. Strangers tend to make me uneasy, especially when Malachi is away, but John—as he invited me to call him—was so young and handsome, with wheaten hair and eyes the color of Navajo turquoise. I confess that for the first moment all I could do was stare at him, my heart fluttering in my foolish chest. I was acutely aware of my wind-tousled hair, my threadbare clothes and workworn hands, but he dismounted and presented himself to me as if I were a princess in a silken gown.

Eternities seemed to pass before I found my tongue and invited him into the house. My husband was away, I told him flinging all caution to the wind. And as I had not the strength to row the ferry across the river and back, especially with the water so high, he—John—would have to wait three more days for Malachi to return.

It would be no trouble at all, he assured me. If I would allow him to pitch his tent in some out-of-the-way spot, he would pass the time taking photographs of the canyon, which he had come to do in any case.

I invited him to lunch with us, and then to supper. The children took to him right away, and he was charming with them. He even took the time to show Joshua his camera while Carrie and I cleaned up the kitchen and washed the dishes.

After the children were in bed he joined me on the front steps. We talked for hours while the moon drifted across the sky. Oh, the places he has been—New York, New Orleans, even California! And the things he has done! How I envy such a free and joyous life! Half joking, I asked him to take me away with him. He looked at me in such a curious manner, I could not help but wonder what he was thinking. "Don't say such things unless you mean them, Elise," he told me, and I blushed in the darkness.

John did not do all the talking. Much of the time he listened to me, to all my silly little dreams. I found myself telling him small secrets I had never told anyone, not even Malachi. For that matter, I believe we exchanged more words in four hours than Malachi and I had shared in eleven long years!

When, at last, we knew it was time to go to our separate beds, he took my hand and clasped it tightly. For a long, breathless moment the stars swirled in my head. I had no power to move as he bent and kissed me, ever so gently, on the lips.

I was paralyzed with astonishment, but as his hands slid around my waist I found I had no will to resist. My response was as natural as breathing. I returned his embrace, and we stood locked together in the shadows, our mouths and bodies melting with desire. Both of us knew what would happen if we did not stop, but my willpower was gone. I could not pull myself away from him.

At last John found the strength to draw away from me. "No, my beautiful Elise," he murmured, gazing down into my face. "Much as I want you, I would not ruin you for the sake of my own pleasure. Go into the house now, and let me return to my lonely tent. In the morning you'll wake up and thank me for this. You'll see."

I turned and fled from him in a state of confusion. Tears blinded my eyes as I slipped into the house and bolted the door behind me. I knew what I wanted, what John wanted. But was I prepared to pay the price? He had left it to me to decide.

That, my nameless paper friend, was two hours ago. It is now past midnight, and I have not been able to close my eyes for a moment of sleep.

The idea that this is all I will ever have—a hovel in the wilderness with a man who cares nothing for my wishes—fills me with the blackest despair. Should I follow the rules and consign myself to a life of drudgery…or should I follow the cries of my lonely, desperate heart?

But I already know the answer to that wrenching question. I am going to John. Tonight. Now. Whatever the consequences.

Whatever the consequences…

Chapter Thirteen

Anna huddled in the light of the flickering candle, staring wide-eyed at the shakily scrawled lines, so unlike Elise's usual precise, elegant script. Malachi's perfect wife had been unfaithful to her marriage vows. She had given herself to a near stranger, a man she had known only a few hours. How could she have done such a thing—to Malachi, to her beautiful children?

But Anna already knew the answer to that question. She had read the frustration written into every line of Elise's journal. The loneliness, the privation, the unfilled needs. Yes, for all her shocked outrage, Anna understood, and she knew better than to cast the first stone. She was in no position to judge what Elise had done.

But what had happened after that fateful turning point? And what connection, if any, did Elise's affair have with her death?

Stop! Anna's instincts warned, but she had come too far along this path to turn back. She had walked in Elise's footsteps. Now she had no choice except to follow them to the very end.

Heart pounding, she turned the page to the journal's next—and final—entry.

June 6, 1888

John has moved his camp to a strip of land a mile downriver, accessible by foot, by horse or by boat. I understand, of course, that he does not want to be here when Malachi arrives. Still, his absence affects me as if a piece of my own flesh had been torn away. Our lovemaking these past two nights has changed my life forever, and I know that, whatever the cost, I can no longer be happy apart from this man.

Last night, for the first time, we spoke of my going away with him, just the two of us. The children, of course, could not be left alone long—for that reason we would have to delay our departure until just before Malachi's return. Even so, it would not be difficult to manage. There is a side canyon below John's camp, with a steep, winding trail that goes all the way to the rim. It is not a good trail, but in taking it, we would avoid meeting Malachi on the road....

Here the writing wavered and trailed off into little spatters of ink, as if the hand holding the pen had fallen into spasms of trembling. The rest of the page was blank, as was the rest of the journal.

Anna sat with her feet growing numb beneath her, the candlelit page blurring in her vision. Questions seethed in the dark recesses of her mind—questions whose answers she had no wish to learn.

She remembered Carrie's heartrending story of her mother's death. Had Elise set out to run away with her lover? Was that how she'd drowned? Was that why her clothes were missing—because, unable to carry them as far as the camp, she'd packed them in the dory and set out by river?

And Malachi—what if he'd known about the tryst? What if he'd arrived unexpectedly and caught the lovers together? He had gone to prison, Anna recalled, for beating a man. Was he capable of murder, as well? Could he have killed them both?

No! her heart screamed. *No, it wasn't possible!*

Anna glared down at the open page with fury and loathing. Why had she ever opened Elise's journal? Why had she allowed it to draw her in, to raise ugly questions that she had no business asking?

And why hadn't Elise taken the journal with her? Had she simply forgotten it? Or did she have some perverse need to leave behind a record of why she had vanished?

Anna's hands went cold as she thought of Josh and Carrie. No—Elise's children could never set their innocent eyes on this book. Its contents would destroy everything they believed about their mother. It would haunt them for the rest of their lives. She could not allow such a thing to happen.

Staggering to her feet, she forced her numb legs to move, to carry her into the dark kitchen where embers still glowed in the belly of the big iron stove. Her hands shook as she lifted one of the iron lids, ripped a page from the back of the journal and dropped it onto the coals. The damp, mildewed paper smoldered for a perilous instant; then the flame died, leaving the page intact save for its blackened edge.

With a muttered curse, she seized the poker and thrust the limp paper into the bed of orange coals. It burned, but with excruciating slowness, sending out a thick spiral of whitish smoke. Hastily now, Anna ripped out a handful of pages and stuffed them into the black maw of the stove—too many pages, she swiftly realized. The musty paper was smothering the feeble blaze. Frantically she stabbed at the smoky mess with the point of the poker. Choking, white smoke had begun to pour out of the stove. It stung her eyes and throat as she struggled to separate the papers.

"What are you doing, Anna?" Malachi's raw whisper exploded out of the silence behind her.

Anna stiffened as if she had felt the point of a blade between her shoulders. Her thoughts whirled like the crown of a runaway dust devil. How much did he know about his wife's infidelity? Nothing? Everything? Enough to murder her?

"Anna?" His voice had dropped to a growl. Goose bumps rose along her arms as she slipped the remains of the journal into the folds of the nightshirt, flattening it against her side. "I asked you what you were doing," he said.

"Nothing." Her voice shook, betraying her frayed nerves. "I—was cold. That's all. Yes—I was just stoking the fire."

"With *this?*" He peeled a soggy scrap of paper from the lip of the hole. "I'd have an easier time believing it if you told me you were sending smoke signals! What the devil is going on? And what's that you're hiding?''

His hand flashed out with the speed of a striking rattler, seizing Anna's wrist and whipping her around to face him.

"Let me go, or I'll scream!" she whispered, meeting the cold, gray moons of his eyes. "I'll wake the children—"

"Go ahead." He called her bluff, then forced the remains of the journal from her reluctant fingers. She stumbled back against the stove as he released her. Fortunately, at this late hour, the surface wasn't hot enough to burn her.

But she forgot about burning when she righted herself and saw his face in the hellish glow of the exposed coals. He was staring down at the tattered remnants of his wife's journal, his faced blanched with the shock of recognition.

"This is Elise's handwriting," he rasped. "Where did you get this, and what the devil were you trying to accomplish by burning it?"

Anna pushed herself away from the stove and squared her shoulders, steeling herself against the withering power of his eyes. She thought of the children, asleep behind the closed doors of their rooms, and she spoke now for their sake.

"What am I trying to accomplish? I'm getting rid of something that should never be allowed to see the light of day. Something with the power to destroy two precious young lives—and you, Malachi Stone, would be a fool to stop me!"

She saw the anger die in him like a blaze doused

with cold water. He slumped in the darkness, his face a rugged slab of pain.

"It was a diary? Hers?"

Anna nodded, hoping he would not demand to know what she'd read. She would not lie to Malachi. The time for lying was over. "I found it beneath a floorboard when I was looking for my earring," she said. "I should have left it alone—"

"But you didn't. You read it."

"Yes, and made up my mind to burn it." Did he know what the journal contained? Was that the reason for the anguish that furrowed his rough-chiseled face? "I was afraid the children might find it," she said. "There were things inside they...shouldn't see."

"Things?" His free hand caught her upper arm, the fingers tightening painfully. "What things, Anna? What did Elise tell you?"

She glared up at him, thinking she would give anything if he would just back off and spare her—spare himself. "Don't," she whispered. "Don't make me tell you. You'll only wish I hadn't."

The papers in the stove had dried out enough to catch fire. The damning pages burst into flame, the orange glow dancing through the grate, casting twisted shadows on the whitewashed wall. Malachi's shadow loomed above Anna's like a beast of prey about to strike. For the space of a heartbeat she was afraid. Then, once more, his shoulders sagged in defeat. His grip slackened on her arm, then fell away, leaving only a tingle where his fingers had so nearly bruised her flesh.

Anna's eyes widened as he turned toward the stove and dropped the last crumpled remnant of Elise's journal into the flames. The pungent odor of burning leather drifted upward as the cover began to smolder.

"Come on." He slid a large, rough hand behind her elbow and steered her none too gently toward the front door. The cool night breeze struck Anna's face as he swept her out onto the porch, leaving the door open to air out the smoky room. "You seem to know her side of the story," he said, sinking onto the step and pulling her down beside him. "Before you pass judgment on either of us, you might as well hear mine."

Anna huddled in the darkness, not touching him, but close enough to feel the tension that emanated from every nerve in his powerful male body. The night was alive with moon shadows, punctuated by small animal sounds and the rushing murmur of the Colorado. The dog sidled up to Malachi and thrust its muzzle beneath his hand. Absently, Malachi scratched the massive head. His eyes gazed outward toward the river. What was he remembering? Anna wondered. Clearly he knew about his wife's affair. But how had he found out—and what had he done about it?

Aching with dread, she waited as he cleared his throat and shifted his weight on the step. When he spoke it was more to the night, more to the sky and the river than to her.

"It took a long time for me to realize that Elise wasn't quite well in her mind," he said. "Oh, she was rational enough when it came to everyday things, like the house and the children, but sometimes—" he exhaled painfully as if groping for words "—there was this rigidity of will that defied all common sense. She'd get a bone in her teeth about something, and when that happened she wouldn't let loose of it until she had her way, no matter what the cost.''

No matter what the cost. Elise's own words echoed in Anna's head as she listened. There were two sides to this story, she reminded herself. She could no more afford to give full credence to Malachi's version than to his wife's.

''I know Elise wanted you to go back to Santa Fe,'' she said. ''And I know the kind of tactics she used to try to persuade you.''

He glanced at her, as if he were startled that she'd spoken. ''Then you also know those tactics didn't work,'' he said curtly. ''I couldn't leave. I'd invested everything I had in this place, in the hope that it would give us a decent life. There was nothing in Santa Fe, no way for me to support my family. But here I had something of my own. A source of pride…and hope.''

''Yes, I know.'' Anna reached over and laid a sympathetic hand on his knee. His muscles tightened beneath her palm, warning her that he was in no condition to be touched. Regretting the impulse, she pulled her hand away and tucked it between her knees.

''We were at an impasse,'' he said. ''I'd tried to make her happy, but there were needs I couldn't satisfy—the need for friends, for society, for comforts that were impossible here. I should have known it would only be a matter of time until she tried to leave me.''

He fell silent for a moment, brooding on his own words. Anna's eyes traced the craggy lines of his profile, cast into stark relief by the moonlight. Yes, it was beginning to make sense—his disappointment in her, his need for a plain, hardworking woman with no illusions about romance. A woman who would be content with her lot in this lonely place. A woman who would not try to leave him for another man.

"I was late getting home the day it happened," he said. "I'd told Elise and the children that I was going to Kanab to buy lumber, but the truth was I'd gone for the piano. I was bringing it back as a surprise, but it was the very devil to haul over that road. Kept shifting on the turns, and the weight of it damn near broke the wagon bed." His voice trailed off as if he'd just realized he was rambling, going on about the piano to avoid the horror of what had happened next.

"I rolled in through the gate to find the children frantic and crying. It was nearly dusk, and their mother had been missing all day. I asked them if anyone else had been here, and they told me about the photographer. When I checked the wardrobe and saw that her clothes were missing, it wasn't hard to guess the rest."

"Did the children know she'd taken her things?" Anna asked, aching for them.

"I don't think so. They hadn't thought to look, and I kept it from them as best I could." His hand raked his sweat-dampened hair, making it stand in peaks between his fingers. "Lord, I was just grateful she hadn't taken them with her!"

"So why did you go looking for her?"

"For the children's sake mostly. I could hardly tell them their own mother had picked up and left." He gazed toward the corral where the mules snorted and stirred, dreaming, perhaps, in the darkness.

"One of the two dories was missing, and the children had traced her tracks to the landing. She would have needed a boat to carry all the things she'd taken with her. The fact that the current was high and dangerous, and that she'd never learned to handle a boat well made drowning even more plausible. I figured, if nothing else, I could search for a while, make certain she'd really gone, and then go back and tell Josh and Carrie she'd drowned. It would at least give them some sense of closure.

"Carrie said you brought her body back, and that you wouldn't allow them to look at her." Anna knew she should leave well enough alone, but the question would torment her forever if she did not ask. Was the body Malachi had found really Elise's? Had she drowned, or had he killed her—and perhaps her lover—in a jealous rage?

"I did bring Elise's body back," he said. "And no, I didn't let my children see her. The memory would have haunted them to the end of their days."

"How did you find her?" Anna whispered, wanting the truth but dreading what she might hear.

His hand had stilled on the dog's head. Doubtful whined and nosed his palm. Malachi, for once, ignored the beast. A shudder passed through his body as he spoke.

"It was the ravens," he said. "I'd gone less than a mile when I saw them, circling the open spot downriver where travelers sometimes camped—where *he* would most likely have camped, and where she would have met him. As I rowed toward the spot, I saw the dory pulled onto a gravel bar. Elise's clothes and other things were still in it, but the camp was deserted. Someone had been there, but the ashes were cold through, the horse droppings two days old at least.''

"And Elise?'' Anna could hear the sound of her own heart, pulsing like a drum in her ears.

"At first I didn't see her. Then I noticed the ravens again, farther back in the trees.'' He spoke with effort, his throat working. ''They were flocking around her, where she—she'd hanged herself from the limb of a cottonwood. The birds had already been at her. Her eyes…''

He trailed off, swallowing hard, sparing Anna the rest of the description. But the image was already there, seared into her mind. She pictured the deserted camp, Elise arriving in the dory to find her lover gone. She imagined the hopeless grief, the despair that would lead a woman to take her own life. What a mad, selfish act it had been. What a devastating waste of all that was precious.

Suddenly she found herself raging inside. Elise had been blessed with two beautiful children and the love of a good man—the kind of love that she, Anna de Carlo, would give anything to know. That a woman could have so much and throw it all away—everything—

Anna became aware that Malachi was watching her. She turned abruptly and caught the naked anguish in his eyes. At that moment she knew, beyond doubt, that what he had told her was true. She knew this man. She had seen his integrity, his tenderness, his strength. Such a man could never have murdered the mother of his beloved children.

"I was going to bury her there,'' he said, his voice

raw with the strain of holding back his emotions. "But I knew it would help the children to have a grave, a spot they could visit and feel close to her. So I burned her clothes, wrapped her body in a piece of canvas and brought her back to the house."

"I know the rest of the story," Anna said, wanting to spare him. "Carrie told me."

"And it doesn't make a nickel's worth of difference, does it?"

Anna stared at him, caught off balance. "No," she murmured, "I don't suppose it does. Not as far as my own plans are concerned." Feeling awkward, she turned away from him and gazed up at the scarred face of the moon. "At least, after I'm gone, I won't waste time puzzling over it."

"The way I've puzzled over you, Anna?"

She glanced sharply around to find him gazing at her, his eyes narrow and probing in the darkness. "I confess you've got me buffaloed, lady. You've pried every secret out of me, made me spill my guts till it hurt. And there you sit, buttoned up tighter than a virgin's underdrawers. You're hiding something, Anna. Something big. And I think I deserve to know what it is!"

Anna willed herself not to shrink from his demanding gaze. Malachi had her cornered this time, she knew. None of her skilled evasions would turn him aside.

But, dear heaven, how could she tell him the truth? Even if he didn't turn her over to the law, he could be implicated for harboring a fugitive. He could go back to prison and never see his children again.

"I was watching your face when that bounty hunter

turned around to stare at you,'' he said. "You looked as scared as a cornered rabbit. You're in some kind of trouble aren't you? That's why you agreed to marry me in the first place. And now, that's why you're so all-fired anxious to leave. You're afraid somebody's going to find out who you are and come after you.''

"That's ridiculous!" Anna snapped, taking the offensive. "I'll admit I was out of money and needed a place to live when I contacted your cousin. But that hardly makes me a fugitive from the law!"

His eyes glittered coldly. "Nice try, lady, but I know when someone's trying to feed me a crock of bull—"

"Oh!" Anna gasped, scrambling to her feet. "That is quite enough, Malachi Stone! If you think I'm going to sit here and be insulted in that kind of crude language—"

"Sit down!" His hand clamped around her bare ankle, its rock-solid grip threatening to jerk her off her feet if she resisted. "You're not going anywhere. Not until you've told me what I need to know.''

"You're hurting me!" Anna whimpered, although it wasn't true. "Take a look at the way you treat women—"

"Sit down!" His fingers tightened. "No more evasions, Anna. No more lies. You give me the whole story now, or, so help me, I'll hog-tie you, sling you over the back of a mule and haul you to the nearest U.S. Marshal myself!"

Anna lowered herself to the step, her mind still scrambling for a way out. "You won't like this," she said, stalling frantically.

"I don't expect to like it," he retorted. "Tell me anyway."

She drew her knees against her chest, fingers rubbing the warm spot where his hand had gripped her ankle. "There's…this man," she said, milking time out of every syllable. "He's after me. I was desperate to get away." All true so far, she congratulated herself. Every last word.

"So why is this man after you, Anna?" he demanded coldly. "Did you take something from him? Swindle him?"

Not even close. "He—uh—wants me," Anna said, still clinging to a thread of truth. Louis Caswell wanted her, all right. He wanted her dead.

Malachi's eyes seared her through the thin nightshirt, their heat touching every inch of her, from her tousled blond hair to the tips of her bare toes. "Wants you? Now that much I can believe. I can't imagine any male with blood in his veins not wanting you." He paused, sucking in his breath. "But I'm not buying it, Anna. Not after that brush with the bounty hunters. You've stumbled over the line somewhere, and unless you tell me—"

"Papa!" Carrie's thin, frightened voice shattered the tension. She burst through the screen door and onto the porch, her eyes huge dark pools in her white face.

"Papa, it's Josh! I heard him through the wall, and when I went into his room, he was crying. He says his head hurts, and his skin feels like it's on fire. Hurry, Papa, he wants you to come now!"

Chapter Fourteen

Malachi's breath caught as he strode into Joshua's bedroom. The air that closed around him was rank with the smell of fever. Josh lay on his bed with the covers flung back. His eyes were closed, his small, sharp-boned face flushed crimson, the skin as dry as parchment. He was burning alive.

The boy stirred and opened his eyes as Malachi bent over him. "Pa…?" he asked with effort.

"I'm here, son." Malachi kept his voice low and calm, betraying none of the churning fear he felt inside. Elise's words, spoken in the heat of anger, echoed in his memory, haunting him now. *What if one of the children takes sick and dies for want of a doctor? It will be your fault, Malachi Stone! Your fault for bringing us to this Godforsaken hole in the earth!* That impassioned argument, above all others, had come the closest to moving him. But for all its implied peril, his children had been as robust as young woodchucks, scarcely knowing a day of sickness.

Until now.

"Pa...my eyes hurt," Josh whimpered, "and my legs hurt, too.... Make it stop. Please."

Malachi brushed his palm across the boy's forehead, smoothing back the tangle of mahogany curls. Dear God, he was so small, so precious, and he was as hot as fire. "I'll do what I can, son," he murmured, feeling helpless. "You lie still now. Close your eyes and rest."

"He needs fluids." Anna had appeared behind him with a tin cup in her hand. Pushing her way to the bedside, she dropped to her knees. "Drink this water, Josh. All of it."

She tipped the cup to his fever-cracked lips. Josh took a tentative swallow, then closed his mouth in tight resistance. "My throat hurts," he croaked when Anna pressed him. "I don't want to drink." His eyes rolled imploringly toward Malachi. "It *hurts,* Pa. Make her stop."

Anna's amber eyes flashed upward, reflecting Malachi's own worry. "He's got to drink," she whispered. "The fever's burning all the moisture out of him."

"Here." Malachi's hand brushed her cool fingers as he took the cup and lowered himself to the floor beside her. Josh lay still on the worn flannel, his eyes half-closed, his bony little body exuding heat like a furnace—heat that Malachi could feel without even touching his skin. Lord, how high was the fever? How high could it go without killing him?

"Drink it down, son," he rasped, forcing the cup between the small, swollen lips. "Even if it hurts. That's an order."

Josh sipped the water whimpering as he swallowed.

The terror of a small, frightened animal flickered in his heat-glazed eyes. "Pa," he whispered, "am I going to die like Ma did?"

Malachi felt his diaphragm jerk as if he'd been gut-kicked. "You know I'd never let such a thing happen to you," he said. "You've got a bit of fever, that's all. You'll be fine once we get you cooled down." His gaze flicked toward Anna. She was watching him, her expression all too sad and knowing.

"Do you know what it is?" She mouthed the words, barely speaking above a whisper.

"Maybe." Malachi bent closer and began to examine every inch of his son's burning skin—the feet, the ankles, the wiry young legs that were always running, jumping, moving. Josh moaned but did not resist as his father slid the flannel nightshirt up the fiery little body, Malachi's fingers and eyes probing for something he hoped to heaven he would not find.

"There." His heart contracted as he found it—a bluish lump the size and shape of a teardrop, nested in the boy's armpit. Malachi cursed under his breath.

"What is it?" Anna whispered beside him.

"Damned tick. I've come to believe they carry fever." He'd gotten a terrible fever himself during those long months alone here—had nearly died from it, in fact. Only after the crisis had passed did he discover the blood-engorged tick clamped on the back of his knee. Over the years, he'd heard stories of men and women dying from similar fevers. The odds of a child surviving the awful ravages were too grim to contemplate. He kept that knowledge to himself as he turned to Carrie, who had crowded in on Anna's right.

"Get my skinning knife and lay the tip of the blade

on the coals," he told her. "When it's red-hot, bring it to me—carefully now."

The girl nodded, looking pale and fearful. It would be good, he thought, for her to have something to do.

"Pa?" Josh's fingers plucked weakly at Malachi's sleeve. "What is it? What are you going to do with your knife?" His eyes were round with terror.

"Nothing that will hurt you." Malachi could have kicked himself for frightening the boy. "We're just going to give Mr. Tick a hot poke in the rump so he'll pull his head out of your skin. If you hold still, you won't even feel it."

He glanced at Anna. "If we just pull the tick off, the head will stay in place...." he explained, the words trailing off into silence as he saw her amber eyes reflecting his own thoughts. Getting the tick out wouldn't make much difference now. Josh's vital young bloodstream was already infected, and the fever was raging like wildfire through his small body.

Carrie appeared in the doorway holding the knife carefully in front of her. "Is it hot?" Malachi asked, glancing down at the blackened point.

"It was red when I took it out of the fire." Only a quaver in her voice betrayed her fear. The girl's courage raised a lump in Malachi's throat. She was trying so hard to be brave and grown-up.

"Josh, do you want me to hold you so you won't flinch?" Anna asked gently, and the boy nodded. She moved to the far side of the bed and, crouching low, slid her arms around him from behind, cradling his curly head against the curve of her throat.

Josh raised his arm without being asked as Malachi approached with the knife. "Be careful, Pa," he said.

Then he clenched his teeth, closed his eyes and waited.

Swiftly now, before the blade could cool, Malachi leaned close. Willing his hand not to tremble, he touched the heated point to the tick. Anna grimaced, holding Josh tightly as the creature loosened its grip and began to squirm.

A dizzying rage surged through Malachi as he plucked the tick from Josh's skin and crushed it hard, again and again against the knife blade. If this tiny bloodsucker had set in motion the forces that would end his son's life...

He became aware of Carrie's startled fawn eyes staring at him from the foot of the bed. Anna, too, was watching him, her soft, ripe lips parting in horror. Probably thought he was crazy. Well, maybe he was.

"You're bleeding," Anna said, and Malachi saw that she was right. He had pricked his own finger on the blade.

"It's nothing." Feeling foolish, he wiped the bead of blood on the seam of his trousers. Josh had relaxed in Anna's arms, his fevered eyes only half-open.

"Did you get all of him, Pa?"

"All of him." Malachi said, wishing fervently that he could trade places with the stricken boy. Josh's life was in the hands of heaven—or fate as the case might be. If his son died, Malachi knew he would never believe in the heavenly powers again.

Anna eased Josh out of her arms and laid him gently back on the pillow. Where his small body had rested, her skin was damp with sweat. It didn't take a doctor to tell her the fever was dangerously high. A young girl at the orphanage—her own friend—had

survived such a fever, but afterward she had a been
a leaden, dull little thing who whimpered rather than
spoke, as if the searing heat had burned away her very
spirit. The thought of Josh suffering the same fate
clawed at her heart with talons of dread.

She glanced up at Malachi, feeling his pain, his
anguish. "We've got to cool him down," she said
quietly. "I'll wet some towels at the pump. We can
use them to wrap him."

"And I'll cut some willow bark for tea. There's
nothing better." Malachi stirred beside the bed, ani-
mated by the hope of doing something useful. "Carrie, you fire up the stove and heat some water—"

"Never mind that," Anna interjected quickly.
"You go with your father, Carrie, and hold the lamp
while he cuts the bark. I can have the kettle on by
the time you get back."

Father and daughter hurried from the house, stopping only long enough to light a lantern. Anna remained in Josh's room a moment longer, watching
the boy from the doorway. He had closed his eyes,
and his lashes lay like dark silk fans against his skin.
Her mind's eye saw him bounding off the porch to
greet her arrival, his welcoming grin lighting up his
face like the Fourth of July. She saw him in motion—
running, swimming, climbing—and at rest, sucking
his lip in concentration as he bent over his sums and
take-aways.

Josh had been her first friend in this hostile place.
He was so loving, so full of life; and now he drifted
in and out of stupor, the fever burning the flesh off
his sturdy young bones.

"Dear God..." Anna's lips moved in the first

prayer she'd uttered since the loss of another child, long ago. "I've tried not to bother you over the years—figured I wasn't fit to ask you for anything. But now I've nowhere else to turn. Please don't take this precious boy. Don't break his father's heart and his sister's. If you have to take somebody, Lord, make it me. I've led a wicked life. I've cheated. I've lied. I've broken most of the ten commandments. And if I live on, I probably won't change much. But this boy...he's got so much promise. He's got a chance to do so much good in the world with his pure, loving spirit. If you'll settle for my life instead, I'm ready, Lord, here and now...."

Anna closed her eyes and stood perfectly still, waiting. Had her prayer traveled beyond the ceiling of the room, all the way to the ear of the Almighty? Not likely, she reasoned, opening her eyes again. If it had, she would already be dead, and Josh would be leaping out of bed, blooming with health. Her time would have been better spent firing up the stove, putting the kettle on to boil, and wetting down the sheets and towels.

As she turned to leave the room, she felt something cool and damp nudge her palm. Doubtful stood beside her in the doorway, thrusting his muzzle into her hand. Anna stoked the great, shaggy head, too preoccupied to wonder at the big wolf-dog's acceptance of her. Through the kitchen door, left open, she could see the lantern bobbing in the darkness, winding toward the willows that screened the river. "It's all right, boy," she murmured to the dog. "Go with them. Go on, now."

Instead the dog slipped past her into Josh's room,

padded over to the bed and laid his chin on the quilt. His pale wolf's eyes, pained and puzzled, watched the feverish boy. His tail wagged, then dropped low, as if in understanding that his young master was seriously ill.

Anna left the two of them together and hurried into the kitchen to fire up the stove.

The sun had risen, crawled across the sky and set in a ball of flame above the canyon walls. Malachi had scarcely noticed the passing of time. The balance of his whole universe hung on the fate of one small boy who lay in a dimly lit room, his young body racked with fever. Again and again, with Anna and Carrie's help, he had wrung out wet cloths and wrapped Josh's burning limbs and body in them to ease the fever. After the morning chores, Carrie had gathered more willow bark and boiled it into tea, which Anna spooned into Josh's mouth while Malachi held him. The taste was bitter, and at first the boy had fought every mouthful. He no longer had the strength.

The routine of wrapping and dosing had been repeated so often during the day that Malachi had lost count. And still the fever raged. Josh was growing weaker by the hour. The progression of his sickness seemed much faster than had Malachi's own bout with tick fever. Maybe this was a different kind of tick, or a different kind of infection; or maybe the tick he'd pulled off Josh had nothing to do with the fever at all. Lord, the uncertainty alone was enough to drive a man crazy! What he wouldn't give for a doctor—but in terms of getting medical help, they might as well be living in the bowels of hell.

It will be your fault, Malachi Stone… your fault… Elise's damning words gnawed at his conscience. If anything happened to Josh, he would never know peace again.

"Papa, I'm going to bed now." Carrie stood in the doorway, looking like an exhausted wraith in her white nightgown. "Will you call me if anything changes?"

"Don't worry, I'll call you. Get some rest, sweetheart," Malachi answered, catching the weary kiss she blew him. If Josh were to die, he would lose Carrie, too, he realized. Not even he could justify raising a young girl alone in a place like this, with no mother and no other child for companionship.

The door to Carrie's room opened and closed. Malachi felt the dog stir beside him, whimpering anxiously. Strange, how animals seemed to sense when something was wrong. Even the noisy mules had been subdued today.

The screen door closed as Anna came in with an armful of firewood. The sounds of her rummaging in the kitchen—rattling dishes, pouring water and poking at the fire in the stove, were oddly comforting, as was the smell of coffee that drifted slowly to his nostrils. Even under the circumstances, it was good having her here.

A few minutes later she walked into the bedroom with two steaming mugs. "You look as if you could use this," she said, handing him a cup of the dark, steaming brew. "Better yet, why don't you get some rest? I can sit with Josh for a while."

"You know I wouldn't be able to close my eyes." Malachi sipped the scalding coffee. She had made it too strong for his taste, but what did it matter?

He studied her over the brim of the cup. The day had been hot, and the plaid shirt and denim pants clung damply to her body. Her hair, hastily twisted and pinned at the crown of her head, had loosened into sweaty tendrils that hung around her haggard face. Her eyes were red with weariness. She had tended Josh all day, fussing and fretting as if he had been her own child.

"You look like the one who could use some sleep," he said gently. "Go on, I'll wake you if Josh needs anything."

She shook her head, staring down at her coffee as if she were about to fall into the cup. After a long moment she took a sip, set the cup on the washstand and gathered up the pile of gingham she was making into a dress for Carrie. She had been sewing off and on for much of the day, leaving her work on the foot of the bed when Josh needed care. Little by little, now, the dress was coming together.

Malachi's eyes followed the quick, sure movements of her hands. There was an undertone of urgency in the way she thrust the needle into the cloth, as if she were racing against time—a race she knew she was going to lose.

She had said she was leaving. Malachi knew that, and had even agreed it was the right thing to do. But how could she even think of going when the children needed her so much—when *he* needed her, damn it.

"Anna." He had not planned to speak, but her name had flown from his mind to his tongue. She glanced up, her eyes meeting his, and in the flickering lamplight, Malachi caught the glimmer of a tear.

"You don't have to go," he blurted, the words tumbling out faster than coherent thought. "Whatever trouble you're in, we can work it out. If you've broken the law, my cousin Stuart can take your case—"

"The same cousin Stuart who arranged for me to come here in the first place?" A bitter little smile twisted a corner of her mouth. "That doesn't say much for his judgment, Malachi, or for his acumen as a lawyer."

"Then we'll find someone better. Stay, Anna—for the children's sake. They—need you."

They need you.

Anna forced herself to look directly at him, to meet his earnestness with the steel of her own resolve— only to find that the steel had dissolved into mist. Dear heaven, how she wanted him—this big, stubborn, awkward, growling enigma of a man! She wanted to share his lonely life, raise his beautiful children and feel his strong, male body clasping her close in their marriage bed. She wanted to grow old with him, to see the sun rise and set on their days in a symphony of color above the canyon walls. She wanted his love, his sorrow, his hopes and fears. She wanted all of him, and all that was his.

But it was an impossible dream, she knew. Even if Malachi were to offer her his love, she could no more stay with him than she could be empress of Russia!

"Anna?"

Struggling to ignore him, she glanced at Josh. The boy was sleeping fitfully, his breath wheezing raggedly in and out of his throat. "There has to be something more we can do," she said, putting off her answer to his question, the only answer she could give him.

"What did they do for fevers in the orphanage?" The question carried an edge. Malachi was no fool. He knew she was putting him off.

"Not much," Anna answered dully, remembering. "Any child who died meant one less mouth to feed. But I remember…" She groped for the memory that had just flickered in her tired brain. What was it she'd heard, and when?

Malachi watched her expectantly, as if waiting for any scrap of hope she might find to toss his way. For his sake, and for Josh's, Anna struggled to push back the edges of her memory, far back, to a time she had long since buried.

"After I ran away from the orphanage," she began, groping her way, "I was taken in by a woman who let me do laundry and kitchen work for my board. It wasn't a good place—in fact, it was the worst kind of place. I left when she wanted to promote me to one of the upstairs rooms." Anna shook her head in frustration. "Why am I telling you this? None of it means anything!"

"Go on," Malachi prodded her. "It's not always easy to remember things. But if you keep talking, maybe you'll find your way."

Anna sighed, slowly remembering. "The cook— she was kind to me—she used to tell me stories about her family while we worked. One story was about the time her younger sister got pneumonia, and they saved her life by making a tent out of quilts and putting her inside with tubs of boiling water. The heat made her sweat, and the steam cleared her lungs.''

''I've seen pneumonia,'' Malachi said. ''I'm no doctor, mind you, but Josh's lungs seem fine. It's the fever I'm worried about.''

''Yes, I know.'' Anna swept her hair back with an agitated hand. ''But we've tried other things, none of which seem to have worked. Short of sending for a Navajo medicine man, what would you suggest we do?''

He hesitated, his silver eyes darkening to slate gray in the lamplight. Then, slowly, he rose to his feet, looming above Anna in the small room. ''We can make a tent in the kitchen, between the chairs,'' he said. ''If you'll sit inside and hold him, I'll haul the wood and water.''

''Wait—'' Anna caught his sleeve as he turned to go. ''I remember something else. The cook said they gave her sister pennyroyal, in a tea, and in the steam.''

Malachi scowled at her. ''There's no pennyroyal here. It's a mountain plant. The canyon's too low.''

''Something else, then. Something to make the steam stronger—''

''Indians use sage. Plenty of that. I'll cut some once the water's heating.'' He strode from the house, clearly relieved to be back in action. Anna had never known a man to be any good at waiting. Waiting tended to be a woman's lot, a woman's own brand of torment.

Moving quietly, to avoid waking Carrie, she

walked into the kitchen and began stacking chairs to support the quilts.

Like beads of desperation strung on a thread of despair, the hours passed. Anna sat beneath the tented quilts, hunkered on the milk stool with Josh in her arms as Malachi shoved buckets of boiling river water, laced with sage, into their tiny chamber. Her limbs had long since ceased to feel their cramped discomfort. As for her mind, it had slipped into a leaden stupor, aware of nothing but the weight of the precious child in her arms, the heat of his small, burning body.

Early on, she had managed to get some tea down him, brewed from more willow bark and a few sprigs of the sage. But now the heat and the steam had sapped her senses to the point where she could scarcely think, let alone take intelligent action.

"I can spell you for a while." Malachi raised the hem of the quilt to thrust in another pail of boiling water and remove the one that had cooled.

"Don't bother," Anna mumbled. "I don't think I could get out of here if I tried."

"How's Josh doing?" The hope in his voice almost broke her heart.

"The same. Hot. Wet. In and out of sleep. He's stirred and tried to speak a couple of times, but I don't think he knows what's happening." She could not bear to tell him the most wrenching thing of all—that for a time the boy had clung to her with small, frenzied hands, whimpering, "Mama...Mama..."

"What time is it?" she asked, shifting Josh's weight in her arms.

"Around midnight." He straightened with a long, anguished exhalation. "Let's give both of you a rest, Anna, get him into the air and see how he's doing."

"All right. But get a dry blanket. We can't let him chill."

He lowered the quilt, and she sat waiting in the steamy darkness, cradling the boy against her chest. The fever had drained him of substance until he seemed no more than a bird in her arms, all hollow bones and weightless flesh.

"Ready—" He tugged away the quilt and she passed Josh into the heavy Navajo blanket. Malachi wrapped his son tenderly, swaddling everything but his small, peaked face. Josh's brown puppy eyes blinked drowsily up at his father, then slipped shut again as Malachi gathered him close.

Anna's legs had lost all feeling. She strained to get up, but only succeeded in toppling sideways off the milk stool onto the floor. She lay there with no will to move, the wood grain pressing into her cheek.

"Anna." She was aware of Malachi's boot toe nudging her shoulder. "Are you all right?"

Anna moaned. As she lay still, wanting only to rest, she felt his hand slipping around her ribs. Then he was lifting her, supporting Josh against his shoulder and, with his free hand, dragging her toward the massive leather armchair that sat before the darkened fireplace. How strong he was, she thought groggily. And how gentle, as he settled her in the curve of one arm, with his son in the other.

"I'm soaked!" she protested weakly. "I'll get you all wet—"

"Hush, Anna." He tugged another dry blanket

around her. "Be still and rest," he murmured, pulling her against the warmth of his chest. "You've done all you can. What happens now is beyond your power or mine."

Anna closed her eyes, letting herself be lulled and soothed by the steady beating of his heart. She could feel Josh beside her, snuggled into the thick Navajo blanket. The woolen folds rose and fell with the light cadence of his breathing.

"How does he look to you?" Anna whispered the question to Malachi.

"Peaceful. Sleeping."

"Good," she muttered through a cloud of exhaustion. "Sleep's the best thing for him."

"And for you." His throat moved against her hair. "Close your eyes. Try not to worry."

She did as he asked, snuggling close against his broad, hard chest. There would be more room on the bed. But she had no will to get up and move. It seemed so right, so perfect being here in his arms. She had never felt more protected, more cherished....

The dog nudged her feet as he made room for himself next to Malachi's legs. Anna felt herself begin to slip away, then stop with a sudden jolt.

This was the time. It had to be. She could hold no more lies, no more evasions between herself and Malachi. She owed him the truth, no matter what it might cost her.

"Malachi?" she whispered, her lips moving against the roughness of his shirt.

"What is it?"

"Earlier you asked me a question." She fumbled

for a way to begin. "I owe you an answer. A lot of answers."

He did not speak, but she felt the tension building in his body as he waited for her to go on.

"There's no easy way to tell you this," she continued, choking on the words. "You're right. I'm wanted by the law—wanted for a crime I didn't commit."

Still he was silent, waiting, probably doubting her words already. Didn't all criminals claim to be innocent?

"So what was the crime?" he finally asked.

Anna willed herself to speak clearly and boldly. "The crime was murder."

Chapter Fifteen

Anna felt his heart jump. His muscles jerked tight, and she sensed the raging struggle inside, as if part of him wanted to shove her off his lap, away from himself and his innocent son. An eternity seemed to pass before he spoke.

"Tell me what happened."

So Anna told him. At first the words came with difficulty, but then, as if a dam had burst, the story came tumbling out of her—how she had met Harry Solomon when she sang at the Jack of Diamonds in St. Joseph, how Harry had asked her to wed, and how she had climbed the back stairs to his quarters on that terrible night and met Louis Caswell and his looming cohort, The Russian.

"I didn't give them much thought at the time," she said. "Not until I walked into Harry's suite and found him lying on the floor with the knife in his back...." The memory surged, its horror threatening to strangle her words. Not once in five long months had she told anyone about that awful moment. Not until now.

"I ran to him," she said, forcing the words. "I

threw myself down beside him, trying to save him, to pull the knife out of his back and stop the bleeding. He was dead by then—I'm certain of that now. But I was in a state of shock. His blood was all over my clothes, my hands, leaving bloody prints on everything I touched. Harry's safe was open. The papers had been scattered on the floor. I remember gathering them up, looking at them, smearing them with blood—''

''Papers?''

''I think Harry must have had some evidence against Caswell—maybe that he was taking protection money from some of the saloons. That would have given Caswell a reason to kill him and go through his safe. At least that's the only explanation that makes sense.''

''And you didn't call for help?''

She shook her head. ''I knew I'd be blamed, especially since Louis Caswell was the law in town. All I could do was run. I left town that very night—that very hour.''

''And you've been running ever since.'' Malachi's flat voice told her nothing. Was he shocked? Disgusted? Did he hate her for the treachery she'd committed against his family? Did he even believe her?

''Yes, running,'' she said. ''And hiding. And dodging. And lying. Anything to stay alive and free for one more day, even marrying a complete stranger.''

That would get a rise out of him, she thought. But it did not. When he spoke again, it was in that same calm, flat voice.

''And you've never thought of stopping long enough to try to clear yourself?''

"Clear myself?" Sweet heaven, did he really believe her? Anna's heart jumped, and plummeted again as she realized it made no difference. "That's impossible," she said. "I played right into Caswell's hands that night. That's why he didn't kill me on the spot. He knew exactly what I would do. I was so frantic to get away that I even left my shawl next to poor Harry's body and my bloody clothes in my dressing room at the Jack of Diamonds. All that evidence! Caswell was in the clear! No one would think of blaming anyone but me!"

"So why do you think he's still looking for you?" Malachi asked quietly. "The time, the expense— Why hasn't he just let you go?"

Anna turned in his arms, so that she could gaze up at him. The lamplight had deepened the lines at the corners of his eyes and darkened the stubble on his cheeks and jaw. He looked unspeakably weary, drained by the ordeal of his son's illness.

"Caswell won't sleep well until he's silenced me for good," she said. "If I'm caught, I'm done for. He'll make sure I never live to tell my story to a judge."

"Then it appears Caswell still has something to fear from you." Malachi hesitated, then continued without waiting for Anna's response. "You saw him and his hired thug leaving the murder scene. You *saw* him, Anna—and who's to say you didn't find something among those scattered papers? Something that would link him to Harry's death?"

"But I didn't!" Anna was losing patience with this hopeless game. "I found nothing, Malachi, nothing at all."

"But does Caswell know that?" Malachi's eyes narrowed like a cat's in the lamplight. "Haven't you ever played poker, Anna? Don't you know the value of a good bluff?"

"When it comes to poker, I could bluff you out of everything you own!" Anna said. "But there's nothing to bluff with here. Caswell is holding all the cards, and he knows it!" She glared up at him, overcome by sudden despair. "Why are you doing this to me, pulling me this way and that, getting my hopes up for nothing? For that matter, why should you even believe me? I may not be a murderess, Malachi, but I'm not a good woman, either. I've lied to you all along. I've even lied to your children—"

She broke off as Josh began to stir. For a long moment he whimpered, then sighed and settled into sleep once more. Anna lowered her voice as she took up the thread of her tirade. "I've lied to all of you, about everything—"

"Hush." His finger, laid lightly on her lips, blocked the rest of her words. "Be still Anna. Close your eyes and rest. Neither of us is thinking very clearly right now."

"But—"

"Tomorrow," he said softly but firmly. "We'll talk then, when we're both seeing things more clearly."

Anna exhaled, willing herself to be silent. He was right, she knew. Her nerves were raw with worry and exhaustion, as were his. Yes, tomorrow they would talk. Tomorrow…

Her mind was already spiraling into sleep. She halted the spinning long enough to remind herself that she should slip off Malachi's lap and go to bed. But the enfolding warmth of the blanket was pulling her into slumber. The strength of his arms made her feel safe and protected. She closed her eyes, fear and uncertainty falling away as she drifted deeper...deeper.

Malachi cradled them both—his slumbering son and the woman he had come to love. Anna's head lay against his collarbone, her hair damp and tangled. Her gold-tipped lashes caught opalescent glimmers of lamplight where they lay against her ivory skin. She slept, now, like a child, her strength utterly spent.

Had she been honest with him this time? Had her wild tale been true, or was he holding a murderess in his arms? By her own admission Anna had lied at every turn. Why should he believe her now?

She moaned softly in her sleep, butting her head into the hollow of his throat like a small animal seeking nourishment. How trusting she was, how needful of love. How could he not believe her? He had seen her kindness. He had seen the devoted care she gave his children, her passionate concern for the lost mule and the mired cow. This woman was no killer. She was not capable of such a violent act.

But, unless he could find a way to prevent it, she would leave him. Malachi felt the certainty of reason as he held her. She was too frightened to take a stand, too fearful of bringing harm to him and his family.

He brushed his lips against her damp hairline, aching to hold her like this forever, to make her his, to bind her to him as the wife of his heart, his soul, his body. What could he do? How could he keep this precious woman in his life?

Josh wriggled against his other arm, sighing in his

fitful sleep. Malachi tested the heat of his fever by laying his cheek against the boy's forehead. His skin felt much the same as it had for the past twenty-four hours. But at least he was sleeping. His body was at rest, gathering strength to fight for life.

Josh needed Anna, too, and so did Carrie. They needed the laughter and music in her and the guidance of her hardwon wisdom. They needed her motherly love.

Malachi's arms tightened around Anna and Josh, even as his thoughts embraced Carrie where she slumbered behind her closed door. He would die protecting these three precious lives. He would do anything to keep them safe, to keep them together.

But tonight an army of adversity was lining up outside the walls of their sanctuary—dark forces, any one of which possessed the power to shatter all their lives.

The dog pressed against his leg, its big body warm and reassuring in the darkness. The lamp wick sputtered and died to a vermilion glow. Malachi felt the peace of the house, the canyon and the river around him. He felt his loved ones in his arms. Treasuring the moment, he drifted into a doze.

He awakened to darkness, his mind a blur. How long had he slept? An hour? Two? And what had awakened him?

Anna was still fast asleep, the arm that held her numb beyond all feeling. Josh, however, was stirring restlessly, his small voice whispering, "Pa…Pa…"

Malachi was instantly alert. "It's all right, son," he whispered. "I'm right here. I've got you. How do you feel?"

"I...had a dream, Pa."

"A good dream?"

The boy nodded drowsily. "I saw Mama. She looked beautiful, like an angel, and she held out her arms to me."

"And did she say anything?" Malachi clasped his son close, suddenly fearful.

"Uh-huh. She said I could come and live with her—that it was nice there and we'd be happy together." His fingers found the front of Malachi's shirt and clutched at the fabric, wadding it in his small fist. "She said that if I stayed with her, I could have anything I wanted. Even a pony."

"And what did you tell her?" Malachi was dimly aware that his heart was pounding—a foolish reaction to a child's dream.

"I told her no—I mean, no thank you," Josh answered. "She asked me why, and I said that I needed to stay with you and Carrie and Anna—and that I wanted to grow up." His dark eyes were round with childish wisdom. "If I stayed where Mama was, I knew I couldn't grow up. I'd have to be a boy, always. Was that all right, Pa, to tell her no?"

Malachi hugged his son close. He had never been much of a believer in dreams, but if this one had brought Josh back to him, he was in no position to argue. "Yes," he whispered, choking on emotion. "Yes, it was all right."

As he held the boy, Malachi became aware of a dampness through the thick wool blanket. His heart leaped as he pulled aside the folds and layers that swathed the small body. Beneath the perspiration-soaked flannel nightshirt, Josh's wet skin was smooth and cool. The fever had broken.

"Am I better?" Josh whispered hopefully.

"Do you feel better?"

"Uh-huh." He yawned like a sleepy pup. "Just tired."

"Want to go back to your own bed?"

The boy nodded. Still dizzy with relief, Malachi turned himself to the task of rousing his own benumbed limbs and waking Anna.

Anna stirred at the touch of his hand on her shoulder, struggling toward awareness like a swimmer rising out of a deep, warm ocean. "What...what is it?" she mumbled sleepily.

"Look." Malachi cupped her chin, turning her face toward Josh. "The fever's broken," he said. "And I think it's time for all of us to go to sleep in our own beds."

"Oh—" Anna's eyes shot open. The room was dark except for the gleam of moonlight through the window and the red glow of embers through the small mica panes on the stove. Josh lay nestled against his father's shoulder, his peaked little face split by a gap-toothed grin. *Thank heaven,* she thought. *Thank heaven.*

Stumbling in her haste, she clambered off Malachi's lap. Her body felt as if it had been broken apart limb by limb and stuck together with corn syrup. She ached in every joint and muscle. Her clothes were plastered to her skin, and her hair was a clammy mass of knots and tangles. She dragged herself upright, clinging to the back of the chair for support while the circulation returned to her limbs.

Malachi's efforts to rise were even more pathetic than her own had been. He lurched to his feet, groaning like a wounded bull elk as his bloodless legs collapsed beneath his body. Laughing in spite of herself, Anna reached out and lifted Josh in her arms. Only then was Malachi able to stagger to his feet and, little by little, recover his balance.

"You need a dry nightshirt," Anna said to Josh. "Let's go in your room and look for one."

"All right," Josh said solemnly. "But you'll have to go out while I put it on. You're a girl, and you mustn't see me."

Anna hugged him. Yes, the real Josh was back. Only now did she realize how much she had missed him.

She waited in the kitchen while Malachi tucked his son into bed, then tiptoed into the next room to whisper the good news to Carrie as he had promised. By the time he came out, closing the door quietly behind him, Anna was dismantling the makeshift steam tent they'd set up. The quilts on the bottom layer sagged with moisture, and even the blankets they'd piled on top to seal in the steam were damp. "These need to go out on the line tonight," she said. "They'll be musty if we leave them till morning."

Without a word, Malachi bent down, gathered up an armful of wet quilts and strode toward the door. Anna followed him with the lighter blankets. The night was cool and moist, almost tropical in the lushness of stars, the mellow gold of the low-hanging moon.

They worked, the two of them, with a quietly shared jubilation. Tomorrow, in the harsh light of day, the realities of the outside world would come crashing in on them again—the bounty hunters and lawmen who haunted Anna's dreams and the court-appointed do-gooders on whose judgment hung the future of Malachi's family. But tonight there was an air of unspoken celebration between them. The fever had broken. Josh's tender young life would continue. Fate and heaven willing, he would grow, learn and become a man to make his father proud.

The joy in this simple knowledge glowed when their eyes met and sang between them when their hands touched. When they stretched the wet quilt to hang it over the line, the feeling rippled between them like an electric current along a telegraph wire. Anna was aware of it in every nerve, cell and fiber of her being—and so, she knew, was Malachi.

Both of them knew how the celebration would end. Every touch, every caress of his eyes told Anna how much he wanted her.

Caution shrilled in her head, telling her that she should run, that she should get away before someone got hurt. But the clamor of warning bells was overpowered by the eager drumming of her own heart. She had nowhere left to run, no time but now. She needed this man's love as she had never needed anything in her life. The future might be filled with heartbreak and separation, but now, in the peace of this night, sheltered by towering canyon walls and lulled by the murmuring river, she would allow herself this one time to remember—for now and for all the lonely tomorrows to come.

They strung the quilts and blankets along the gleaming line and fastened them into place with the wooden pins. Their task done, they turned to each other without a word and he gathered her into his arms.

For a long moment they simply held each other, both of them trembling. There were no more secrets between them. She knew about his time in prison and the nightmare of his wife's death. He knew about the orphanage and the baby, about Harry and Caswell and her desperate, fugitive life. Tonight none of it mattered. Nothing mattered except love and need.

"Anna—" In Malachi's rough whisper she heard the all his fears and uncertainties, all his longing to be loved.

"Don't start talking now," she whispered. "No explanations, no apologies. There's nothing to be said."

"In that case…" he chuckled, a low rumble in his chest that dissolved the tension between them "—I'd just like to remind you that something else needs to be on that clothesline as well."

Anna stared into his laughing silver eyes. "I don't see—"

The words died in her throat as his hand brushed the curve of her waist, skimmed her breast through the damp flannel, and slipped upward to the button below the collar. "You'll catch your death if we don't get you out of these wet clothes," he muttered, his fingers working the button free of its hole. "And after that, we need to get you warm."

Anna had dressed in urgent haste that morning. She was naked beneath the sodden flannel shirt and denim pants, and he knew it…oh, sweet heaven, he knew it.

His long, callused fingers worked their way downward to free the next button and the next. She gasped as his rough hand slid through the open front of her shirt to cup her breast, molding her eager flesh, stroking, caressing her until the blood in her veins shimmered with heat. He was doing this for her, Anna knew, taking the time to rouse her to a fever pitch of pleasure. But didn't he know she was ready for him *now?* Didn't he know how much she wanted to feel the length of his hard, naked body against hers, wanted him to take her, to fill the aching core of her need with his love?

"Malachi…"

"Hmmm?" He had lowered his mouth to her breast while his hands liberated the rest of her buttons. His tongue brushed the exquisitely sensitive circle of her aureole, teasing the nipple to a hard berry, which he drew slowly into his mouth, sucking lightly, each tug sending freshets of desire surging downward into the moist center of her body.

"The children…" she murmured giddily. "They could wake up. They could see…" But even as she spoke she realized that she and Malachi were screened from the house by the solid line of quilts. No one could see them but the mules in the corral, who were discreetly minding their own business.

"Someone could come…they could see…"

"And what would they see?" His hands freed the buttons of her pants with the skill of a magician. "A man making love to his wife? Could anything be more right or natural, Anna? My touching you like this, loving you like this?"

As he undid the last button, the pants collapsed over her boots in a soggy ring, hobbling her ankles. The stars spun and blurred as his exploring mouth nibbled downward, his tongue darting into the hollow of her naval, then skimming lower, lower…

Anna whimpered aloud. Her frenzied fingers furrowed his hair, pulling him into the thick, golden nest. Her mouth opened in a silent cry of ecstasy as his tongue probed her moistness, awakening the tender bud, the tingling petals of flesh. She was floating now, on the verge of shattering like a bubble.

"Malachi—" She arched against his cradled head as her body throbbed, yearning for his thrust, for all of him. He paused in his blissful torture, but only long enough to replace his mouth with his fingertip.

"Is there something else you want, Anna?" His eyes flashed up at her in the moonlight.

"Just…" She struggled against the wave of sensation that threatened to sweep her over the brink of sanity. "Just, please, get me out of these pants!"

He chuckled, then swept her up in his arms, the bunched pants still dangling over her booted feet.

"Where are we going?" she whispered as he strode across the yard, away from the house.

"Not far." He reached the barn and ducked inside the tack room, where his bedroll lay spread on a pile of clean straw. She caught his head as he lowered her onto the thick mat of blankets, kissing him wildly, hungrily, her free hand tugging at the buttons of his shirt.

"I want to see you," she whispered as he crouched above her, bathed in a shaft of silver moonlight that filtered between the planks. "All of you. Take off your clothes, Malachi. Now."

"You little wanton! You shameless little hussy!" His words teased her, but his eyes did not. His gaze was raw with need, his voice thick with yearning. She lay back on the bedroll as he stripped off his clothes and stood above her, the moonlight defining every ridge and muscle of his rough-chiseled body, honed by a life of hard outdoor work.

Anna's gaze traveled boldly from his massive shoulders to the patina of dusky hair that shadowed his chest, tapering down along his rock-hard belly to the tangled nest that framed the splendor of his aroused manhood. He was beautiful, she thought. But he could have been potbellied and bandy-legged and it wouldn't have mattered. He was her love, her life. And she was his.

"Take off my boots," she murmured, her voice husky with desire. She ached to have him, to hold him, to feel that great, hard length of him all the way inside her.

Did his hands tremble as he tugged at the damp leather laces? No matter. Impatient as he was, she curled to a sitting position and helped him, their fingers bumping and tangling, until, at last, he jerked the boots off her feet and the denim pants with them, freeing her ankles. "Now!" she whispered, unable to contain herself any longer. "Malachi, hurry, please—"

He entered her in one long, gliding thrust that sent a shimmer of joy through her body. Her legs caught him, and for a long, breathless moment they held each other in perfect silence, lengthening the moment— that precious, perfect moment when two lovers join for the first time. Would it be the last time? But Anna could not think of that now. She could only think of

Malachi, close against her, as she had wanted him, needed him, for so long.

"I love you, Anna," he whispered, and the words broke her heart. A truthful reply would bind him to her forever—and destroy them both.

Keeping her silence, she arched upward, deepening his path and heightening the fire bursts of sensations that coursed between their bodies. His eyes glazed with need as he responded, pushing deeper, deeper. She moved with him, loving him, touching every part of him. She wanted to melt into him, to drown in him. To go on and on to the end of existence.

More…more…she met each thrust as the singing arose deep in her body, growing, swelling, sweeping her away in its power.

Malachi…oh, Malachi, I love you so….

They shattered together in a burst of love so intense that Anna felt a surge of tears. She held him close as he quivered against her, kissing his bare shoulder, his throat, his face, never wanting to let him go.

They lay joined as the madness drained away, clinging to each other in silent gratitude. He was her love, her husband. Whatever might lie ahead, they would have this night, this simple place, and a few precious hours before dawn.

When she awakened to thin rays of pewter light, he was gone. Her pants and shirt, still slightly damp, lay spread on the straw at the foot of their makeshift bed. Anna scrambled into them and raked hasty fingers through her tangled hair. It wouldn't do, she thought, for the children to awaken and discover that she'd spent the night in the tack room.

Carrying her boots, she walked to the door of the barn. The corral was empty, as she had feared it would be. Malachi could not spare another day from clearing the road, even if it brought their day of reckoning closer.

Her body responded with a raw twinge as she bent to pull on her boots. She and Malachi had made love again, then yet again in the hours before dawn, each time more tender, and more wrenching than the last. Malachi had said little, as if, in the course of their loving, he'd come to understand that this heaven could not be forever. That realization, so deeply shared, had only made their time together more bittersweet.

She would leave this place. She had to leave for the safety of these three precious people. But first she would keep her part of the bargain she had made with Malachi.

A wren piped its early-morning song from the limb of a tamarisk as she studied the house, the uncurtained windows, the cluttered porch. She thought of the children in their shabby, outgrown clothes and the piano, waiting for the touch of a young girl's fingers. Yes, she had a great deal of work to do, and she could wait no longer to begin. Time was growing short.

Chapter Sixteen

"Wait—this note's an F. See, right here. You played an E." Anna leaned close to the piano, guiding Carrie's eager young fingers over the chipped ivory piano keys. "Yes...that's it," she urged her protégeé. "F, then G, then back down to D again—hear the melody? Once you know which key to play for which note, you can figure out any piece of music ever written!"

Malachi watched them from the doorway as they studied the open music book, Anna's tousled, tawny mane bent toward Carrie's sleek, dark head. Carrie was wearing the muslin pinafore Anna had made for her to wear over her old dress. The simple, apronlike garment, which Anna's magical fingers had whipped together in less than a day, hid the dress's deficiencies in length and breadth, making it wearable, around the house at least, for yet another season.

Two more new dresses hung in Carrie's wardrobe—not comparable to the fashions of London or Paris, to be sure, but Anna made up in speed what she lacked in finesse of detail. Carrie would be respectably clothed for the visit of the Children's Aid Society people, and for many months to come.

At Carrie's insistence, Anna now had a dress for herself nearly finished, as well as three new shirts for Josh. Fresh curtains hung at all the windows, and the house fairly sparkled with cleanliness. Anna and Carrie had even made soap from the lye and drippings that were stashed behind the coop. She was a wonder, his Anna.

His Anna.

Emotions churning, Malachi slipped out onto the moon-washed porch and sank onto the top step. These past two weeks with Anna and the children had been the happiest time of his life; but it was a happiness as fragile and precious as a rose in the desert. How long would it last? How long *could* it last when all the forces of hell were conspiring to tear his family apart?

After hours of passionate arguing, Anna had finally agreed to let him contact Stuart Wilkinson about the charges against her. Stuart was no great shakes as a lawyer, but he had some powerful friends in the legal system, friends who might be willing to protect her until she could tell her story. Malachi had every reason to trust his cousin. Even so, for Anna, it was a terrifying step, fraught with peril. Her willingness to take the chance was a testament to her courage, her faith and her love for him.

He had grilled her mercilessly about the murder scene, emerging, finally, with one thread of hope. Harry Solomon had been a tall man, close to six feet. The knife had been thrust into his back from a high angle, and with considerable force. If an exhumation of the body bore this out, it could be argued, quite convincingly, that a woman of Anna's small stature could not possibly have inflicted the fatal wound. They had a chance—a fighting chance. Even so, the thought of exposing Anna to the risk of a trial made Malachi's stomach churn. She was so precious, so vulnerable.

Doubtful padded across the porch and nosed at Malachi's hand, wanting to be scratched. Malachi massaged the great, flat skull, rubbing his fingers absently behind the ears, sending the dog into a paroxysm of tail thumping.

The motion of his arm crackled the folded paper in his pocket, an ominous reminder of the message a rider from Kanab had brought him today while he was clearing away the last of the slide. He had read it once and thrust it out of sight, barely overcoming the temptation to tear it into a hundred pieces. The moment of truth was close at hand. Days, even hours from now, that truth could explode and shatter his whole world.

"Pa?" Josh's voice called to him from the kitchen. "What's seventy-one take away forty-eight? I can't seem to work it out."

"I'll be right there." Malachi eased himself to his feet and ambled back inside to teach his son a lesson in borrowing. How much longer would he be able to help Josh with his studies? How long would he have any of them—Josh, Carrie or Anna?

How would he endure a life alone in this place?

"Love, oh, love, oh careless love,
Love, oh, love, oh careless love,

> Love, oh, love, oh careless love,
> Just see what careless love has done…''

Anna was playing the piano now, urging Carrie to join her in the mournful ballad about love gone wrong. Some would say it wasn't any kind of song to teach a young girl, but the radiant joy in Carrie's eyes overcame any objections on Malachi's part. Anna had been good for his daughter. She had been good for both his children.

If they lost her, it would break their hearts.

An hour later Anna slipped outside, closing the screen door behind her without a sound. Malachi was sitting on the porch, gazing pensively toward the river. He looked so tired, she thought, as if the weight of worry was enough to crush his massive shoulders. He had, in fact, been silent all evening. Something was eating at him, troubling him deeply.

Stealing behind him, she sank to a crouch and slid her hands up the backs of his shoulders. An anguished shudder rippled through his body. The thick ropes of muscle that buttressed his neck were knotted with tension. Wordlessly she began to knead them, pressing the heel of her hand against his taut flesh. Even then, he did not speak or even turn to look at her.

For a time, Anna held her tongue. Fate had given her two precious weeks with this man and his children. It had given her the memory of a love that would warm her for the rest of her life. And, despite the fearful odds, it had given her hope—the hope that her troubles could be resolved and this beautiful dream would never end.

She had held happiness between her hands like a rainbow bubble. Now, she sensed, that bubble was about to shatter.

"Do you want to tell me about it?" she asked at last, breaking the silence between them.

Malachi responded with a ragged sigh. "Are the children asleep?" he asked.

"Yes, both of them. I checked before I came outside."

"Let's walk." He rose to his feet and ambled distractedly across the yard, just wandering at first, then moving toward the river. Anna walked beside him, biting back the probing questions she knew would only deepen his natural stubbornness. Whatever the trouble, Malachi would tell her in his own way, in his own time.

The ferry landing was bathed in moonlight. He paused on the bank and stood staring at the current. "Where did you learn to play the piano?" he asked as if making idle conversation. "I wouldn't think the orphanage would have offered music lessons."

Anna forced a laugh. "I learned from an old man, a freed slave, who worked a riverfront saloon in Natchez. Shadrach—that was his name. And the way he played, you'd think the man had signed a contract with the devil. One night when business was slow I offered him ten dollars to teach me. He gave me a few lessons, and I taught myself more over the years. Carrie should be able to do the same after…"

After I'm gone. Anna choked on the words, unable to speak them aloud. Hope was a two-edged sword. If Malachi's plan worked, she would be free. If not, she would be facing the gallows, or worse, perhaps, life in the rotting hell of prison.

Without a word, Malachi turned and caught her in his arms, holding her as if he never wanted to let her go. As Anna's hands crept around his ribs she could feel him trembling against her. She pressed her face to his chest, wanting only to lose herself in his manly warmth and the sound of his beating heart.

That was when she heard it—the crackle of the folded paper in his pocket. And that was when the thing she had only suspected became a dreadful certainty.

"The people from the Children's Aid Society. They're coming, aren't they?"

She felt him nod.

"When?"

"Any day now, I'd guess. The wire is dated nearly three weeks ago. It gathered dust in the telegraph office waiting till somebody could get out this way and deliver it. Now that the road's open—"

He did not finish the sentence. As she held him, Anna sensed the war of self-recrimination that raged inside him. "You had to open the road," she said gently. "You couldn't have shut the world out forever. Not for any of us."

"Couldn't I?" His voice rasped with bitterness. "Do you know how many times I was tempted to blast that damned road into kingdom come? To chop the ferry into kindling or burn it to the waterline? Lord, there've been times when I would've done anything to keep things the way they've been these past two weeks! Now it's too late!"

"Don't." Anna's fingertip brushed his lips. "You

know a thing like that would never have worked, especially with the children. We have to face this. And we've got to believe we have a chance!''

"No.'' He gazed beyond her, toward the ferry and the rushing, tumbling river. "You've done a fine job here, Anna, with the house and the children. But we're both fooling ourselves if we think it's going to make a nickel's worth of difference. The decision's already been made. It was made weeks ago, maybe months ago, back in Santa Fe.''

"Don't say that!'' Anna argued, holding him fiercely. "There's still time, Malachi. Even if the Children's Aid people find against you, they have to report back to the judge and get a ruling. In the meantime, your cousin could file an appeal—''

"No, Anna.'' His body quivered against her, racked by a rage he had no way to express. "The wire made that one point clear. If our visitors decide against me, they have written, legal authority to take the children at once.''

"Oh,'' Anna whispered. "Oh, Malachi.'' Her arms tightened around him, even as her mind struggled to blot out what they both knew. Malachi loved her deeply, but without his children his heart would shrivel and harden. The warmth, the tenderness in him would die forever.

"Make love to me,'' she whispered, clasping him close. And her heart echoed, *Make love to me as if it were going to be the last time.*

The visitors from the Children's Aid Society arrived the next evening, just as the sun was sinking behind the vermilion cliffs. It was Josh who looked up and saw them coming around the farthest visible bend. The shout he raised brought everyone to the front yard—Malachi from the barn, Carrie and Anna from the house. They stood in a tightly drawn circle, all gazing up the road.

"I recognize Ephraim Snow's rig." Malachi squinted into the blazing sunset. "And there's old Ephraim driving it. Looks like they must've come into Kanab on the stage and hired him to bring them out here." His eyes strained to see the two prim-looking figures seated on the back bench. He couldn't make out many details at such a distance, except they were both holding parasols.

"I don't want them to come, Pa," Josh's hand tugged at the edge of Malachi's vest. "Tell them to go away and leave us alone. I don't want to live in Santa Fe with Grandma and Grandpa."

"Hush, Son," Malachi said, his own heart bursting. "Go wash your face and hands, and put on that new shirt Anna finished for you today. Make me proud of you tonight."

Anna, still in pants, pressed close to him, shading her eyes against the glare. "Two women," she muttered. "Look at the way they sit, with their backs as straight as stove pokers. Oh, dear..."

Malachi could feel the apprehension in her taut body. He understood. Anna would have suffered much from such women—so-called decent folk who looked down their noses at her careless beauty and her way of earning a livelihood; the kind of women whose husbands had likely put down hard-earned cash to bask in the vision of Anna's golden beauty and drink in the warm, sweet honey of her voice.

Malachi felt the fear in her as, for a long moment, she lingered beside him, her fingers twisting a lock of hair into a tawny rope. Then she exploded into action like a nervous little wren. "Carrie—check the stew! Make sure it's not scorching! Then give me a minute to change, and I'll braid your hair. Thank goodness we made bread and churned butter this morning! Josh, get a broom and sweep the porch—oh, and Malachi, shouldn't we shut the dog up somewhere? He scared the life out of me when I came here—"

Malachi stood for a moment watching the frenzy of preparation around him—watching his beloved Anna doing her best for a cause he knew to be hopeless.

Then he turned and, squinting into the glare once more, let his gaze follow the buckboard as it rolled down the winding trail like the herald of an oncoming apocalypse.

"Well, I must say that was a tasty stew." Miss Sophronia Hull, tall and racehorse lean, dabbed at her mouth with the folded calico square that passed for a napkin. Her companion, Miss Lucy Bigler, who reminded Anna of a plumply risen yeast roll, buttered a tidbit of bread and popped it daintily into her mouth.

"I should say it is!" she warbled. "Yes indeed, you should give me the recipe, Mrs. Stone. Really, you should."

Anna glanced hesitantly from one woman to the other. They were middle-aged, both of them, and clad in nearly identical navy-blue bombazine gowns that covered every inch of skin except their hands and faces. How on earth, she wondered, had they survived the withering midday heat?

So far, the visit of the Misses Hull and Bigler had been nothing but a chain of calamities. Doubtful had started the show by escaping from the barn and barking like a fury. Malachi had been glowering and withdrawn, and Anna's own efforts at playing lady of the manor had fallen as flat as a biscuit without soda. Her game might have fooled a pair of men, but these maiden ladies were far too shrewd to be taken in. Within minutes, their sharp, knowing eyes had reduced her to quivering jelly. Even Josh, the very soul of charm, had farted during grace and been too flustered to say "excuse me."

"Mrs. Stone?" Lucy Bigler gazed at her now, one pale eyebrow raised condescendingly. "I asked you for the secret of this delicious stew! Pray tell, what did you use for seasoning? Some wild herb, perhaps? It couldn't have been common onions and parsley!"

Anna swallowed, playing for time. In truth, it was Carrie who had made the stew—and much as it might enhance her standing with these women, she was not about to lie and claim credit.

"Well?" Miss Lucy's plump finger drummed on the tablecloth as Anna cleared her throat.

"To tell you the truth—"

"The recipe's an old family secret!" Carrie interrupted sweetly. "Anna's promised it to me on my wedding day, and not a minute sooner! I fear you won't succeed in talking her out of it. But she's teaching me to cook other things, and to sew and to play the piano."

"A secret recipe!" Miss Lucy sipped tea made

from the small stash she had brought along in her portmanteau. "Well, I never!"

"And what was it you did before your marriage, Mrs. Stone?" Sophronia Hull impaled Anna with a bespectacled gaze that took in her too new calico dress and hastily pinned-up hair.

"I was…a seamstress," Anna sputtered, fumbling for an acceptable answer that wasn't an all-out falsehood.

"She made all our clothes!" Carrie added brightly. "All except Papa's of course. And she made the curtains, too!"

"And how, might I ask, did you come to meet Mr. Stone?"

"Through…a relative of his. A cousin. He, uh, thought we would get on well and put us in touch." Anna felt a tarry weight in the pit of her stomach. Things were not going well at all. And Malachi just sat there scowling, blast him, as if he'd already given up and refused to compromise his pride. Only gristly old Ephraim Snow, who'd driven the buckboard, seemed at ease. He sat at the foot of the table, making little slurping sounds as he shoveled stew and bread into his mouth.

"The Reverend—the children's grandfather—was quite concerned about their education." Miss Lucy fingered a mole on her powder-white chin. "It's quite obvious they can't attend school here—"

"We have our own school!" Josh piped up. "Carrie's read 'most every book on those shelves, and I practice my sums and take-aways every night. Anna helps me." He glanced at his father, as if seeking support. "Papa says I have to study hard enough to go to college and be a doctor or an engineer or some such thing. And Carrie—maybe she'll be a teacher, or something even better!''

''Well and good, young man.'' Sophronia Hull smiled coldly, showing her big, horsey teeth. ''But, Mr. and Mrs. Stone, it's the children's *spiritual* education we're equally concerned about here. Are they getting regular bible study?''

''There's a bible on the shelf.'' Malachi spoke up for the first time. ''They can read it whenever they choose.''

''But do you *instruct* them, Mr. Stone? Do you teach them to fear the Lord? Do you discipline them for spiritual sins, such as vanity, pride and careless speech?''

''Discipline?'' Malachi's left eyebrow twitched.

''Spare the rod and spoil the child!'' Lucy Bigler chirped piously.

''Pa spanked me good and hard when I lit a fire in the barn once,'' Josh volunteered. ''Dang near blistered my rear end.''

Carrie groaned out loud. From the foot of the table the elderly driver chuckled between slurps. Neither Miss Sophronia nor Miss Lucy looked amused.

''I discipline my children as I see fit,'' Malachi said in a chilly voice. ''And I can't see that it's the business of anyone outside the family.''

''Well,'' said Sophronia, drawing herself up in her chair. ''Well.''

''Who's ready for custard?'' Anna broke in desperately. ''It was made fresh this morning and chilled in the spring.''

''Me!'' Ephraim Snow declared. ''Bring it on!''

"I'm much more interested in hearing Mr. Stone's opinions on child rearing," Sophronia said, folding her arms across her bony chest. "And, despite his protests, I fear that his views are indeed our business. That's precisely why we're here."

Malachi frowned. Anna could sense the desperation seething behind that stoic mask. She had never known a better father than Malachi Stone, but he was a man of action, not of words. And there were no words for what Josh and Carrie meant to him.

"Well, Mr. Stone?" Sophronia's gaze impaled him like a Kiowa lance. "We're waiting."

"I...believe in giving children the freedom to grow and learn for themselves," he said, struggling with every word. "When they make mistakes, I usually stand back and let them take the natural consequences...." His jaw tightened as he fought to keep his emotions in check. "But I sure as blazes don't beat them for so-called spiritual sins! And as for anybody who'd so much as lay a hand on either of them—" He choked on his own words, unable to go on.

"Carrie managed the house on her own before I came," Anna interjected. "And Josh is responsible and obedient. He always does what he's told."

"Please don't take us away!" Josh burst out. "I don't want to live with Grandma and Grandpa! I want to stay here with Pa—and with Anna!"

Sophronia froze him with a stern glare. "Young man," she said, "didn't anyone teach you that it's not polite to interrupt grown-ups while they're talking?"

Josh's lower lip quivered. In the silence that hung

over the table, he glanced at his father, seeking reassurance. Malachi strained forward, his own temper
perilously close to the snapping point.

"Hell's bells, stop yammerin' and bring on that
cold custard!" Ephraim Snow shouted from the foot
of the table. "Then let a man eat in peace. Supper
table's for eatin' not for arguin'!"

The old man scraped the last of the stew into his
bowl and, in the shocked silence that followed, began
sopping it up with the bread and stuffing the soaked
pieces into his mouth. Sophronia dabbed at her pursed
lips with her napkin. Lucy concealed a ladylike belch
behind her hand. Malachi had frozen in place like a
rough-hewn granite statue.

Anna slid back her chair and stood up to fetch the
bowl of custard from the spring. As she turned to go,
her glance fell on Carrie. The girl was sitting rigidly
in her chair, her hands in her lap. Tears trickled freely
down her beautiful, young face.

The disastrous evening ended in retreat—on everyone's part. Malachi, with Josh clinging to him like a
shadow, went out to look after the animals, a chore
Anna knew he would stretch out for as long as possible. Anna and Carrie cleaned up the kitchen while
their two female guests planted themselves in straight-
backed chairs next to the fireplace, Lucinda knitting
a long wool sock and Sophronia inspecting the books
on the shelves—probably looking for something dirty,
Anna groused, keeping her silence. What would these
so-called ladies say if they knew how she'd really
earned her living?

Maybe she ought to tell them. Their shock might

at least provide some entertainment. Oh, Malachi had been right! Why had they bothered to stage a show for these two straitlaced, judgmental women? There was only one way this tragic farce could end!

Yes, maybe she ought to give them a piece of her mind! Why not? What did she have to lose? What did Malachi and the children have to lose that wasn't already lost?

The moon was just rising over the canyon when the two visitors excused themselves to prepare for bed. The sleeping arrangements had been decided on earlier. Lucy and Sophronia would take the double bed in Anna's room. Anna would bunk with Carrie. Josh would spend the night with Malachi in the tack room, freeing his bed for Ephraim Snow—and, if the worst happened, allowing Malachi a few last precious hours with his little son.

Carrie, red-eyed and silent, had gone to bed. Lucy was standing on the porch, waiting for her turn at the privy, when Anna decided to speak her piece. Wiping her hands on her apron she stepped out onto the porch. Lucy turned to look at her, one eyebrow arching suspiciously.

"The nights are quite refreshing here, compared to the days, wouldn't you say so, Mrs. Stone?"

"Yes, I suppose I would." Anna nodded in polite agreement. Then, forcing all pretense aside, she turned her full desperation on the short, plump woman. "You can't take those children away! Malachi is a wonderful father! Those two youngsters are his whole life—and they love him! Can't you see that?"

"Indeed we can." Sophronia came around the

house adjusting her ample skirts. "And frankly, Mrs. Stone, it's not your husband's suitability as a parent that concerns us. It's your own!"

Anna stared at the two women, too stunned to reply.

"We're not the cruel monsters you seem to think we are," Lucy said. "Sophronia and I truly have the welfare of those two children at heart. The judge ordered us to determine whether this place was a proper home for them, and we are duty-bound to do just that."

"It's perfectly understandable that Mr. Stone doesn't like us," Sophronia added. "The fact that he doesn't try to hide that dislike speaks well for his honesty. He appears to be a good man and a loving, if rather lenient, father. Now, you, on the other hand—"

"We contacted Mr. Wilkinson in Salt Lake City." Lucy snatched up the thread of the explanation. "He told us about the circumstances of your marriage to Mr. Stone—that the two of you were wed by proxy just a few weeks ago, without ever having set eyes on each other. Is that true?"

"Yes." Anna felt as if she had stepped into quicksand and, like the cow, was sinking out of sight. "Malachi needed a mother for his children, and he had no other way of finding one. It wasn't his fault that Stuart Wilkinson didn't come up with someone more...suitable."

"Indeed." Sophronia swatted at a mosquito that was buzzing around her long face. "We also investigated your history, Mrs. Stone."

Anna felt herself sinking deeper, felt the quicksand closing around her throat, strangling her with fear.

"We found...nothing." Sophronia crushed the insect smartly against her cheek. "No birth certificate, no parents, no past marriages. Nothing of public record. It's as if you didn't exist before you contacted Mr. Wilkinson in Salt Lake City."

"Which led us to suspect that you were hiding something," Lucy interjected.

"Quite." Sophronia snatched back the conversation like a cat pouncing on a string. "When we met you, we knew our suspicious were well-founded. No woman with your looks would be desperate enough to wed a total stranger. Not without a very good reason."

"Again, it's the children we're concerned about," Lucy said. "Take Carrie...a lovely child, but so impressionable. Exposure to the wrong kind of influence—especially from a woman—could wreak havoc on her character. As for young Joshua, that child is so love-hungry he'll follow anyone who'll give him a pat on the head. He needs—"

"Wait!" Anna reeled amid the wreckage of her fragile world, struggling to understand what she'd just heard. "Are you saying that if I weren't here, Malachi would have a better chance of keeping his children?"

Lucy stared at her, blinking, while Sophronia seemed to be plucking at an imaginary lint speck on her skirt.

"You said *I* was the problem!" Anna persisted, talking fast, afraid of stopping long enough to think. "What if I were to leave—now, with you, first thing tomorrow? Malachi could get a divorce—maybe even an annulment—on grounds of desertion. He could find another wife, a proper mother for his children...."

Anna choked on the throbbing lump that rose in her throat. She'd been happy here, so happy that she'd almost let herself believe this brief heaven could last forever. Why hadn't she thought ahead—and held back her heart?

"Let us make sure we understand you," Sophronia said. "You would leave with us and never return? You would allow Mr. Stone to divorce you?"

Anna twisted the thin gold band on her finger, her heart pounding. "I would, but only in exchange for your promise—your *written* promise to Mr. Stone— that the children would be allowed to stay here with their father."

The two women glanced cautiously at each other.

"Please!" Anna begged, tears springing to her eyes. "I'll do anything, sign anything! Just don't take those children! Please, it would break their father's heart!"

Again the two women exchanged glances, as if communicating by some secret, silent code. Anna waited in slow agony, telling herself this was the only way—for Malachi, for the children and for her. The chance to clear herself had been no more than a will o' the wisp. It was time to cut and run.

An eternity seemed to pass before Lucy cleared her throat and spoke. "This is where we stand, Mrs. Stone. The judge has given us two options. If we see fit, we have the authority to take the children back to Sante Fe with us—or we can recommend a year's

probation, after which the judge will review the case
and make a final ruling.''

''As we've already made clear, our first and only
concern is the children's welfare,'' Sophronia added.
''If you'll sign a paper consenting to the divorce and
agree to leave the canyon with us tomorrow, we will
let Carrie and Joshua remain here with their father.
The probationary year should give Mr. Stone enough
time to, let us say, get his life in order.''

Get his life in order.

Anna nodded, knowing what the well-couched
phrase meant. Malachi would have time to find a suit-
able wife, a good woman who would share his days,
mother his children and, perhaps in time, come to
know his love. Yes, a year would be enough.

''Very well,'' she said, forcing herself to sound un-
caring and hard. ''I'll want both your signatures on a
paper for Malachi, in case anyone challenges his right
to keep those children. Just get me out of here first
thing tomorrow morning. My time here is finished,
and I don't believe in milking a dry cow!''

''I have some writing materials in my valise.'' Sophronia's bombazine skirts rustled as she mounted the
steps and swept over the threshold. ''Let's get this
matter taken care of so we can get some rest, shall
we? I daresay it's been a very long day.''

Anna tiptoed into Carrie's room, closed the door
softly behind her and, at long last, allowed herself to
collapse against the wall. Every nerve in her body was
quivering, and her stomach felt as if she had swallowed a cup of lye. It was done. The papers were
drawn and signed and folded into her apron pocket—

her own agreement to a swift legal divorce and the two women's promise to Malachi that they would prevail upon the judge to delay his decision for one year.

The time for make-believe was over. She would be leaving this place tomorrow morning with no money, no tickets and no resources except her own wits. She had no idea what she would do when the buckboard reached Kanab, especially if the bounty hunters were waiting. But somehow she would survive. She was good at surviving.

Her trembling fingers touched the thin gold ring that adorned her left hand. Slipping it off over her knuckle, she squeezed it tightly in her hand. Men had given her jewelry before, glittering baubles, most of which she'd sold to tide her over the lean times. But this small, plain band meant more to her than anything she had ever owned—and now she had given up the right to wear it.

Sliding open the drawer on the washstand, she dropped the ring quietly inside. Then, as an afterthought, she removed her pearl earrings and placed them beside the wedding band. They would look pretty on Carrie when she was grown.

Turning, she gazed down at the moonlit form of the girl who had so nearly become her daughter—who was, in fact the very age her own daughter would have been if she'd lived. Carrie was curled beneath the quilt, her arms clutching her pillow. As Anna leaned over her, she stirred and opened her eyes.

"Anna, is that you?" she whispered.

"Yes. I was just coming to bed."

"Are those two old biddies asleep yet?

"They're not old biddies, Carrie. Just two well-meaning women trying to do a very difficult job."

"Why can't they just leave us alone?" She sat up, and Anna could see from her blotched face that she'd been crying. "I don't want to go away! I want to stay here in the canyon with Papa!"

Anna sank onto the edge of the bed and gathered the distraught girl into her arms. Carrie began to sob again, her tears soaking Anna's collar and pooling in the hollow of her throat. "It's all right, Carrie," she murmured, aching. "No one's going to take you away. I won't let that happen."

"Promise?" Carrie hiccuped.

"I promise." Anna eased her back onto the pillow. "Go to sleep now. Things will be better in the morning. You'll see."

"Don't leave me." Carrie clung to Anna's shoulders, reaching up, pulling her down. "When I'm alone, bad thoughts come into my head. They scare me, and I can't make them go away."

"Shhh…" Anna lay down on top of the covers and gathered the girl close. "Don't be afraid. I'm here. I'll be here all night."

"Thank you," Carrie whispered closing her eyes. "I love you, Anna. I love you almost as much as if you were my real Mama…." The words trailed off as she dropped into exhausted slumber.

Anna lay awake in the darkness, cradling her close, for the rest of the night.

Chapter Seventeen

Behind the eastern buttes, the light of the unborn day paled the indigo sky. Streaks of pewter and opal glowed across the landscape, casting rippled shadows that flowed like water in the waxing light. Jutting spires of rock caught the first rays of the sun. Sandstone and shale flamed to life in hues of bronze, amber and amethyst. Against the sky, a lone raven circled, spiraling downward to perch on the roof of the barn like a black omen.

Malachi stepped outside, his eyes stinging with weariness after a long, sleepless night. He had passed the hours in the tack room lying next to his still-slumbering son, agonizing over the day ahead. Now that day was here. What would it bring?

The two women had said nothing about when they would announce their decision, but there was no need to wonder what it would be. What would he do when he heard the news? Would he curse fate and heaven and the pair of harpies who'd come to rip his world apart? Would he seize his precious children, keeping the visitors at bay with his rifle while he fled with them up the canyon, out of reach?

No. He had taught Carrie and Josh to eschew violence and to respect the law. For their own sakes, he would have no choice except to let them go.

And after that… Yes, he would seek out every possible means to get them back. He would fight for them, just as he meant to fight for Anna. Whatever the cost, he would not rest until the four of them— his family—were together again.

Glancing toward the house, he caught sight of the smoke curling from the chimney. He could smell the rich aromas of coffee and bacon. He had been doing chores in the barn since first light, so it came as no surprise that Anna was already up and cooking breakfast. All the same, the sight of Ephraim Snow, hitching up his team outside the corral stopped him like a solid punch in the face.

"Ephraim, what the devil—" He willed himself to move, sprinting across the yard to the old man. "You're going? Already?"

Ephraim hawked and spat on the ground. "Looks like it. Ladies woke me up and gave me my marchin' orders. Said they wanted to get an early start, afore the sun gets too hot."

"But they just got here! What did they decide?" Malachi reeled between hope and desperation. "What about my children? Are they going, too?"

Ephraim scratched his bony rump. "Don't rightly know about the young'uns. But I'd get in that house and find out what's goin' on if I was you. From the talk I heard, I got the idea your missus was fixin' to go with 'em."

* * *

Anna, dressed in her denim pants, was pouring the last of the flapjack batter onto the hot griddle when Malachi came storming into the kitchen. Her heart faltered at the sight of him—so angry, so hurt, so bewildered.

"What in blazes is going on?" he demanded, letting the screen door slam behind him. "Ephraim says you're leaving!"

"Ephraim is right." Anna forced herself to speak calmly, keeping a grip on her churning emotions. "We'll be leaving right after breakfast."

"The children! What about the children?" His gaze darted to her ringless hand, then back to her face. He was wild-eyed, a wounded beast, his hair uncombed, his face unshaven. In his frantic state, he did not even appear to have noticed the two women seated at the table.

"The children will be staying with you, Malachi," Anna said quietly. "You'll be given a year to convince the judge you can provide a good home for them. That was the best bargain I could make."

He stared at her, uncomprehending, like a man in the grip of a nightmare.

"Here," she said, fumbling in the pocket of her apron. "Maybe this will make things clearer."

He snatched the paper from her and unfolded it. Anna turned the flapjacks while he read, her heart bursting with things she had no right to stay. Sophronia and Lucy stared down at their plates, picking at their food, pretending to eat.

"Where's Carrie?" Malachi asked, his voice harsh with strain.

"In her room. She knows. Leave her alone, Malachi. Carrie will be all right once she's had time to think things through. So will you."

"The devil!"

"Malachi, please—" She glanced toward the table, fearful that his outburst of temper would destroy her hard-won victory.

"We have to talk," he said, catching her wrist.

"There's nothing more to say."

"Outside." His grip tightened. "Now."

"The flapjacks—" she protested. "They'll burn!"

"Let them," he growled. "Are you coming, or do I have to shock these proper ladies by dragging you out the door?"

"You're already dragging me!" Anna could sense the two women watching her. The last thing she wanted was to make a scene. "All right. Five minutes, Malachi. No longer—"

"Come on!" He jerked her out the front door, yanked her down the steps and whipped her around the corner of the house, away from curious eyes. "Now what is all this?"

Anna gained her footing and forced herself to meet his heartbreaking gaze. "Don't you see? It isn't you those women are worried about—not you as a father. It's me as a mother. They're on to me, Malachi. They know I'm not what I pretend to be. So last night I did the only thing I could do for you and the children. I struck a bargain with them—I leave, the children stay. For one more year. That was the best I could do." She blinked back furious tears. "Let me go, Malachi. Your children are safe. I've kept my part of the bargain!"

He caught her close then, crushing her against his heart. Anna clung to him in spite of herself. Holding him, feeling his warm masculine strength—for the last time, she told herself. The last time.

"No, damn it," he whispered against the tangle of her hair. "It doesn't have to be this way. I'll talk to those women, tell them how much the children need you—how much *I* need you! You're my wife, Anna! I can't just stand back and let you go without—"

The loud, metallic twang of a rifle shot, ricocheting off the canyon walls, shattered the world around them.

"The ferry—" Anna glanced toward the river, but even as she spoke she knew the shot had not come from the far bank. The sound had been too close for that.

Malachi had made a lightning-quick turn and was sprinting toward the front of the house. He halted at the corner, caught Anna's arm as she hurtled past him, and swung her backward against the adobe wall. "Stay back!" he warned. "We don't know what's happening out there."

Cautiously now, they peered into the front yard. Ephraim Snow was hunkered behind the buckboard, cursing but unharmed. The dog, gun-shy like many of his wild hybrid kind, cowered under the steps. There was nothing else in the yard but Ephraim's horses and a few startled chickens. Then Anna saw it—the glint of sunlight on polished metal in the high rocks that jutted above the ranch and ferry, separating the road from the river. Silently she nudged Malachi and pointed. He nodded grimly. They both knew what it was—and perhaps even *who* it was.

"What in heaven's name is happening out here?" Sophronia burst through the screen door onto the porch, followed by Lucy, then by Carrie, who was still in her nightgown. "Mr. Stone, what do you mean by this, scaring us half out of our—"

"Shut up and get back inside!" Malachi hissed. "All of you! And keep away from the windows!"

"Where's Josh?" Anna whispered as the two women hustled Carrie back inside the kitchen.

"I left him asleep in the barn. Just pray he's got the sense to stay put!" Malachi inched forward. He had no weapon, Anna realized. The pistol and rifle would both be in the tack room, where he had spent the night.

"I see you, Mr. Stone!" The oily voice that rang out from the rocks was sickeningly familiar. "Now that I've got your attention, we can talk."

"Anyone you know?" Malachi glanced back at Anna, his eyes narrowed like a wary cat's.

"It's Caswell," Anna said, feeling her stomach clench.

"I figured as much. Stay back."

"Come on out where we can parley!" Caswell shouted. "I've got no quarrel with you. It's your woman I've come for. Did you know Anna was wanted for murder back in St. Joseph, Mr. Stone?"

"I don't know what you're talking about!" Malachi bluffed, stalling for time.

"Well, Mr. Stone, perhaps my young friend here can jog your memory."

There was a pause, followed by a scuffling sound amid the rocky ledges. Then a small, terrified voice called out, "Pa! I'm up here, Pa! They've—" The rest of the words were abruptly muffled.

"Dear God," Anna muttered. "He's got Josh!"

Malachi's face had turned ashen. "Stay here," he said, inching back around her. "Talk to Caswell. Try to distract him while I work my away 'round the back. I'll try to get a gun and get behind them somehow."

Anna moved forward to take his place at the corner of the house.

"Be careful," he said.

"You, too," she whispered. "Remember, Caswell wouldn't have come alone. He'll have others with him."

She watched, holding his image as he disappeared around the back of the house. Then, taking a deep breath, she edged forward, just short of Caswell's view.

"Let the boy go, Caswell!" she shouted. "It's me you want, not an innocent child!"

"Is that really you, Anna?" Caswell's unctuous voice dripped pleasure. How long could she bait him, she wondered, before he moved in for the kill?

"That's right, you lying, murdering skunk!" she shouted. "If you want me, come and get me!"

"Tut, tut, now!" Caswell chuckled darkly. "Is that any way to talk to an old friend, especially one who's come such a long way to see you? It was Mr. Samuel Johnson who recognized the poster and wired me that he'd found you. I was a bit skeptical at first, but I changed my mind when these two gentlemen wired, as well. I instructed them to wait in Kanab for my arrival, of course. I know you, Anna, and I know the persuasive effect that face and body can have on men—I certainly know what a fool you made of my poor friend Harry. I wouldn't trust anyone but me to bring you to justice.''

Anna squinted up at the ledges, taking time to weigh what she'd heard. The two men he'd mentioned—that would be the bounty hunters, she was certain. Such men would owe no special allegiance to Caswell, and neither of them would be eager to risk trouble by harming a child. They were here only for the reward—for her.

"Let Josh go!" she called out again. "You're already guilty of kidnapping. If you lay a hand on him, there are people here whose testimony will send you to jail!"

"Anna, my dear you misjudge me!" Caswell shot back. "I would never do anything to harm Mr. Stone's little boy. But accidents do happen. What if the child were to become frightened and try to run away? He could slip and fall, perhaps all the way to the river. What jury would hold me responsible for such a tragic mishap?"

Anna's fear darkened as she realized he was right. Caswell was a monster. If things didn't go his way he was quite capable of shoving Josh off a ledge. And with the jutting rocks blocking their view, no one watching from below would know what had really happened.

"Your time's run out, Anna!" Caswell shouted. "Harry Solomon was my friend. When he was murdered, I swore I'd track his killer to the ends of the earth—Lord knows, I never realized how literal that vow would become! You've led me on quite a chase, Anna DeCarlo, or whatever your real name is. But it's all over. You killed Harry, and the time has come to bring you to justice!''

"Liar!" Anna shouted, stalling desperately. "Harry was the kindest man I've ever known! He treated me like a queen! We were going to be married—why would I want him dead?''

"You're asking me to explain a woman's thinking?'' Caswell's laughter echoed off the canyon walls.

"You're the one who killed him—or hired your ugly Russian friend to do it for you!" Anna countered. "I saw you on the stairs that night. Why did you do it, Caswell? Did Harry know something about you—something he threatened to reveal if you didn't stop squeezing him for money? Did he want to come clean before he married me? Was that it?''

Caswell hesitated, but only for an instant. "You're stalling, Anna. There's only one way this is going to end. The only question is, how many people are going to get hurt before you give yourself up?''

Anna's gaze darted to the steep, circuitous route Malachi would be taking up the side of the ledge. She could see him now. He was climbing stealthily, the rifle, which he'd evidently retrieved from the barn, slung over his back. If no one spotted him, he would emerge above the road, behind Caswell and the bounty hunters.

But someone *had* spotted him. Her eyes caught a flicker of movement in the rocks, and her heart stopped cold. Someone was waiting just a few yards ahead of him, hidden behind a jutting boulder. Anna's blood congealed as she recognized the hulking form of The Russian, Caswell's companion on that terrible night in St. Joseph.

Her first impulse was to scream—but no, a scream might trigger a hail of gunfire. She could not put two precious lives at risk for her own sake. She could not put *any* lives at risk. If she wanted Josh free and alive, there was only one thing to do.

"I see you brought your bloodhound along!" she shouted. "I see him, Caswell, right up there in the rocks above the road! You can call him back now. I'm the one you want, and I don't want innocent people hurt on my account."

"Are you saying what I think you're saying?" Caswell all but chortled the question.

"Yes. It's over, you slimy, murdering bastard. You've won."

Malachi glimpsed the movement in the rocks above him, checked his climb and squeezed back into the shadow of an overhang. Anna's discreet warning had saved his life, he realized. He had counted on Caswell and the two bounty hunters, but not on the fourth man—Caswell's man—who had evidently seen him coming and moved into ambush position.

He pressed deeper into the rocky cleft, cursing under his breath. He was safe for the moment, but what now? His whereabouts was no longer a secret. Caswell still had Josh. And what in thunder was Anna up to?

"Come on out!" Caswell shouted. "Put your hands above your head and walk toward me!"

"Not until you let Josh go!" Anna yelled back, and Malachi groaned out loud, feeling helpless and sick. He knew what she meant to do, and he had no way to stop her—not without endangering his son's life. Right now his only hope of saving anyone lay in staying put and keeping quiet.

"Send the boy out!" Anna shouted. "When I can see that he's all right, I'll come out in the open. As soon as he's safely back in the house, I'm all yours!"

Malachi felt his heart swell and shatter. She was a glowing flame of courage, his Anna. He could only hope the two old harpies who'd judged her an unfit mother were hearing every word.

In the brief tick of silence Malachi could hear the song of a canyon wren and the rushing sigh of the river. Then his chest jerked as Joshua appeared at the crest of the rock. The boy appeared white-faced and shaken, but otherwise unhurt, thank heaven. Anna had come out into the yard, making herself an easy target. Caswell or one of his cronies probably had a bead on her right now. Malachi's tightly clenched jaw sent darts of pain up his face. A drop of sweat trickled down his temple as he willed himself to keep still.

"Come on, Josh," Anna called, gently encouraging the terrified little boy. "That's it. Down the rocks and into the yard. Nobody's going to hurt you. I won't let them!"

Malachi watched, his heart in his throat, as Josh reached level ground and broke into a headlong run. Anna was moving toward him now, reaching out as he stumbled, catching him, enfolding him fiercely in her arms. Josh clung to her like a frightened little animal.

For a moment she held him tightly. Then slowly and gently she lowered him to the ground, saying something that Malachi could not hear. Suddenly Josh leaped on her again, his small arms locking around her neck. The lump in Malachi's throat all but choked him as she eased the boy away from her and turned him firmly toward the house.

"Run!" she commanded, and Josh did, his sturdy little legs devouring the distance to the porch, where Carrie waited to snatch him into the safety of the house.

Malachi's eyes stung with unshed tears of relief. "So help me, I'll make this right," he whispered. "I swear it, Anna, on my life."

Head high, Anna walked slowly toward the rocks. Malachi seethed helplessly, knowing he could not interfere now. Caswell would not murder her outright in front of so many witnesses, but if a gunfight broke out, with everyone shooting, Anna would be the first to die.

As she reached the foot of the ledges, the two bounty hunters stepped out of hiding, seized her roughly by the arms and half marched, half dragged her up the rocky path. She made no outcry, and Malachi knew that she would face Caswell with proud defiance. Anna—*his* Anna—would spit into the very eye of death.

How long would Caswell keep her alive? Would he wait until they got out of the canyon? Until the bounty hunters went their separate way? Or would he arrange an "accident" at first opportunity on the steep trail? Malachi could not predict what a monster like Caswell would do. He only knew that time was already running out.

Taking swift advantage of the distraction caused by

Anna's capture, he slipped back the way he had come. Where the rough trail forked upward, he paused to glance back toward the clump of rocks where she had vanished. The thought of her there, at Caswell's mercy, tore at his heart.

Suddenly he felt something cool and damp push into the palm of his hand. He swore softly as he looked down into Doubtful's pale, wolfish eyes. The last thing he needed was the fool dog following him, giving his presence away. "Go home, boy!" he ordered, pointing furtively to the house. "Home!"

Doubtful's tail wagged hesitantly. He whined, then, when Malachi did not relent and scratch his head, he slunk off in the direction of the house, disappearing behind a clump of mesquite. Malachi waited an instant longer to make sure the dog was not following him. Then, praying for time, he struck out for the high, rocky ridge that ran parallel to the road.

Anna sprawled in the gravel at Caswell's feet, where the two bounty hunters had flung her. She was bruised, scratched, dirty and sick with fear—a fear she masked with defiant rage.

"There's your murderer!" She pointed at Caswell but her words were meant for the two cold-eyed hunters who'd dragged her up the rocks. "He killed the man I was going to marry—he and his big, ugly stooge! Then they blamed me when I walked in and discovered the body! Why don't you—"

Her words ended in a whimper as Caswell's black, high-heeled boot slammed into the side of her head. Sparks exploded in her brain as she fought to stay conscious.

"Save your breath, you little whore!" Caswell spat out the words. "Nobody's going to believe your lies!" He jerked his head toward the bounty hunters. "We've got what we want. You two go back up the road and bring down the horses. We're getting out of here!"

Anna lay still, gathering the last of her strength as the bounty hunters trotted off toward the road. Her vision was blotchy from the impact of Caswell's brutal kick. The ringing in her ears blended with the rushing sound of the Colorado, where it swept below the ledges, no more than a stone's throw away.

Caswell stood over her, smiling his oily smile. "Well, my dear," he said, "it seems we've come to the end of the trail. Sorry we didn't get to know each other better. I might have found you...amusing." His hand lifted a lock of her hair, his fingers slowly twisting it into a tawny rope.

Anna knew, then, that he was going to kill her. He would do it here. Now. That was why he had sent the bounty hunters away. All he had to do was throw her over the ledge into the river. Then he could claim that she'd drowned trying to escape.

Caswell glanced at his hulking companion. "Do it," he said. "Then let's get out of here before that big lout she married decides to make a hero of himself."

"Why did you do it, Caswell?" Anna stalled desperately as The Russian moved toward her, his eyes as cold and flat as a snake's. "At least I'm entitled to know that before I die."

Caswell smiled. "My dear, you are not entitled to anything—except the satisfaction of knowing I'll sleep better after you're gone.'' Again he nodded, and the big man caught Anna's wrists, whipped her upright and began dragging her toward the precipice.

''Stop right there.'' Malachi stepped into sight from behind a rock, the barrel of the rifle leveled at Caswell's heart. ''Tell your plug-ugly friend to let her go, or you're a dead man.''

Caswell froze, his hands inching upward, his small, black eyes darting nervously from the rifle to his hulking cohort. ''Do it,'' he croaked. ''Let her go.''

The Russian flung Anna roughly to the ground. She landed sprawling, the rough gravel cutting into her hands. Malachi caught a flash of crimson—was she hurt?

He glanced toward her, distracted for a split second. Too late, he realized his mistake as the enormous figure of The Russian hurtled down on him, slamming into his body with the force of a runaway locomotive. The rifle flew into the air as Malachi went down under the crushing weight. ''Run, Anna!'' he gasped, struggling. ''Get out of here!''

A giant fist seized his throat, and Malachi found himself fighting for his life. His adversary was an immensely powerful man, but Malachi's own arms, the muscles hardened by years of backbreaking work, fought free, allowing him to scramble to his feet. Now, with both of them standing, their fists came into play. Malachi was outweighed by a good forty pounds, but rage and desperation gave him strength. The soulless monster would have killed Anna. He would likely have killed Josh, as well.

Chest heaving with fury, Malachi drove his enemy back toward the ledge that overhung the river. The

Russian swung hard, landing a glancing blow that threw his own huge body off balance. He stumbled, his arms waving grotesquely like the wings of a fledgling vulture. Then, with a hoarse, animal cry, he pitched backward over the precipice.

The drop was not far, but here, where the canyon narrowed, the water was deep, the current too strong for any swimmer. By the time Malachi checked his own forward momentum and glanced over the edge, his foe had vanished beneath the swirling brown water.

The rifle—he saw it, then, wedged where it had fallen between two rocks. Wrenching it free he swung around—only to find Caswell a dozen paces away, holding Anna against him with one arm as he pressed the blade of a long, sharp knife to her throat.

"Drop the rifle, Mr. Stone," Caswell said. "Do exactly as I say, or Anna dies here and now."

Anna watched as Malachi's expression froze in shock. Carefully he lowered the rifle and let it drop to the ground. "You were about to have her killed anyway," he said. "Now your hired killer is gone. If you want her dead, Caswell, you'll have to bloody your own hands. Are you ready to become a murderer?"

Caswell did not answer. Anna willed herself to keep perfectly still. She could feel the razor edge of the knife against her jugular vein. She could feel the fear, the exquisite tension in Caswell's trembling body. Her slightest motion could be enough to send the blade slicing into the tender flesh of her throat.

Her gaze locked with Malachi's across a distance that had suddenly become too great to bridge. She could feel his fear for her, his helpless rage. *Go back,* she would have told him if she could speak. *Go back home, my love, and be a father to your children. Be a loving husband to the new mother you'll find for them. Forget me, Malachi. It's all over....*

Caswell's grip tightened around her ribs. The cold steel slipped against her throat. She felt it slice through her skin, felt the first thin trickle of blood.

"You don't have to kill her!" Malachi's voice rasped with desperation. "We have no proof against you, Caswell. Let her go and leave us in peace."

Caswell's laughter was tinged with madness. "Why, Mr. Stone, you can't really expect me to—"

His words ended in a gurgle of astonishment as a snarling, snapping ball of fury erupted from the direction of the road, hurtling into his legs and throwing Caswell off balance. The knife flew out of his hand, but he had not lost his grip on Anna. As they staggered like drunken dancers toward the ledge, with Doubtful's huge canine teeth locked into the flesh of Caswell's leg, she heard Malachi shout. He flung himself forward—but too late. In one last desperate act Caswell spun Anna toward the precipice and shoved her away from him, toward the river.

Anna's feet slipped over the rocky edge. Then she went down, clawing and fighting as she slid over the lip of the rock. Her flailing hands caught the end of a tree root that twisted outward from the side of the cliff. Reflexively she seized it, clinging frantically as the root sagged with her weight, sending a shower of pebbles into the boiling river below.

Above her pandemonium reigned. The air rang with Doubtful's snarls and Caswell's terrified screams. "Get him off me, Stone! I'll tell you any-thing—anything you want to know! It was the Rus-sian who killed Harry—the Russian, I tell you, not me—"

Anna felt the root giving way. "Malachi!" she screamed. *"Malachi!"*

Suddenly he was there, his fingers reaching down toward her, his eyes dark with love and with fleeting shadows of terror. "Catch my hand, Anna," he said in a calm voice. "It's all right. I won't let you go—not for as along as I live."

Paralyzed with fear, Anna willed herself to move, to reach upward. Their hands brushed. Then caught. Then locked tightly in a clasp that would never be broken again.

Little by little he pulled her upward into his arms.

Epilogue

May, 1890

Anna and Malachi sat close together on the front steps of their home, watching the twilight shadows steal across the canyon. Among the rocks and willows, a thousand tiny night creatures were awakening to a cool night. Swallows swooped above the river, their iridescent wings catching the clear amber light. Frogs croaked in the shallows, singing in a hundred different keys, life calling to life.

From within the house, the wistful notes of "Beautiful Dreamer" floated on the evening air. After only a year Carrie was becoming a fine pianist; but the song, which the girl had learned so eagerly, never failed to take Anna back to that terrible night in St. Joseph when she had passed Louis Caswell and The Russian on the dark stairway.

Caswell was in prison now, serving a life sentence for murder, attempted murder and extortion. As Anna had long suspected, the oily little police chief had been collecting protection money from every saloon in St. Joseph, including the Jack of Diamonds. Harry Solomon had died for threatening to expose Caswell's crimes.

Anna herself had been cleared of all charges. Her bad dreams had eased over the past months, but there were still nights when she awakened in the darkness, needing the comfort of Malachi's arms. Always, Malachi was there.

"Look, Pa! Look, Ma!" Josh raced across the yard with Doubtful at his heels, chasing the stick the boy had tossed. "Doubtful almost caught it this time! Maybe next time he really will!"

Malachi chuckled, drawing his wife closer. "I'll wager the blasted dog will never learn that trick," he said. "But then I guess nobody's perfect."

"No, and that's all right," Anna murmured, grateful that Sophronia and Lucy had been willing to accept her own imperfections. The sacrifice she'd made to rescue Josh had been enough to change their minds about her. "No one but a true mother would offer her life to save her child!" Lucy had declared, settling the matter once and for all.

Only a few weeks ago, word had come from Santa Fe that the judge had granted Malachi permanent custody of his children. They were a true family now, all five of them, in every sense of the word.

The tiny bundle in Anna's arms stirred and whimpered drowsily. Anna smiled a tender smile, her heart all but bursting as she cradled her baby close. Little Susan Jeanette Stone, to be called Jeanie, had entered the world in the midst of an April storm. She had her mother's golden curls, her father's silvery eyes and a double dose of stubborn temperament from both parents. Hers would be a life of warmth and security, Anna vowed. A life of laughter, music and boundless love.

"I'll take her." Malachi's huge hands worked their way beneath the blanket, lifting his daughter into the light of the rising moon. Anna wrapped her arms around them both, her joy too great for a solitary heart to contain.

* * * * *

Author Note:

The location of Stone's Ferry is fictitious. My imagination places it somewhere near the lower end of the lost Glenn Canyon, now covered by the waters of Lake Powell. The characters are also fictitious. Any resemblance to actual persons is coincidental. Only the canyon, the Colorado, and the town of Kanab, Utah, are real.

AWARD-WINNING AUTHOR

GAYLE WILSON

presents her latest
Harlequin Historical novel

ANNE'S
PERFECT HUSBAND

Book II in her brand-new series

The Sinclair Brides

When a dashing naval officer searches for the
perfect husband for his beautiful young ward,
he soon discovers he needn't search any
further than his own heart!

Look for it in bookstores in March 2001!

Available at your favorite retail outlet.

CELEBRATE VALENTINE'S DAY WITH HARLEQUIN®'S LATEST TITLE— *Stolen Memories*

Available in trade-size format, this collector's edition contains three full-length novels by *New York Times* bestselling authors Jayne Ann Krentz and Tess Gerritsen, along with national bestselling author Stella Cameron.

TEST OF TIME by **Jayne Ann Krentz**—
He married for the best reason.... She married for the only reason.... Did they stand a chance at making the only reason the real reason to share a lifetime?

THIEF OF HEARTS by **Tess Gerritsen**—
Their distrust of each other was only as strong as their desire. And Jordan began to fear that Diana was more than just a thief of hearts.

MOONTIDE by **Stella Cameron**—
For Andrew, Greer's return is a miracle. It had broken his heart to let her go. Now fate has brought them back together. And he won't lose her again...

Make this Valentine's Day one to remember!

Look for this exciting collector's edition on sale January 2001 at your favorite retail outlet.

HARLEQUIN®
Makes any time special ™

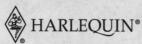

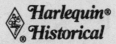

PRESENTS

SIRENS OF THE SEA

The brand-new historical series
from bestselling author

Ruth Langan

Join the spirited Lambert sisters in their
search for adventure—and love!

THE SEA WITCH
When dashing Captain Riordan Spencer arrives in
Land's End, Ambrosia Lambert may have
met her perfect match!

On sale January 2001
THE SEA NYMPH
Middle sister Bethany must choose between a
scandalous highwayman and the very proper
Earl of Alsmeeth.

In June 2001
THE SEA SPRITE
Youngest sister Darcy loses the love of her life
in a shipwreck, only to fall for a man who
strongly resembles her lost lover.